Peace on Earth & Mercy Mild

Nikki Elizabeth

Published by Nikki Elizabeth, 2024.

PEACE ON EARTH & MERCY MILD

First edition. November 13, 2024.

ISBN: 979-8227224606

Written by Nikki Elizabeth.

To TGATG. You guys keep me laughing when the Hellmouth is spewing demons, possums, ants, and moles. May we continue to slay the day, even long after we've moved to a less hellish plane.

Chapter One

Mercy walked along the icy Connecticut street, her scarf blowing over her shoulder as her boots brushed across fresh snow. There was an intoxicating stillness about the night. At one point in her life, she might have reveled in the beauty of the winter evening.

Of course, her life was essentially over now.

The town felt sleepy, just as it always had. As a child, she'd found the town boring. As a novelist, it never even crossed her mind as a potential setting for a story. It was beautiful, sure, but otherwise unremarkable. She much preferred her adult life in New York. It was just two hours away, but it was worlds away from this quaint community.

Of course, big city life can come with some minor inconveniences. For one, she didn't own a car. In a place like NYC, you simply didn't *need* a car. She had taken a Greyhound bus into Hartford and then a taxi into the Commercial District as a result, and she now found herself walking across snow-kissed small town streets.

She had her scarf drawn up over her mouth. The few passersby she encountered were blowing clouds of steam with every exasperated breath, but she wouldn't do the same. She didn't want anyone to notice.

Mercy had grown exceedingly talented at blending in.

She walked from the Commercial District to residential streets, which were more abandoned than the small downtown. Each home was garnished with holiday decorations, emanating warm light and cinnamon-soaked scent into the night.

It was peaceful. Peace on earth and Mercy Mild. Peace on earth. Mercy Mild. It wasn't just peace on earth... it was peace on earth, excluding Mercy.

Every holiday, she was reminded of her horrible namesake. Mercy Mild Harker. She sounded like a Christmas carol. It made a small ball of resentment form in her tummy as she approached her childhood home.

As always, the holiday was promising to be anything but peaceful.

She approached the door, then lifted a hand to knock. Before her fist could meet the door, it opened. Mercy allowed her hand to fall.

"Hi, Mary."

Mary Olive squealed and pulled her sister into an embrace that might have sucked the life out of her. "Mercy! We've missed you. I was hoping you'd come this year. Get in here! You're as cold as death."

Mary's perfume was intoxicating, a sickeningly sweet aroma that made Mercy want to gag. Combined with the peroxide blonde hair and orange skin (which somehow grew oranger with each encounter), Mary was truly a sight to behold. A product of the times.

A pretty, dumb young woman who'd never left her hometown.

"We just made cookies," Mary explained as Mercy removed her coat and situated it on the banister. "They're shaped like ornaments and bells. Come warm up by the fire and munch, sis."

Mercy followed her sister deeper into the house. It had wallpaper that hadn't been updated since the Eighties, Hummels, other knickknacks that clashed with the Christmas décor, and ever-stagnant photos that were accruing a thicker layer of dust with each passing year.

"It's so cozy," Mercy said. The house hadn't changed at all over the years. Truth be told, neither had she.

Mercy could tell it bothered her family. While Mary grew more physically mature, Mercy hadn't changed since she was roughly twenty. When she left home, she was a petite girl with delicate features, including black hair and blue eyes. While the girl in the family photographs had matured emotionally, her features today were the same.

Like that one Britney Spears song – not a girl, not yet a woman. The reference was already dated, and it would only grow more so as her life stretched onward. It wasn't quite right to describe her anyway. She'd never be a woman, not like most girls were, eventually.

Her mother approached and embraced her. "We've missed you, baby. Let's get you warmed up by the fire. Did you walk all the way from the bus stop?"

"Yeah," Mercy said as they moved into the living room. She settled into a recliner by the fire and eyed the tinsel-coated Christmas tree with disinterest. "I see you got a live tree this year."

"We did," Mom said. "We got to cut it down ourselves and everything... there was hot chocolate, and we sat by a fire. It was magical. I wish you could have come with us. Mary did."

Mercy shifted to pop off her snow boots and pull her ankles under her legs. "Me too, Mom, but you know the publisher has me working like a dog. I'm already running behind, and I've only been here for a minute."

Mary snorted. "Tell them they need a dose of Christmas cheer."

"Those people only need money." Mercy chuckled. "Literal lizard people."

Mary and Mom sat down, chuckling. Neither understood Mercy's lifestyle, and she didn't expect them to. However, they at least feigned sympathy. Mercy's father eventually joined the ruckus, and his face hardened when he spotted his eldest daughter.

"Hello, Mercy."

"Hello."

While he settled down wordlessly, he seemed content to let his wife carry the conversation. She spoke of everything and anything, which was the norm. What was unexpected was Mercy's father's clear hardness. He hadn't ever been incredibly fond of her, but now he just felt foreign.

MERCY'S MOTHER JABBERED away until nearly midnight, at which point she was taken aback by the hour. She sent her children to bed, and Mercy ascended the stairs numbly. Not a soul spoke to her as she changed into her pajamas and brushed her teeth.

One floor down, however, she could hear her parents bickering. Her mother was nagging her partner for not being welcoming. Her father suggested the mood was ruined by Mercy rather than him, but she kept arguing, her voice rising as her temper flared.

"There's something wrong with Mercy," he finally barked. "For fuck's sake, Beth, can't you see it? She's always in a foul mood. All she wants to do is run from responsibility and live her party-centric life. She's using drugs or something."

"*Something*?"

"You know what alternative I'm implying. Don't make me say it again."

Mercy rolled her eyes and approached her old bedroom. As she reached for the knob, a chill tore through her. She took a deep breath, opened the door, and snaked behind it quickly, taking care to lock it before she turned to face the room.

As she suspected, there was someone in the bed, reclining with one leg bent and the other propped atop it. His eyes were closed, but a sly smile broke across his face.

"Welcome home, Mercy, dear."

"Levi."

At the sound of her voice, he rolled onto his side and gazed at her. "It's been a while. Far too long for my own liking, personally."

"What are you doing here?"

"I own you, darling. You forgot to tell me that you were coming into town."

"You don't own me."

"I do, in fact," he said. "I made you. You're a scion."

Against her better judgment, Mercy impulsively reached up to touch her neck. She'd had a pulse when she met Levi. Now, there was none.

"I thought so," he mused. "You're getting hungry, aren't you? Staying with your family brings it out."

Mercy's back instantly bristled. "What do you mean? I haven't felt hungry all day."

"Your eyes are dull, darling. You're tired. They take all your energy. They're the real vampires, don't you think? They feed on you. You're not a monster until they drag the monster out of you. I see it all over your face. You're struggling to keep it in."

Mercy dropped to her knees and covered her face. It was all she could do to not scream in frustration. She knew she risked encountering Levi if she came back home, but she longed to bask in the once-cherished bond of family every so often. This was her first time in town in over a year, but he'd surely sensed her as soon as the Greyhound rolled over the border.

"The only monster here is you, Levi."

He moved with soundless grace and pulled her to her feet. "Now that's not fair, love. I'm a perfect gentleman. I only turned you because you asked. Remember?"

"I was young and dumb then."

"...And because you know how I feel about you." He gazed at her with red-hued eyes, then snaked an arm around her shoulders and pulled her into an embrace. "I'll take good care of you now that you're home. You should rest."

Levi's voice trailed off as he pulled back.

"And you're planning on staying the night?" she demanded, with no hint of uncertainty or doubt.

"Of course. It's been over a year, right? That's mere moments in my long life, but it has been rather lonely."

Mercy got up and moved to the bed, pulling the covers back and settling in. "Don't you dare come near me. I'll kill you if you touch me again."

As if to challenge her, he approached and tucked the blanket around her. "You're adorable. So fiery. Again, Mercy, I'll remind you: I own you. I'll sleep on the floor, as any owner would sacrifice comfort for their sick pet. You're sick, darling. Pretending you're something you're not isn't healthy."

Mercy stared at him coldly. He was handsome, but he was also a killer. He had dark hair and dark eyes, and had at first seemed mysterious. Levi had a faded accent, the remnants of which were barely noticeable. He intrigued her when she was young. Now, he was nothing more than a burden. She hated his stupid curly hair and the way his beard and mustache shifted when he smirked.

Levi had a devastating glimmer in his eyes as he gazed down at her. "They can't understand you, Mercy. You're not like them anymore. Once they realize you're dead, they'll distance themselves. I've seen it happen, dear, but you're not alone. I'm always here for you, and nobody will ever be able to love you as I do."

Mercy hated him. She couldn't act against him, though. In the vampire world, those who are turned are often in the debt of their sire – the vampire who made them. Oftentimes, that debt turns them into servants, more or less. A strong vampire could create an entire coven of underlings. Sometimes, though, a vampire might turn a human because they're destined soulmates. That was what Levi insisted – they were destined to be together, and he'd known as soon as they met. Once she asked for immortality, he'd been far too eager to give it... he was lonely, he'd said.

She didn't understand that he expected *eternal* companionship.

She'd found that to be rather in the vein of Lestat de Lioncourt. Lonely, pathetic, insane. She would never have willingly accepted immortality if she knew it would bind them together as it had. After all, she didn't believe in love at first sight, soulmates, or anything of the like. At the time, he was attractive, and she wanted immortality. That was enough for her.

Mercy had initially left with his permission. Levi gave her his blessing to explore the world, to build a career. Her wanderlust wouldn't last, he insisted. As soon as she settled into her new place, she understood why – she could hear him calling. In the dead of night, his voice would drift to her. He'd call her home every week or so. As she resisted his call, it became more desperate and more frequent.

Eventually, she came. It was near Easter, so she visited him briefly just to silence his persistent calls, then headed to stay with her family. He expected her to come back. Mercy returned home to New York.

For the past year or so, he'd speak to her every day. She never so much as picked up the phone to call him, but she couldn't escape his eternal presence. Levi owned her. He'd made sure she couldn't go far.

There are a few ways to break the hold that a master vampire has over their creations; one way is to kill them (Levi was far too powerful to be easily taken down), another is to have them personally give you your freedom (which Levi would never do), and the last was to become their equal, and that was achieved by time and companionship (yuck). Levi – crazy, ancient Levi – never stopped hoping that Mercy would love him. He said that in all his years, he'd never felt for anyone what he felt for her.

Bull*shit*.

Staring up at him, she felt like she'd never escape. But she could force some distance between them.

"Go home, Levi."

"I'm home when I'm with you, Mercy."

"Oh, just fuck off already," she muttered. "Get out of here so I can get some decent sleep."

He left through the window, and peace on earth seemed possible in the blissful silence following his departure.

VAMPIRES HATE MORNINGS for a good reason – they're smart and prefer to sleep in. Mercy had never been a morning person, but her aversion to early hours grew far worse as vampirism aged her.

"Mercy, Mom made breakfast!"

Too early. Too much sun. Too much sunshiny sister.

The door opened. "Mercy!"

She sat up. "Mary Olive, can you not see that I'm trying to sleep?"

"You can't sleep in on Christmas!" she exclaimed. "Don't be ridiculous, night owl! Mom and Dad are already eating and aren't happy that you don't want to join them."

Mercy stretched groggily. "Mornings suck."

"Yeah. So does Mom's cooking, but we'll both pretend to like it. Look, sis, we only have to do this one day a year. Believe it or not, I don't want to be in this passive-aggressive Hell either. But I ignore their jabs and comments for the sake of tradition... and because I want to spend time with you."

"Really?"

Mary crept into the room and sat at the foot of the bed. She took a deep breath. "Yeah. You know something? I brag to all my friends about you. You've done so much with your life. I know I'm a lot younger than you, and I know our town is uncool, but I always love spending time with you. I look forward to that more than anything else."

Mercy smiled slowly. "Truth be told, me too. I'm glad I never have to face this alone."

"Think you can manage a smile at breakfast?"

"Yeah, I'll try."

Mercy was, at the very least, comforted by the abundance of cloud cover as they entered the window-filled kitchen. Their parents were already eating when they arrived, and Mary dug into her meal ravenously. She was stick-thin, so Mercy understood the hunger. Mercy politely ate a pancake, even though the taste of most food sickened her nowadays.

As Levi had mentioned just a night before, she was *hungry*. She needed real nutrients.

Mom swallowed her pancake and brushed her hair from her face. "Dear, did you get holy water for our Christmas blessing?"

"Yes," Dad said. "We'll do the blessing before we open gifts."

Mercy frowned. She'd touched holy water just once, curious to see what it felt like. It burned. "I respectfully decline from your blessing. I'm Buddhist."

Mary frowned. "Since when?"

Since I needed to save my skin. "A couple years. More diversity and opportunity to learn in New York, ya know?"

Her father's eyes bored into her. "Why are you celebrating Christmas, then?"

Mercy had to breathe deeply to keep her eyes from turning red. It was hard when she was hungry. "Mom insisted that I come this year."

"Thank goodness you did!" Mary exclaimed.

Breakfast concluded, and a blessing commenced. Mercy watched from the sidelines patiently, then eagerly engaged in the merrymaking as they opened presents.

When all was said and done, Mary and Mom retreated to the den for cheesy Hallmark movies. Mary, though sunshiny and enthusiastic, shot Mercy a look that revealed her exasperation. Mercy sympathized, but clutched a novel gratefully as the ladies left. She curled up by the fire while her father situated himself nearby with a magazine.

After a few chapters of blissful silence, Dad cleared his throat. "Mercy..."

"Yes?" She dog-eared a page and closed her book, meeting his gaze with unwavering confidence.

"Don't think I haven't noticed. You haven't aged."

Mercy, bored, tapped the cover of her book. "Storytelling and Botox, pop. Keeps me young and effervescent."

"You're a vampire," he nearly choked. It hurt him to say it, Mercy realized.

Despite her initial irritation, she laughed. "Vampires are fictional, Dad. They live in stories, not reality."

He took a deep breath. He suddenly cast a cup toward Mercy, who was mercilessly splashed with holy water. She screamed as her skin sizzled and scorched. Then it began to heal, and in half a minute, she was completely unmarked. Dad narrowed his eyes as her mother appeared in the room to check in on the ruckus.

"I'd recommend that you leave soon," he said. "Pack your bags. It would be best if you didn't come back."

"I thought it would be safest if I stayed away, but Mary and Mom keep bringing me back."

"If you really loved them, you would leave them behind."

"Honey!" Mom chastised. "Don't be cruel. Mercy may be Buddhist now, but she's – "

"She's not our daughter anymore," he spat. "Our daughter is dead, Beth. That *thing* is a shell of its former self."

Mom shrunk back as his face turned red and his jaw clenched. Though not a naturally empathetic person, she stepped toward him. Mercy watched her mother's features twist with frustration as she attempted to protest.

"Holy water burns her!" He reached for another cup to demonstrate, but Mercy stood.

"Don't," she whispered. "I'll pack."

"But honey – "

"Mom," she said. "Please. He's right. I should go."

As Mercy departed, she turned to gaze at her father with fury. Her eyes were red now, she knew, and the look on her parents' faces said everything she needed to hear.

Mercy ascended the stairs with a jacket slung over her shoulder, then marched toward her old bedroom to pack. The bathroom door opened, revealing a tear-streaked face that stared out at her with wide eyes. Mercy felt her frustration wane, and her eyes must have faded back to blue. Mary cautiously stepped into the hallway.

"I heard. Oh, Mercy! You won't really leave us, will you?"

"I have to." Mercy closed her eyes. "He asked me to leave, Mary. This is his house. I can't stay if I'm unwanted, just as I can't enter a house without permission. I must go."

"Don't!" Mary protested. "You can't leave on Christmas!"

"I have no choice."

"You'll come back," she almost pleaded. "Please say you'll be back. Call me and keep in touch."

"I will," Mercy promised. "Tell anyone that asks that I had to address an issue with my publisher."

Mary wiped tears from her face. "And you're... you're really a vampire?"

"Yep. For eight years or so now. Nearly nine."

Mary's eyes wandered past her to the windows. "It's an absolute blizzard out there. Where will you go? I can take you back to my house."

While Mercy and her sister were getting along, being stuck in Mary's house felt more hellish than their childhood home. Mercy shook her head.

"I'll be okay, sis. I have a... *friend* I can lean on for support."

Mercy walked to her old bedroom and opened the door. Of course, said "friend" was seated inside reading a novel that she had written. Mary's footsteps faltered behind her sister as she tiptoed up.

"Levi?"

Mercy sighed. "Tell me you don't know this man."

"He owns the café I work at."

Levi marked the page he was reading and stood gracefully. "Hello, Mary. Merry Christmas, it's good to see you! It seems, Mercy, that we'll be spending this holiday together. It's long overdue if you ask me."

"I hate to say it, but you were right. They loved Mercy Mild, but I'm not the same innocent girl I was. Who could ever love a vampire?"

His gaze answered her question, which made her stomach churn. "I could. I will always love you and everything you are, beautiful Mercy."

"Aw!" said Mary. Sweet, clueless Mary.

Levi, always the gentleman, helped Mercy put on her coat. Mary gave her a sad smile as she retrieved her purse.

"Ready, my love?"

Mercy nodded.

He took her hand, and the pair retreated through the window. Mary waved, then mimed a telephone and mouthed, "call me." Mercy waved back.

Levi pulled her close as the icy wind whipped around them and plunged into her skin like needles. They withdrew to his vehicle, where they departed without exchanging a single word, enveloped in a heavy silence.

When they finally arrived at their destination, it turned out to be a massive Colonial. The interior, Mercy would soon find, was warm and homey. This was thanks in part to a fire, which was already blazing in the fireplace. Levi eagerly drew an oversized pillow close and patted it. Mercy settled beside him, taking in the glittering wealth of the surroundings with wide eyes.

"This is stunning."

"It has been rather cozy for the past few centuries," he said. "It's yours now, my love. I will give you anything and everything if only you'll stay."

His eyes were full of an emotion that Mercy had never seen before: raw passion. She had seen the faded remnants of past romance in the eyes of many adults, and she'd encountered lust firsthand in the horrid halls of her university. This, though, was raw, barefaced adoration.

Mercy leaned into him, resting her head against his chest where a heart would have been beating. She gazed up at him, then arched her neck for a kiss.

She'd grow stronger, she reasoned, and she might even learn a thing or two about his weaknesses during her stay.

She hoped *desperately* that she'd learn of weaknesses, because she planned to kill him. As soon as she did, there would be peace on earth for Mercy Mild Harker.

Chapter Two

Mercy had attended a party back in the day – perhaps a decade ago, she thought. Maybe just over nine years back. There was a community college in town, albeit a small one, and some local kids threw a party. Her first rager.

That was where she met him.

He was sitting in the corner, sipping a drink, taking in the activity with sparkling eyes. Mercy had been abandoned by Kaitlyn, her best friend at the time, and found herself people-watching, just like him.

Levi had approached her with sparkling dark eyes, and she was taken aback by his beauty – his skin was flawless, his eyes deep and complex though brown, and his lips were perfectly smooth and full. Mercy, a self-professed Chapstick addict, couldn't imagine a life without chapped lips.

As time would tell, Kaitlyn had snuck off for a boy, which ultimately ended their friendship. Mercy felt betrayed that her friend abandoned her while she was drunk and vulnerable. Kaitlyn had argued that "nothing went wrong," and she couldn't imagine why Mercy was accusing her of endangering a friend.

Ironically, Kaitlyn's absence had endangered Mercy, but she wasn't immediately aware of the peril. Levi drove her home that night and left her with his phone number. He told her to call him.

She did. She didn't particularly *want* to, but she felt compelled to follow his instruction.

Within a few weeks, maybe months, he'd brought her up to speed on his condition. Mercy found herself asking for immortality.

She didn't particularly want that, either. She did, to a degree, but she wasn't exactly ready to ask for it.

It had taken a lot of strength to stay away since she'd last left. Levi's influence never waned. Now that she was back, he didn't want her to leave. *She* suspiciously didn't want to go. Mercy knew she did, however.

She had to keep reminding herself of that. *I am not here by choice. Don't believe him.* She knew he was in her head, just like he always was. Everything was confusing. It all felt oddly cyclical – he called, she came, he tried to lure her into staying. She'd consider staying, though she didn't *want* to. They'd likely do this artful dance through the final stretch of eternity.

Mercy shook the thought away and eyed the closet distastefully before selecting a black polo shirt. She pulled her hair up, using her camera as a mirror, and frowned when Levi appeared in the space behind her.

"Mercy, please. It's the day after Christmas. Must you work?"

"It's just a quick conference call, Levi. My agent is off until after New Year's and wants an update on this book before she unplugs. It won't be long."

He slinked up beside her, so she pivoted to face him. He took her hands in his, stepping back to extend their arms out long in the space between them. "It's been two years since you stayed with me, Mercy. I want a few uninterrupted days, just the two of us."

She pulled her arms back and crossed them, attempting to close herself off to his influence. "I know, Levi. My career comes first. That's why I left in the first place."

His face fell. "And what will you do when you don't *age*? You can't keep publishing forever."

"Pen names exist," she said as she turned her face toward the flashing computer screen. "Crap, Ann is calling. Go away. Please."

Levi stepped back, escaping the view of the camera but refusing to leave. Mercy glared at him before she accepted the call and turned her camera on. "Ann! Good to see you. How was your holiday?"

On the screen, a pixelated Ann adjusted her blonde bun. "We can skip the formalities, Harker. Tell me about the draft. How's it coming?"

Mercy shifted. "The working title is *Water Wars in the Wild West*. In a mining town where the landscape has been changed dramatically in a short time by workers, flooding is a new problem. Clean water is suddenly more valuable than gold, and one man – Wager Watkins – has an idea to harvest it. And he knows where to get the funding: the head of Shaft Town Saloon, the brothel that built the town, is willing to help him in exchange for joint ownership of his business."

"A lot of W's in that story." Ann leaned back and studied Mercy thoughtfully. "Water Wars in Wager Watkins' Wild West. Damn. So, it's a historical fiction?"

"Not exactly," Mercy admitted. "It's slightly goofy so far. The tone is modern in many respects. Silly. It's a serious story, but it doesn't take itself seriously."

"A cowboy romance, then?"

"When have I ever written romance, Ann?"

Ann nodded. "Alright, that's fair. At least it's an original idea. Get me your work-in-progress before my flight takes off this afternoon so I can skim it over. I'll connect with some editors and shop around to find a fit when I get back."

"Okay," Mercy offered. "Have a good trip."

"Don't let me down with this one, Mercy. I can't take another retelling of a Greek myth. Artemis and her vrykolakas friends still haunt my nightmares, and not because *they* were scary. Enjoy the rest of your day."

The call ended. Mercy closed her laptop, then put her head down with a defeated sigh.

Levi stepped forward, cautious in tone and body language. "I was there, you know."

"I know, you didn't leave the fucking room."

"Not in your call," he said. "In the Wild West, as you called it. A lot of vermin on the frontier. I didn't particularly like that. The brothels were nice, though. You might not expect that, but they really *did* build up towns, as you mentioned. Whether or not you came for the girls, it was a clean place to grab a drink, usually. But, like I said, vermin were a problem. They're ultimately why I came back East."

Mercy lifted her head. "You know, maybe you can help. Want to talk through a few plot points with me?"

A SOFT CRUNCHING BOUNCED through the still, chilly air as their feet scraped across well-trampled snow. Mercy shot an uncomfortable look at Levi, whose arm was intertwined with hers.

"So that was the biggest tree in Connecticut this year. I wish we'd seen it before the holiday. Next year, perhaps."

Mercy pulled her scarf tighter around her neck and adjusted her sunglasses. "Maybe next time I'm in town. But it won't be anytime soon."

He stopped walking and turned to face her. Red and green string lights illuminated features etched with concern. "Mercy..."

She met his gaze and lifted her chin. "Please stop trying to make future plans with me, especially here. I left my hometown for a reason. If I don't have an obligation to see my parents, I don't really plan on coming back."

"But Roxbury isn't – "

"It's right around the corner. Come on. Being here isn't necessarily awakening pleasant memories for me. I'm not interested in coming back on any regular cadence."

His look softened. "I understand, and I'd happily follow you anywhere. But I've lived here for nearly three hundred years, darling. I don't want to leave."

"Then don't," she said gently.

He ran his eyes over her face. "This isn't about disliking small-town life, is it? It's about me. You don't want to stay with me, here or anywhere else."

"No, I'd say it's about both."

He sighed resignedly and trapezed forward, dragging his feet across the hardened snow.

Follow me, Mercy. You must. You're mine.

At the sound of his voice in her mind, Mercy inched after him, scowling at herself for giving in so easily. As she fell into stride, she ran her eyes over him. "I'm not trying to hurt you, Levi, but... It's nothing personal, exactly. I just don't want this. But you have this hold over my mind, and... Who am I kidding? You know what you're doing. Just set me free, dude. It's what I want."

When his eyes met hers, they were a rich textured scarlet, almost reminiscent of a carnation petal. "This isn't just a tradition thing, Mercy. Scions aren't allowed to run amuck unsupervised for good reason. I've already given you much freedom, which you don't seem particularly grateful for."

"*Freedom*?" she demanded. "Your voice follows me everywhere I go. I don't know how you do it, but it's unsettling. That's not freedom."

He raised his eyebrows and was quiet for a moment, deeply pondering that statement. "I don't have that power, Mercy. You know my power – control. That's the extent of what I can do. I'm sorry to say, but that voice is a figment of your imagination."

"Powers? Vampires have *powers*? I thought most sires could just influence their scions!"

His eyes faded back to brown before he laughed. "You're joking, right? After all these years, you haven't figured it out? That alone shows me that you still need guidance. You have powers, too, love."

Mercy blinked. She opened her mouth, about to ask what he meant, but decided against it. She feared it was something obvious, like her incredible balance, or perhaps something she'd never dare try, like necromancy.

"You're a cloud maker, Mercy. The storm formed as soon as you crossed into Connecticut. That's how I knew where to find you. You always cause storms when you return to that home."

Mercy looked up to the now-clear sky in amazement. She was skeptical, of course, but... Before she found success as an author, she remembered that it would rain when she was running late to work. It would snow when friends bailed on her. One time, it flooded after an especially embarrassing date. That was the day she learned that rats can swim.

"You have so much to learn," he said. "Like I said, you can't keep pretending you're human. You're not, Mercy. Stay for a while. Learn from me. You might decide to make your stay more permanent. After all, the sun is out."

"How do I know you're not using your powers right now?"

"You don't." A slow, intentional smile bloomed across his face. "But that makes it fun for you, doesn't it? I know, but you get to guess every time. It's like a game."

"You're *actually* insane."

⁓ ❧ ⁓

MERCY OPENED HER NOTEBOOK and touched a pen to the page.

"You're not actually taking notes, are you?"

"No," she lied. "I'm just... jotting some stuff down. Okay, weather. I'll think about that one, though I still don't believe you."

Levi smiled patiently. "You don't have to believe me. But you won't learn to control it until you do. Now, what can I answer for you?"

Mercy tapped her lip with the pen and leaned back contemplatively. "How about this one – why am I so pale while you still look flushed and not dead?"

He chuckled and walked to the window, looking out at the snow-covered landscape with amusement. "Because I was darker in life, love. Some of my ancestors were from the Umayyad Empire, though just through one grandparent. My skin tone suited me well in the Mediterranean climate."

"You're... Italian, right?"

"Spanish," he said, turning to face her. "I'm many things now, I suppose. Lived in many places. But I was born in Spain in 1469."

"And the Umayyad Empire was..."

He scratched his chin. "Countries, I'm so bad with those. They're always changing. Um, the Northern tip of Africa into modern day Turkey, I think. Following the Spanish conquest, ethnic groups settled and stayed in their own communities, for the most part. After a few hundred years, one couple broke away and assimilated into a melting pot of a city. Their son married a Jew – those two were my paternal grandparents. I was raised Sephardic."

Mercy tilted her head. "Why didn't you tell me this before?"

"You never asked." He shifted to lean against the window's frame, allowing him to peek out at the landscape between glances at her. "Besides, I thought you wanted to learn about vampirism rather than me. After all this time, you *should*."

"Okay. When were you turned, then?"

He chuckled and shook his head. "Two birds with one stone, I suppose. Things grew hostile when the Catholic Monarchs took over." He paused, then cocked an eyebrow. "Wait, you were raised Catholic, right?"

"I was. Why?"

"I'll refrain from slurs, then," he said with a guarded smile. "The Catholics didn't like us, though our Islamic neighbors considered us to be People of the Book. When their *Decreto de la Alhambra* came, we suddenly had to leave."

"Why?"

"Religious wars. Stupid, silly human things. But horrible things were unfolding in our own backyard, so we were on the run when I was turned."

Mercy closed her notebook and leaned forward. "We? Who is *we*?"

He pursed his lips. "My family, Mercy. My wife and kids. Those three became meals. I don't know why our attackers chose to sire me, but... they abandoned me and left me in the carnage of my loved ones."

Mercy didn't know what to say to that. "Thank you for at least making my experience feel like a choice."

"It was a choice. Is this why you were running from me? Do you really believe I coerced you into making that choice?"

"I do, Levi. I remember that I didn't particularly *want* this, and yet I asked."

"You know what I think?" He slowly paced toward her, sauntering with each ragged step. "We're soulmates, darling. You were scared because – I mean, vampirism is a scary commitment, but – you *knew* you wanted to be with me. You were so certain for the first time in your life that it *terrified* you. You're a writer. You're just inventing a story right now to justify your running."

"I am certain I do not want to be with you."

"You've never stayed for more than a day or two," he said. "Stay this time, Mercy. You'll understand then. At the very least... you're hungry. You shouldn't travel in this state."

"Then let me hunt."

"We'll get blood," he promised. "Tomorrow. Until then..."

Levi moved to a bookshelf, picked up something small and metallic, and then flicked it, revealing it as a pocket knife. He drew it down the side of his neck.

Mercy felt her fangs protract, brushing against her lower lip with startling sharpness. Almost hypnotized, she inched toward the edge of her chair as she stared at the red stream dancing down his neck.

"Hurry, before this heals."

"Levi, no. There's so little iron in our blood, it wouldn't satiate me." Nevertheless, Mercy was transfixed by the blood's siren song. She found herself rising to her feet and creeping forward.

As she approached Levi, he opened his arms. She melted into him, wincing as her tongue flicked past her lips. She could taste the blood in the air. Against her better judgment, Mercy stood on her tiptoes and sunk her fangs into his neck.

MERCY SHIVERED AS THE bells on the shop door jingled – Café au Levi was never her favorite place, even before she'd met Levi. It was rather cottagecore, full of plants and sparkling surfaces yet seemingly eternally dusty. Cobwebs clung to the shiplap ceiling. The blonde behind the cash register turned to face them, and her face lit up.

Mary Olive.

Mercy's sister rushed over to scoop her in a hug. "Mercy! I'm so glad you're still in town. Are you okay?"

"I've kept her safe," Levi promised, patting his employee on the shoulder. "I always will. I'm proud of you for standing by her, dear. We don't all have people who continue to support us after things change."

Mary smiled at him warmly, then returned her eyes to her sister. "How long are you staying in town? We should get drinks or something."

"I..." Mercy hesitated when her sister's smile dimmed. "Sure, sis. I'll text you."

"Mary," Levi commanded. The power in his voice – his *mind control* tone, Mercy had learned – caused Mary to snap her head in his direction. "Show your sister where the clean aprons are. You can stay in the kitchen and bake for a bit. We'll run the register."

"I am *not* free labor," Mercy protested, which earned her a glare from the older vampire. She recoiled at his coarseness as her sister grabbed her hand and dragged her toward the back. Though she knew Levi could likely still hear them, she dropped her voice and leaned close to Mary Olive. "He's controlling your mind, you know."

"He's certainly persuasive," Mary Olive said as she inched toward a coat rack and picked up a green apron. She offered it to her sister with a smirk. "Handsome, too. How long have you been seeing him?"

"I'm *not*, Mary."

She blinked. "But he said he loves you."

"Yeah, he does that."

"So he just... professes his love to you? Regularly, and despite it being unrequited?"

Mercy nodded as she pulled the apron on and fastened it around her waist. Mary studied her before making her way to the baking station. With a graceful motion, she reached for the flour and delicately sprinkled it over the counter.

"Why do you hang out with him then, Mercy? That's weird as Hell."

Mercy hovered behind her sister for a moment before she shrugged. "I don't. Not really. But I'm a scion – I'm not, like, a mature vampire. Until I am, he's sort of responsible for me, to a degree. And for the record, I'll also point out that he's probably listening to our conversation. I've noticed that he has heightened hearing."

Mary Olive shivered. "Okay. I'm still confused about the frequent expressions of love, but I guess I'll settle on not understanding vampire culture as an explanation."

"Honestly, Mary, I can't say I understand that one, either. But I do think I have to stay for a little while longer... I've learned quite a bit this time, and I think I should learn it sooner rather than later. I need just a few more days. And I *desperately* need to feed before I can confine myself to a bus ride full of people for hours on end."

"So the sex must be pretty good, then." At Mercy's glare, Mary laughed. "Come *on*, sis. Don't give me that look. I wouldn't have guessed vampires can get hickies. How does that work?"

Resignedly, Mercy reached around her back and adjusted the apron's tie. "I need iron for DNA synthesis, and I need amino acids to repair my tissue and heal. Or so I've heard. I haven't eaten in a while, so I'm not exactly healing. The older vamps don't have an issue with that."

"How often do you, uh, eat?"

"It depends on how much I drink," she said. "A pint can keep me going for a month or so – I burn about eight milligrams a day sustaining my body, so you do the math. More is better, obviously, but we don't *have* to feed often."

"And... the last time you ate, Mercy?"

"Five weeks ago." Mercy turned her back to her sister. Her eyes were red, she knew. Thinking about it made her hunger feel unbearable. "The weather was bad leading up to Christmas, so I didn't get a chance to get more before I came. I better go keep Levi company."

"Wait," Mary said. "I'm still trying to wrap my head around this. So you're sleeping with him, but not seeing him? And you don't *like* him?"

Mercy sighed. "I mean, I find him attractive. I like him, at least a little. He's just... he's *obsessed*, Mary Olive. I don't believe in that old trope – an ancient immortal falls in love with some young human, he turns her, and they live happily ever after. That's weird as Hell. It's not normal. His obsession is out of line and unacceptable."

"Have you asked him why he's obsessed?"

"He thinks we're soulmates." Mercy bit her lip when her sister shifted to glance over her shoulder and cock an eyebrow at her. "I know, I'm a bad person for leading him on. But I've been perfectly clear about where I stand – his love is unrequited. He knows I'm not interested."

Mary tilted her head. "For what it's worth, I like Levi. And I believe in soulmates."

"I don't." Mercy shifted toward the door. "I'll see ya later, sis."

Mary didn't even say goodbye as her sister left the back room. When Mercy pushed past the swing door, Levi turned to look at her expectantly. He met her gaze and lifted his chin, so she approached without faltering.

When she came to stand beside the register, he studied her for a long, silent moment.

"You're my trainee," Levi finally said. "Play the part. I'm going to show you something. See that building across the street?"

"The hospital?"

He nodded. "Wait until a worker comes over alone. It happens all morning – they trickle in on lunch breaks, sometimes to grab group orders for the nurses on their floor. You've found ways to hunt, I know, but allow me to show you an easy way to stock up. Keep in mind that blood only keeps for about a month before it loses its flavor, and we don't know how old their samples are. It's a gamble, but an easy one to make."

"Are you saying you steal from *hospitals*, Levi? That doesn't sound ethical."

He shook his head. "You're not human, Mercy. It would do you well to remember that."

"It would do *you* well to remember that my sister is in the room behind us. Whether I'm human or not, people I love are. Before you turned me, you could have said the same thing."

He tightened his jaw, causing his mustache to flatten from an arc into a straight line. "I concede – you're right. We won't make a habit of this, love."

Soon, someone came in – a doctor, if the formal dress was any indication – and approached the register. After he ordered a large caramel macchiato and paid, Levi leaned forward and met his gaze as he returned the debit card. "Tell me when your shift ends."

"Two more hours," the doctor said. "I'm on break right now."

"Here's a free tote." Levi had that tone in his voice – the one that scared Mercy. You *had* to follow his direction when he used that tone. "Place two bags of whole blood in here when your shift ends. Make sure nobody can see you doing it. Bring your haul back here and return it to me, then forget about this whole encounter. Tell no one in the meantime."

He moved to make the macchiato. Mercy stared at his back with wide eyes, then trailed him in awe. "It's really that easy, is it?"

Levi grinned at her as he put the lid on the drink and met the doctor's gaze again. "Have a great day. I'll see you soon."

The doctor wished him well, and as he retreated, Mercy leaned against the counter. "So now we have blood."

"*I* have blood," he said. "Just under two pints, if I'm lucky. If one bag is bad, I pray the other is fresh enough to sustain me until I hunt or get more. Now, it's your turn. I see a nurse coming. Command him, Mercy."

She blinked. "I don't have your power, Levi!"

"To the contrary," he said with a wink. "You consumed my blood just last night. You'd be surprised what that can do. Give it a try."

Mercy gulped as the nurse opened the door, the musical twinkling of bells announcing his presence. With each step he took toward the register, Mercy swore her heart might jump back to life and start pounding in her chest.

As per usual, however, her heart stayed motionless.

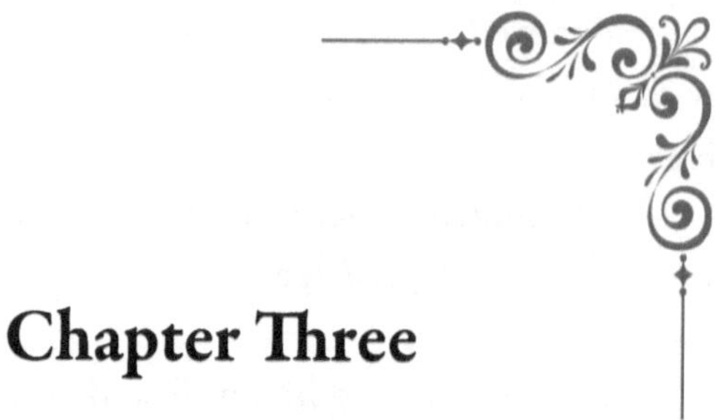

Chapter Three

Mercy cradled the chalice, eyeing its emerald insets curiously. Knowing Levi, it was equally as likely to be a prop or the real deal.

They'd been successful in this haul. All four bags contained relatively new blood samples, meaning there was plenty to keep them sustained. Levi advised they take it slow, though. Savor it.

Blood had to be heated on the stove, and he used a digital thermometer to gauge its readiness. Once it was close to feverish levels, he ladled it into their cups. Now, they were sitting across from each other at a vast mahogany table.

"So that was your first lesson," Mercy said. "And one you knew I wouldn't learn on my own."

"It's hard to learn on your own," he said, lowering the chalice from his lips. He wiped his sleeve across his mouth. "Not all of us *get* gifts, and those who have them rarely advertise it. And assuming you do consume a vampire's blood, the odds of you deciding to test weather manipulation or calling a swarm of bats on a whim is low. The effects are temporary, too, but it's a skill you should know you have. We all have it."

Mercy sipped her drink and stared down into the ruby redness with fascination. In the chalice, the fluid looked almost like wine – it was thicker, however, and nearly syrupy in its consistency. "How is that possible, Levi?"

He shrugged. "Scientific study around our kind is a rarity, my dear. We're reclusive creatures, and for good reason. I've seen persecution time and time again, and I'm not interested in being a victim ever again. But the theory I've heard is that some of us produce more of certain types of proteins, ultimately influencing which, if any, special skills we acquire. When you consume blood from those vampires, your body temporarily has a boosted supply of those proteins until they're used up. I mean, we're supernatural, though, so who knows. Could just as easily be a blessing from the Devil himself."

She studied him. "How did you learn this?"

"I found a coven when I was young," he said. "The elders taught us a lot. They often took blood from us fledglings to acquire *all* our powers. It helped them keep charge but also educate us. And it protected them from beings like me who can control minds."

"What do you mean by that?"

He leaned forward. "For the time being, Mercy, you're immune to my influence. And you have been since you consumed my blood."

Mercy downed the rest of her drink, which made Levi smirk patiently as she wiped her mouth. "I'm well-fed now, so I won't be making a habit of that."

His lips stretched into a full smile, revealing two pearly fangs. His red-hued gaze ran over her face before landing on her lips, and then he leaned forward and kissed her very softly. "You might surprise yourself, dear. I think with time, you'll find that keeping me company is your favorite habit."

She lifted her chin as she held his gaze. "What makes you think we're soulmates, Levi?"

That question caught him off guard. Levi looked surprised, but he slowly lifted his chalice, took a drink, and cleared his throat. "When I look in the mirror, I see myself. I know myself intrinsically; I've been this man for a very long time. Looking at you, Mercy, is like looking in a mirror."

"I look like a man to you?"

He threw his head back and laughed. "Not at all, love. You're beautiful. But I recognize myself in you. I see it all around you – you complete me. I've waited a very long time to be complete, which is why it drives me crazy to have you living so far away. I'm incomplete without you."

"I'm already complete."

"I know you are, love. But you'll eventually realize we belong together. And I'll be patient with you until then."

Mercy stood and walked the chalice to the sink. As she washed it out, she could feel his eyes boring into her back. "I think you should temper your expectations, Levi."

"I simply cannot. You're mine, darling, and you always will be."

She set the chalice on a drying rack and turned to face him. "And I have no say in the matter?"

He was solemn as he met her gaze, but then he looked away and chuckled. "I regret to say that neither of us do. It is what it is, love."

"I disagree," Mercy stated. "You've chosen to believe this shit, Levi. Stay out of my head in the meantime, or I'll make you a habit, and I'll make you come to regret that."

Levi laughed again. "I adore your fire, Mercy Mild, but I'm not *in* your head. I told you – I don't have that power."

MERCY KNEW HE WAS LYING. His voice in her head wasn't a figment of her imagination. After she drank his blood, his silent commands didn't consume her thoughts. There was blissful silence at all times of the day.

Then, after another day of peace, she heard it.

Wake up, Mercy. I need you.

It was back, and it *was real*. He'd lied. He could control her, near or far. And if she was distant enough to resist his urging, he could at least consume her thoughts.

"And that's why I have to kill him," Mercy explained.

Mary leaned back in her chair, then thoughtfully picked at her charcuterie board. "Yum, this is delicious. You can still eat cheese, right? You should try some."

"Mary Olive..."

She sighed. "Look, Mercy, I get it. I'd go crazy, too. But, he's nice to me. And I don't really want to be an accomplice."

"You don't need to be," Mercy said. "I just need someone to talk through things with me. Think of it like sisterly therapy hour."

Mary averted her eyes. "Okay, but *killing* him seems extreme, right?"

"He's lived long enough. Over five hundred years... who knows how many people he's entrapped like this? It sucks, sis."

"Damn, five hundred." Mary sipped her wine. "That's quite the sprint. He could have been friends with Chaucer."

Though it didn't satiate her, wine did give Mercy a buzz. She drank greedily, taking a big chug that wasn't quite ladylike, but not quite rude, either. "Chaucer would have died before he was born, but you're in the right era."

"And..." Mary trailed off, then traced the rim of her glass with an almond-shaped acrylic nail. "I mean, Mercy, I just don't see the case for killing him. The mind-voice thing is *weird*, sure, and annoying, I'd bet. But he also showed you how to stop it."

"But that entails..." Mercy dropped her voice. "Drinking his blood. I mean, Mary, come on. Would you want me to drink *your* blood?"

Mary raised a hand to her neck with wide blue eyes. "No, that sounds... intimate? Is that the word I'm looking for?"

Mercy shrugged. "That's a good one for it, yeah. I mean, you saw *my* neck."

"The hickies," she said. "*Right*. I don't understand, Mercy. Why don't you just leave when you're done learning and ignore his voice, as you have been? Like, just put your time in with Yoda until you master the Force. Then you can go off and be a Jedi."

"Because I'll still have a Force ghost watching me sleep, telling me to return to his swamp planet. There are three ways to break his hold over me, I've learned. He can grant me my freedom before I'm a mature vampire, which sires rarely do... They consider themselves responsible for their fledglings. They're supposed to teach us. It's tradition, or a liability, or something. I learned Levi was abandoned and left to fend for himself, so I don't think he'd leave any fledgling vampires he makes."

"Okay," Mary said. "I think I'm tracking. And the other way is killing them, right? What's the last one?"

"I mature out of needing a mentor. I remain under his tutelage and command until I obtain autonomy. Master the Force, in your words. His command can translate to absolutely anything. I will do the most unspeakable things if he demands it – a fledgling vampire shot JFK, you know."

She snorted. "*That* I don't believe. You learned that from him? Or in New York?"

"In the city. There's a lot of us out there. But we can always learn more from our sires... like weaknesses our more experienced contemporaries wouldn't dare reveal. I just need him to trust me enough to open up about that." Mercy took another sip of wine and cleared her throat. "You're taking this all suspiciously well, Mary."

Mary shrugged, letting a nervous chuckle escape. "Dad's been saying it for years, you know. I thought it sounded crazy, but I figured if there *was* any truth to it... well, you're the same old Mercy. And you've always been aspirational. I'm rooting for you, in a weird *I hope you don't kill him and find peace, but I also accept I can't stop you* kinda way."

"I won't find peace, Mary. He's made it more than clear that he won't let me go. I feel trapped."

Mary studied her sympathetically. "I'm sorry, sis. You don't deserve that. But, I have to say... you and I have such different perceptions of Levi. I mean, he's kind of a weenie. Like, this is the guy I watched experiment with blueberry cookie recipes for two months last summer. I just can't see him as this monster you're painting him as."

"That's what the families of serial killers always say," Mercy stated. "They never see it until it's too late. I see through him. And that's why I'm gonna get rid of him."

Mary picked up a cube of cheese, studied it, and then slipped it in her mouth. As she chewed thoughtfully, Mercy had to look away. While she needed support, she felt guilty for bringing her sister into this mess. Mary Olive was totally innocent.

I just need to get rid of him, Mercy thought. *Then, I can go home and live a normal life. I'll be free of his influence. I'll be free of this anger.*

I just need to escape.

I KNOW YOU'RE NOT THINKING of leaving, Mercy.

Mercy stared out at the frozen world beyond the window. Freezing rain fell upon the landscape, encapsulating trees and shrubs in ice sculpture-like compositions. She scanned the snow, wishing it was pretty like a snow globe.

Perhaps Levi could help her make the world beautiful. He said she could control the weather... that sounded like bullshit, quite frankly, but she *had* looked a man in the eyes and demanded blood that was soon freely received.

She was starting to doubt her faculties. Nothing that she believed was real necessarily was... but she knew Levi's annoyingly consistent presence was an absolute fact.

Come to me, Mercy. I'm here.

Frustrated, Mercy spun on her heel and marched toward the door. She walked down the stairs and found Levi sitting in the living room. A collection of silver trinkets was spread across the table before him. One was presumably wrapped in the cloth he was toying with, being shined despite already shimmering without an ounce of tarnish.

He lifted his eyes to gaze at her, then smiled mysteriously as she trailed into the room. "I like silver quite a bit. You know by now that it doesn't harm us, nor does it prevent us from having a reflection. Nonetheless, I find the myths amusing. I've collected quite a bit of it over the years."

"Silver is such a silly thing to assume hurts vampires," Mercy said.

"It used to be seen as pure and, therefore, something that could harm or refuse to reflect impure and sinful creatures like ourselves. Humans are superstitious. Always have been."

Mercy settled beside him on the couch, then leaned forward to see what piece he was polishing. He shifted to pull the cloth away from it, showcasing a small silver tree frog statue.

"I like frogs," he explained. "Fascinating little creatures, and they're said to be lucky, too."

"So silver's not a real threat," Mercy said. "And I know that stakes through the heart are a threat because – hey, we still need our hearts to function even though they don't beat."

"Only stakes of acacia wood are a threat, my love," he said. "Whatever this disease is, there's a Biblical element to it. Although, a part of me wonders if acacia isn't just some silly metaphor. The wood is fairly resistant to decay, just like we are. Curious, isn't it?"

Her eyes followed his hands as he leaned forward, set down the tree frog, and scooped up a silver statue of a fly. "What else can hurt us, Levi?"

He lifted the tiny sculpture and studied it. "You ever read *Dracula*?"

Mercy shook her head.

"There's a character," he began, "Renfield. He's compelled by the count, so he sets out to consume life. He eats flies at first but then feeds them to spiders, which he *then* feeds to birds. He eventually consumes the birds, effectively accumulating more life to fuel him. Oddly, that's one myth that has some truth to it. Life that doesn't consume life can't quench you. People with plant-based diets don't make the best snacks."

"The *weaknesses*, Levi," Mercy pressed. "Come on, now. I need to know this for my own protection and longevity."

He tucked a hair behind her ear. "Just avoid stupid situations. You'll be fine, love."

"Why won't you tell me?"

He set the fly back on the table. "You're too young, Mercy. I'm sorry. You've still got at least half a decade as a fledgling, and you need to spend that time *learning*. This knowledge has emboldened fledglings to make dumb decisions, so it's truly not the safest thing to pass on. And you're still so impulsive."

"I am not!"

"You moved two hours away the day I told you to explore the world. And you'd have moved further if I hadn't demanded you stay local. That is *absolutely* impulsive." He met her gaze, then smiled slowly. "Go get us some blood, Mercy."

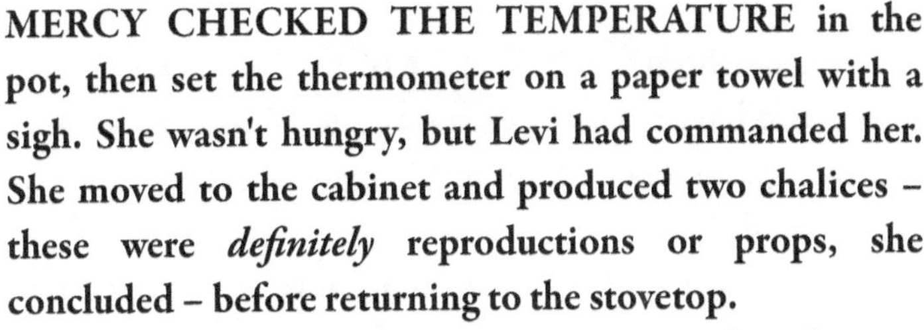

MERCY CHECKED THE TEMPERATURE in the pot, then set the thermometer on a paper towel with a sigh. She wasn't hungry, but Levi had commanded her. She moved to the cabinet and produced two chalices – these were *definitely* reproductions or props, she concluded – before returning to the stovetop.

He won't tell me our weaknesses, Mercy thought. *But perhaps he will tell me his. Vermin. Those are a problem. Perhaps that is a weakness? At the very least, they'll annoy him, which will be funny.*

There was a pet store in town, she recalled. She had walked past it in the Commercial District. Mary would probably love to accompany her on a trip there, and hamsters weren't super expensive.

Mercy double-checked the temperature before turning off the burner. With two servings in hand, she obediently returned to the living room. There, she found that Levi had cleared the table of his knickknacks and was staring out the bay window.

"Ah," he said as he accepted the cup. "Thank you, darling. B-positive."

"Be positive? I'm being as positive as I can be, considering I'd rather be home right now. But you've either convinced me I need to stay and learn from you, or you've subtly commanded me to do so. Hard to find anything but a net negative there."

He lowered the chalice from his lips and licked them. "It's B-positive... the last was O-negative. You opened a different bag."

"Oh."

He set his cup on the ledge of the bookshelf beside him. "You haven't considered staying? Mercy, you live in a tiny apartment out there. Isn't this nicer? More comfortable?"

"Perhaps if I came here of my own accord. I don't know how to explain it to you, Levi – you don't know what it's like being under your spell."

"I won't sugarcoat this, love. When we're young, we're prone to suggestion. And we can easily become weapons. I will not allow a member of my bloodline to fall victim to that fate. *Especially* not someone with such dangerous abilities. I know you don't understand, Mercy, but it's for the best."

Mercy sighed and lifted her chalice. She downed it in thick, greedy chugs, then wiped her mouth on the back of her hand. "So you've done this before?"

"Made others? Yes, I have. You likely will, too, one day. It strengthens us. Like a pyramid scheme, I suppose."

"Jesus Christ," Mercy said. "What a depressing way to boil down my existence. I'm just the newest Avon lady."

Levi laughed. His fangs caught the light as he recovered. "Oh, Mercy. Not at all. The others were made for various reasons – the first was a dying soldier I saved. One was just a man who wanted to keep living, and I thought he had potential. Another was a ballerina whose career was threatening to reach its conclusion if the troubles and toils of age caught her in its grasp. I'm a strong proponent of preserving the arts."

She waited for him to finish his thought before she huffed and looked away. "And I'm your soulmate. I know."

He leaned forward. "How can I possibly convince you that you genuinely *like* me? You did before you changed. As soon as I turned you and told you what my gift was, you grew cold. I understand why you're skeptical, and I understand why you're always running. But I cannot fathom how you will not allow yourself to trust and like me."

Mercy traced the lip of her chalice and looked down at her reflection. Though the image was distorted, she could tell she was flushed. She looked lively. Maybe even alive.

"And I've *told* you how to block my power," he said. "What is the *problem*?"

She cast her eyes across the room, avoiding eye contact even with herself. "The problem is that I *hate* this, Levi. I didn't understand what I was getting into. I don't like being immortal. I should be searching for my first gray hairs and electing to get my tubes tied like a normal almost-thirty-something woman. Sure, I found you charming back then. But now, I look at you and see..."

His face twisted with pain. "You see regret. You're mourning what you thought you might be. Who you thought you might be if you'd never met me. And you're *wishing* you never met me."

Mercy met his gaze for a second, then tore her eyes away.

He scoffed. "Great to know where I stand in your life."

"You're joking, right? I was *running* from you, Levi. You said it yourself. I was running and you understand why."

He turned his back and marched away. "Then go back to New York. I don't care anymore."

MERCY STARED AT THE blank page before her. She moved a single fingernail over her keyboard, then sighed and stood. The words just weren't flowing today.

She closed her laptop and marched into the hallway. She could hear a noise down the hall, so she walked toward it.

As she approached, she heard the melodic hum of a strange instrument. When she found Levi alone in his study, he was cranking a knob on an instrument that looked a bit like a flattened violin. She sat and watched as his hand danced across the fingerboard.

His eyes flashed up at her briefly before returning to his instrument. The tune never faltered.

He finished playing the song before he sighed, rubbed his forehead, and looked up at her. "I thought you were leaving."

"Yeah, well..." Mercy trailed off, then cleared her throat. "Can we talk?"

"It appears we already are."

"Ah, right. So..." She bit her lip. "Sorry for what I said. And for considering killing you."

His eyebrows rose. "You... what?"

"Come on. I think all fledgling vampires have been there."

He chuckled, then moved the instrument to the side. "Yes, I suppose we have. It's unfortunate you were driven to that point."

"You said it before," she muttered. "I'm sick. You were right, Levi. I've been mourning my humanity this whole time and taking my anger out on you. I need to accept what I am, and I understand I need your help to get there. You're my Yoda."

"More like Qui-Gon," he corrected. "I understand, though. I was... over half a decade, I think, into my condition before I sought a coven. It takes time to adjust. We were both lucky, Mercy, that we survived our rebellious phase. Not all of us are quite so fortunate."

"So I've heard. I have a few friends in New York who are like us. More like me, I suppose. Young. But I've heard stories. They're nothing like the stories you could tell, I'm sure."

"And nothing like the stories *you* could tell, Miss Sylvia Plath."

Mercy blinked. "The... writer... with the *oven*?"

"A woman driven to madness," he said, shaking his head. "We'll help you find yourself. I have to wonder, though... How have you been sustaining yourself all these years?"

She stared at him blankly.

"How have you been getting blood while at war with yourself? How have you been *hunting*, Mercy?"

She hesitated. "Um, in this current century, we have this thing called the inter–"

"I swear to God, Mercy, you better not be posting on Craigslist."

She shrugged. "I haven't."

"Look me in the eyes and tell me you haven't been posting on Craigslist."

"I haven't, Levi. I've been answering Craigslist ads."

He put his head in his hands. "Oh my God, you've single-handedly brought our bloodline to shame. Where's the *class* in that? Where's the *thrill*?"

"Oh, it's fairly thrilling if you pick the right ones."

Still cradling his head, he exhaled. "Jesus Christ, I have to start from scratch with you."

"So you're still going to teach me?"

He slowly smiled. "I think we could both use a bit of time and space first as you come to terms with your realization. But, yes. We'll start in a couple days."

MERCY ONCE AGAIN LIFTED her hand to knock at the front door on a snowy residential street in Winsted, Connecticut. The wind whipped her scarf around her, and it didn't do anything to ease her nerves. To her relief, the door inched open.

"Mary Olive," she said with a smile. "Hi. Any chance you still want to hang out? I'd love your couch for a few days if you don't mind."

The door opened, and with it, Mary's eyes widened. Then, a smile tore across her face. Worse yet, she started bouncing. "Yes! Sister sleepover! And perfect timing... I'm off all weekend, so we can stay up late doing girly things."

Mercy resisted the urge to gulp as she stared at her enthusiastic sister. "Yeah, sounds like fun."

Mary opened the door wider and ushered her sister in. Mercy scanned the room distastefully – farmhouse chic. Out of date, and a trend she'd never particularly liked. She was gazing at a *Live, Laugh, Love* sign when her sister pressed, "Should I order a pizza?"

Mercy turned to meet her gaze with an apologetic smile. "If you want one, sis. I don't eat people food."

"Oh," she said. "Right, I keep forgetting. So... things didn't work out with Levi?"

"They did, actually," Mercy said. "I told him I was thinking about killing him, so that plan is on pause. He's agreed to keep mentoring me, but... I needed some space. There are some things I personally have to work through. I should have addressed them after I changed."

"Like what?"

"It's a bit difficult to explain, but... I just want to find some peace, Mary Olive. And I think this will help me get it."

Mary grabbed her sister's hand and pulled her into the living room. Her couches were lavender, a surprising splash of color against cool-toned white walls. She directed her sister to a couch, disappeared, and returned with two beers. She offered one to Mercy.

When Mercy stared at the beverage, Mary asked, "What? You drank wine, didn't you?"

"Well, yes. I'm a lightweight, that's all." Mercy took the can and popped it open as her sister settled on the bigger couch and leaned to face her.

"Can I ask... how'd it happen, Mercy? How'd you change?"

"I asked for it," Mercy said quietly. "And I did that despite knowing I didn't really want it. There was this inner conflict between my sensibility and this desire for power and immortality – I realize now those were *his* desires. He controls minds. That's his special power."

"I remember you said that," she said with a nod. "So you... didn't want this?"

"I *don't* want this, Mary. God, seeing Dad's discomfort over the years as he realized I wasn't aging... it's horrible. Food still *smells* good, but eating it makes my tummy sick. Sunlight hurts my eyes, which, by the way, also turn red. I've been mourning my humanity for a long time, I think."

Mary opened her beer and took a drink. "I understand why you don't want to deal with Mom and Dad, but... I'm here, sis. You're my best friend. Whatever situation you're facing, I still see the humanity in you. I always will, and I'll always hear you out."

Mercy smiled warmly. Her sister was a half-decade younger than her, and while they weren't *particularly* close, Mary's loyalty was heartwarming. "I love you, Mary. Thank you for being there. And thank you for accepting me when I don't accept myself."

"But you're still *Mercy*."

"Mercy Mild. Which I've never loved. I've been typecast into this jolly character that I just can't be."

"You've always been serious and contemplative," Mary said. "But *so* imaginative. And smart, savvy, and fearless. Those things I've always adored about you are still there. I don't think there's anything to mourn here, sis. You're still Mercy."

"I guess." Mercy shifted. "Levi said he's going to help me learn to be a vampire. A *real* one, not just a girl who's running and avoiding confronting what she is. That might change me."

"It won't," Mary said confidently. "You'll still be you. I'm going to order a pizza, then we can watch a movie. What do you say?"

"No Hallmark movies."

"Thoroughly, fuck that," Mary said. "I can manage *one* a year with Mom. That's it. Any more and I might just die and become undead myself."

Chapter Four

Mercy hadn't brought enough clothes for more than a couple days, but Mary was gracious enough to allow her sister to raid her closet. Now clad in skinny jeans and a black tank top with text declaring that "*blondes have more fun*," Mercy pulled her leather jacket closer to her skin as the two women walked through the Commercial District.

"I haven't shopped out here since I was a kid," Mercy said, running her eyes over the Victorian storefronts. The small city center was charming, in a way. It was also dreadfully mundane and tired. "I see the town hasn't changed one bit."

"Just like you." Mary followed her statement with a giggle after her sister stopped to glare at her. She looped her arm through Mercy's and pulled her through the door of a consignment boutique. Without a moment's hesitation, she made her way to a display and carefully chose a pair of vibrant red wool stockings. "What about these? Thigh high, very sexy."

"When have those *ever* been my style, Mary?"

Mary rolled her blue eyes and returned them to the shelf. "*Whatever*. I'll just look for something more gloomy and depressing."

"Perfect," Mercy said as she walked past her sister and ventured deeper into the store. She stopped by a display with gloves – those might be beneficial to have while she was staying in town. The cold air truly made her hands feel colder than death... well, more frigid than they usually were. Mary had already complained about that a few times.

"Let me know if you need help finding anything."

Mercy turned to thank the cashier but paused as their eyes met. "Kaitlyn?"

"*Mercy*?" the woman said with recognition. "Oh my gosh, it's been years! You haven't aged a day."

"You haven't either."

"Black don't crack, baby," Kaitlyn said with a wink. "Last I heard, you were in the big city. I've read some of your books."

"Really?"

She chuckled. "Yeah, you're kind of a legend around here. The bestselling author that escaped a small town while the rest of us put down roots."

Mercy chuckled politely, then scanned the shop with realization. "Wait... you put down roots. Is this *your* store?"

"Sure is. She's small but mighty. I'm proud of her. You back in town for the holidays?"

Mercy shifted. "Yeah. Back in town until the New Year, at least. Maybe longer."

"We should meet up!" Kaitlyn said. "It's been, what, *nine* years?"

Mercy, in a moment of blind social panic, smiled and nodded.

"How about Café au Levi for coffee? My shop is closed on Sundays if you'll be free then."

Out of nowhere, a lightning bolt and grumble of thunder shook the world beyond the windows. Kaitlyn's eyes flashed toward the front of the store.

"That's odd, lightning in winter. It was clear just a few minutes ago. Anyway, what do you say? Sunday?"

"Are there any other coffee shops in town?"

"In terms of *good* coffee? Just that one, I'm afraid. A newcomer opened a few months ago, but they're not great."

Mercy smiled. "Sunday it is. By the way, I'm definitely getting the gloves – can I leave them with you while I keep shopping?"

"Sure. Go wild – I'll hook you up, girlfriend."

Mercy smiled and handed the merchandise over before she wandered deeper into the store. Mary was easy to spot as she stood alone in the clearance section, examining a black sweater. "What about this?"

"Better." Mercy grabbed her arm and pulled her close, dropping her voice. "That's Kaitlyn up front. She cornered me and asked me to get coffee. I panicked and said yes."

Mary cocked an eyebrow. "Weren't you two school friends? I don't see the problem."

"We had a fight a long time ago."

"When you were literal kids?"

Mercy sighed and snatched the sweater from her sister. "Sheesh, I can't talk to you about Levi or my social problems."

"Because I challenge your existing biases and make you confront ways you can grow as a person?"

Mercy spotted a loose black strand of hair and brushed it out of her line of vision with a huff. "You really bring down the vibe sometimes, you know. I'm starting to think that sitting next to a literal hurdy-gurdy was a better option than this."

"I have *no* idea what that means. Now, go try on your gloomy and depressing sweater, dork."

ARMED WITH A SLIGHTLY expanded wardrobe, Mercy thankfully now had a jacket with a hood. She needed it, as a winter thunderstorm was dropping hail on the small community. Frustrated, she huddled into her hood as she was pelted by tiny ice pellets.

She pushed through the doors of the coffee shop and took her hood down. Across the storefront, Levi cocked an eyebrow at her. She hesitantly made her way toward him, her steps slow and her demeanor guarded.

"Hey, Levi. It's been a minute. You've been quiet."

He ran his eyes over her features, his countenance stoic. "I've been giving you space. Time to clear your mind of Craigslist bloodplay and thoughts of killing me. I see you're in a foul mood."

"What makes you say that?"

His eyes flashed past her toward the windows, and she followed his gaze and smiled guiltily at the storm.

"I'm meeting up with an old friend. I'm nervous. I wasn't really trying to tie up loose ends while I was in town. I was just planning on learning from you, but..."

He leaned against the counter and studied her, his rich brown eyes sparkling with interest. "How's it going with Mary Olive?"

"Fantastic. I'm an excellent roommate. I don't touch any of her food, I don't wake up early and make a ton of noise, and I've effectively washed all the windows with this storm, assuming the weather actually *is* linked with my mood."

He chuckled. "I had a feeling you girls would have fun. Perhaps, if you'll be around this afternoon, we can work on that weather control thing. Looks like you could use a bit of help with that."

She shrugged. "Yeah, I guess. You're not working then?"

"Nah, the staff will be here this afternoon. I never make them come in early on a Sunday... I'm not a monster."

"And you were nagging *me* for clinging to my humanity," Mercy said as his eyes flashed past her. She turned and made eye contact with her old friend, who lit up and rushed toward her.

"Hey!" Kaitlyn exclaimed. "Were you just ordering? Let me buy for you!"

"It's on the house," Levi said with a wink. "Whatever you want."

"Okay," Kaitlyn said, squinting at the menu. "Two caramel macchiatos. Large, please."

Mercy had forgotten about her former friend's annoying habit of ordering for her. Levi's eyes met Mercy's before he turned and prepared the drinks.

Kaitlyn shifted to face her friend. "Not to be forward, but... I don't even remember why we stopped talking. Do you?"

Mercy flicked her eyes away as thunder roared outside. She shifted. "I remember. You left me alone at a party for a boy."

Kaitlyn chuckled nervously. "Oh, yeah. Um, I'm gay now. Guess I was back then, too. Kinda makes it worse in retrospect. Yeah, that one was shitty of me. Sorry about that."

Mercy resisted the urge to touch her neck, where there was once a pulse. She forced a smile instead. "It's fine. We were kids. I'd be lying if I said I wasn't dumb back then. I like to think I'm better nowadays."

"Me, too. I'm glad you're home. This town is a little less dazzling when you're absent. Hey, I recognize that shirt – from my store, right?"

"It is. You're killing it, by the way. I always knew you were a fashion icon."

Kaitlyn laughed as Levi brought the first drink to her. She nodded to him in thanks before she turned back to Mercy. "Yeah, in Podunk Town, USA. What a title. Your life must be *so* much more glamorous."

Mercy hated when people made that assumption. She wasn't a starving artist by any means, but her average advances equated to a pretty typical salary. She lived comfortably, but she wasn't rich, and she definitely didn't live a particularly glamorous life. Truthfully, her biggest flex was not having to spend money on groceries in a high-cost-of-living area.

Levi approached her with the second drink. When he reached forward to hand it off, her nostrils flared against her will. Their fingertips briefly brushed and their eyes locked as the drink passed from his hand to hers. She glanced down at it, then up at Levi in surprise.

It smells like blood.

Levi nodded slowly, then returned to the register without a word. Kaitlyn was already heading toward a table, so Mercy followed.

Behave, Mercy, came his voice tearing through her thoughts. *Don't cause a scene in here.*

Mercy settled at the table and looked down at her coffee. There was *absolutely* blood in it. The challenge, she realized, was to consume it without letting her eyes change. In just one drink, they'd be a bright shade of scarlet.

And, of course, there was the whole *fangs* thing.

Outside, the storm raged. A flash of lightning lit the sky.

"This weather is so strange," Kaitlyn said, following Mercy's gaze. "I can't remember the last time we had thunder and lightning in December. With any luck, it'll blow past before New Year's Eve. I'm hosting a big party. What are you doing?"

Against her better judgment, Mercy looked back at Levi. The old vampire, clearly listening in, shook his head.

"Oh, taking it easy with my family," Mercy lied. "I don't come into town often, so..."

"I get it. Now that you're a big success, it's hard to find the time, I'll bet."

"Believe it or not, it's not too difficult. Mostly podcasts and virtual appearances. The publisher does most of the heavy lifting for me. My agent helps, too."

"Ooh, an *agent*," Kaitlyn cooed. "That's so cool."

"Not really," Mercy admitted. "Ann is... pretty damn uncool, to say the least."

Kaitlyn took a drink. "That's got to be frustrating. I know you've always hated when people cramp your style. Hey, this coffee is really good. Did you try yours?"

If Mercy had a pulse, her heart would have been pounding. As she raised the coffee to her lips, she could feel her fangs protracting. She closed her eyes.

A large crack of thunder boomed, and lightning flashed so brightly that Mercy could see its luminescence through her eyelids. When she opened her eyes, the room was dark, save a few glowing exit signs. The gloom outside didn't allow any natural light to slip in.

The exit signs cast a faint red glow through the room, but it didn't reach their table. Mercy gratefully lifted her coffee to her lips as Levi announced, "I have candles – hang tight, everyone."

WHEN THE DOOR OPENED, Levi looked pleased. "Well done today, Mercy. You're sharp as a tack."

Mercy pushed past him, storming into his home and immediately crossing her arms. "Why'd you serve me blood? How did you even *get* blood in there?"

"Relax." He closed and locked the front door. "It wasn't human. I bought it at the grocery market. Perfectly legal."

"What the Hell was it, then?"

"Pig blood," he said. "A common cooking ingredient in many diverse immigrant communities. It smells like human blood, though, doesn't it? It triggers an instinctual response, as you noticed."

"You could have exposed me! In the city, it would be no big deal. I'd just be some weirdo with bad red contacts. But in a community like *this*, Levi? In front of someone I've known for a very long time? What were you thinking?"

"I was thinking you could handle it, and you did. You've been underestimating yourself." He turned, gesturing for her to follow as he headed toward the kitchen. "You learned a valuable lesson today – you got to test your instinct. One instinct threatened to reveal your true nature, but you fought it. The other cut the power, and you correctly trusted that one. You created a diversion to protect yourself."

"What if I *hadn't*?"

"I could have ensured she'd keep quiet," he said. "It was a controlled test that revealed something very important – you can manage your power to some degree."

Mercy raised her eyebrows as he opened the refrigerator and pulled out a blood bag.

"And I think you've earned this."

Mercy could sense the hesitation in his voice. "Unless...?"

"Unless you want to opt for a fresher source again today." He took a few steps toward her. "Personally, I find it's easier to teach when we're using the same powers, anyway."

Mercy took a step back and raised a hand to her neck protectively. The last time he'd consumed her blood, she died. She took a deep – and deeply unnecessary – breath. "I don't know about letting you take my blood, Levi."

"Then just take my blood again. We can train with my power first if you prefer. At least until you're personally ready to share your power with me."

Mercy raised her eyebrows. The thought of fully mastering control over *Levi's* powers hadn't even crossed her mind... it simply wouldn't be a useful skill to have.

Unless she stayed. And regularly drank his blood.

Neither thought was particularly appetizing.

Rather than answering immediately, she pressed, "Share my power with you? Why'd you make it sound like this could weaken me?"

"Because it makes you vulnerable. When you had my powers, Mercy, I couldn't control your direction. If you were naturally stronger than me, for example, and you wanted to hurt me, I wouldn't be able to direct you to stand down. If I want to hurt you and I can control the weather... Well, it wouldn't be difficult. It's dangerous and shouldn't be pursued without absolute trust."

Mercy smiled, though just slightly – the amusement was only a brief shadow passing over her lips. "So you trust me, then?"

"With my life."

"Even though I wanted to kill you?"

Levi chuckled, then looked down at the blood bag he was still holding. "Sometimes, Mercy, I think I know you better than you know yourself. Yes, even then, I trusted you. What do you say?"

Her eyes landed on the porcelain skin of his neck, unblemished beneath a closely-trimmed but still curly black beard. The thought of toying with his powers again intrigued her. It felt safer than exploring *her* gifts, though the natural skeptic in her still denied she had any.

"Well, Mercy?"

Slowly, as if entranced, Mercy inched toward him. His blood *did* taste different than human blood – sweeter, more potent. And she remembered the wave of lust that came over *both* of them when her lips last met his skin.

She caught herself with one hand outstretched toward Levi, but she hesitated and allowed her arm to drop. He studied her for a long moment, his irises slowly shifting from brown to red.

Something unsaid passed between them, and she finally felt secure enough to give into the bloodlust. Cautiously, she stepped forward and ran a finger over the ivory skin of his neck, admiring how it was every bit as flawless and unmarred as his eternally unchapped lips.

MERCY PULLED A SWEATER over her head and brushed down her hair without a word, then glanced at the blood-soaked sheet with disapproval. This didn't look like any living thing's blood – it was already rusty.

Behind her, Levi was also getting dressed. His eyes, as red as a carnation, slinked toward her to catch her gaze. He followed it to the bloodied sheets, then chuckled.

"Oh, bother the sheets. They never last, anyway. Such a disposable thing... blankets last for years, but these things wear out so quickly. A skilled vampire should really invent a longer-lasting solution."

Mercy cocked an eyebrow, stupefied by his comment.

Levi laughed awkwardly. "Ah, I take it you don't care about the sheet, then. This is about something else."

She sighed and rubbed her temples. "That was really dumb, Levi. I came here to *study*, not to... *that*."

"Eloquent as always." He stood and stretched. "For what it's worth, it's not your fault. We're soulmates, Mercy. Whether or not you're feeling love in the moment, our souls are intertwined in Hell or whatever plane they exist in. We'll get to what that means eventually... let's get your grasp of control situated first."

Mercy stood. "Alright. Train me."

"I will, darling, but mind control can't work on either of us right now. We'll need another subject."

About an hour later, Mercy and Levi were seated side-by-side on a lavender couch as Mary Olive Harker sipped tea. She smacked her artificially plump lips and loudly clinked the teacup against its saucer as she leaned forward to set it on the coffee table.

"So let me get this straight," she said. "You... want to use me for a mind control test? I'm supposed to just agree to let Mercy do *whatever* she wants to me before the last big party day of the year?"

"It sounds more sinister than it will be," Mercy promised. "I need to practice on someone, and I'm not really interested in doing it without consent like *some people* suggested."

Levi smiled apologetically and shrugged.

Mary studied him before she turned to her sister. "You promise you won't hurt me?"

"You have my word. I won't cause any physical pain."

"Even if I point out that your lipstick stained Levi's pale-ass mouth?"

Levi scrubbed at his lips with frustration as Mercy covered her eyes. "Yeah, even then, Mary. But please, for the love of God, *don't* point it out."

Levi, ignoring her suggestion, turned to Mercy and asked, "Did I get it?"

She put her head in her hands again as Mary laughed. "You two confuse me, but it's kinda fun to watch. Weird, but fun. Okay, let's do this."

Levi gestured for Mercy to initiate a command, so she leaned forward and met her sister's eyes. Mercy held her gaze for a long moment before sighing and turning to Levi. "This is uncomfy. What the Hell am I supposed to do?"

He shrugged ambiguously, and Mary immediately suggested, "Ooh, I can give you a manicure. Just say the word, and I'll take our sisters' sleepover weekend to the next level."

Mercy's eyes darted toward her sister's lackluster acrylics in horror, but she swallowed past the urge to comment and cleared her throat. "No, that doesn't feel right. Um... how about this? Go grab a snowball from the front yard, no jacket or gloves."

"*Ew*, no way."

"Levi!" Mercy complained. "It's not working!"

He leaned backward, melting into the cushiony bulk of the couch. "I see that. Tell me, Mercy, what's different now than when you used my power at the cafe the other day?"

"Well, for one, I'm not skeptical and terrified out of my mind," Mercy said. "So there's that."

"And when you used your power earlier today, love?"

Mercy shrugged a shoulder. "I was also terrified then."

"Okay, so you learned that emotional intent has to be there to carry out the compulsion."

"I did?"

"*Yes*, because I just told you," he nagged. "Mercy, please. Try again. Focus and put some intent behind it. Feel that you desperately need this to work, then *make it work*."

Mercy drew in a slow, deep breath, allowing the air to fill her lungs. She closed her eyes, shutting out the world around her, and focused on clearing any distractions from her mind. With a sense of certainty, she lifted her gaze to meet her sister's, her mind now clear and focused on a specific vision. She knew what she wanted, and she *desperately* wanted to see this one to completion. "Mary Olive, you're going to obey my command. Go take that *Live, Laugh, Love* sign and throw it out the front door."

Mary blinked, stood slowly, and ventured toward the front of the house. Mercy watched excitedly as Levi, bored, raised an eyebrow at her. The front door opened and closed, and then Mary Olive marched back toward the couch. She settled.

"Now," Mercy said as she leaned forward with a wicked grin. "Forget you just obeyed my command."

Mary blinked, then shifted and sighed. "No, Mercy, I'm *not* taking down my sign. I happen to *like it*. It matches the infinity loop hand towels in my front bathroom."

"Oof. Yeah, go online and order some black ones instead. They're less visually offensive and won't clash with your décor."

Mary robotically lifted her phone. As she unlocked the screen and scrolled through her apps, she paused to glare at her sister. "Okay, this one is mean. I don't *want* to follow through with this."

"You can pick cheap ones," Mercy offered helpfully.

As a frustrated Mary completed the online order, Levi stretched. "I thought the point of getting consent was to *not* do something evil. Respectfully, love, you're wading into mad-with-power territory."

"Yeah," Mary protested.

"I said I wouldn't *hurt* you, Mary Olive. I didn't say I wouldn't fix your décor."

"Semantics," Levi said dismissively.

"I'm a *writer*, Levi. I care very deeply about words and was very straightforward with how the situation would play out. I said I wouldn't hurt her."

Yeah, well, maybe you hurt my feelings.

"Feelings don't count, Mary. You *absolutely* knew what I meant when I said I wouldn't cause any physical pain."

"Are you *responding* to me? I didn't say that out loud, Mercy."

Mercy blinked as she processed her sister's words. Slowly, she turned to Levi with her mouth agape. "Oh my God, you fucking pervert. You can *read thoughts*? What the Hell?"

He smiled apologetically. "You figured that out sooner than expected. I... ahem. Yeah. That's a thing I can do."

"Oh my God. How often do you listen to my thoughts?"

"Often enough to never be surprised by your actions."

"You knew I was thinking about killing you?"

"Well, yeah. Obviously. Why do you think I *didn't tell you* how to do that?"

Mercy rubbed her temples. "Oh my God. Oh my *God*, Levi. Jesus Christ, this is such a violation of – "

"Read my thoughts!" exclaimed Mary, cutting her sister off.

Levi glanced in her direction, then furrowed his brow. "I don't get pictures, I get like a mental alt-text description. That's... whatever that *thing* is, it's weird."

"Did you not live through the Nineties? It was a game. I don't remember its name, so I was low-key hoping you might." Mary looked down at the phone in her hands as if just remembering that she was holding it. "I guess a search engine is more useful than a mind-reading vampire. Go figure."

Mercy waved her off dismissively. "Okay, ignore her. What the *Hell*, Levi? How does this power work?"

He glanced at Mary, then returned his gaze to the other vampire. "Well, I can hear the thoughts of people near me if I focus. Sometimes they come to me even when I don't, especially if I've recently compelled the person. Mary Olive is a horrible worker on her own, so I control her direction fairly regularly. I'm unfortunate enough to hear her thoughts with some regularity. She has some strange body issues."

"I absolutely do *not*!"

"There's nothing wrong with the way your knees look," he returned. "For fuck's sake, it's a *knee*. It's a weird body part. It's weird on everyone. For the love of all that is beautiful, *relax*. I've heard that word more in the two years I've employed you than my entire lifetime before that."

Mercy snapped in front of his face, so he turned his attention toward her with wide red eyes. "Okay, Count Dracu-Listening-To-People's-Thoughts. *Ignore her.* So... Were you able to read my thoughts when I initially left with you?"

"You're a bit of a different case," he said slowly. "Yes, I could hear you then. The truth is, I always can. I've always been able to read my scions' thoughts, whether near or far, if I focus. But, apparently, you can hear mine, too, if I put enough emotion behind the thought."

"Are you implying that *I* can read thoughts, Levi? I mean, outside of using your powers?"

His eyes flashed toward Mary, who had just pocketed her phone and was now sipping her tea and watching the exchange unfold. "Mercy, I... can we not do this in front of your sister?"

Mary loudly slurped her beverage. "Oh, no, don't stop on my behalf. There's probably nothing on TV right now, so I'm content here."

Mercy nodded in agreement, so Levi turned his attention back to her. He bit his lip. "Well, I've never had a soul tie before you. I told you – I don't have the power to make you hear *my* thoughts in your mind. And yet, you do. These spiritual ties do weird things... you haven't wholly given me the opportunity to explore what that means yet, so I can't say I understand it. But I do understand that it's not *your* power. It's *ours.*"

Mercy ran her eyes over his face, a million thoughts dancing through her head. He could probably hear them, perhaps all at once like a wall of noise. Articulating them was the challenge. She settled upon what felt like the most concise summation of her feelings. "So... tell me again why you think we're soulmates. I still don't understand what that means."

Chapter Five

Mary politely stepped out of the room to order food – Indian cuisine, she said – which left Levi and Mercy alone. They sat in a state of silence that Mercy couldn't help but remind herself probably *wasn't* quite so silent to Levi.

"It's rare," Levi said. "Believe me – I've only seen this happen once in my half-millennium, and it affected a vampire much older than I am now. I've heard a few different words to describe it. Soulmates is obviously the one I ascribe to. There's a theory I've heard, and I've never stopped thinking about it."

"Okay," Mercy ventured nervously. "What is it?"

"When we die, *something* happens to our souls," he said slowly. "Some people – and some media, for that matter – believe a vampire's soul is damned. We become husks. You know that's not true... you feel like *you* at the core. We are still the same."

"Okay," Mercy said. "That checks out."

"Other people believe the soul *shifts* after we change. Transmutates into something not quite human, but not inhuman. Which also can't be true, because you hate Mary's *Live, Laugh, Love* sign every bit as much as you would have when alive. Nothing changed."

"Right. That *also* sounds correct."

"Which leads me to the third theory. The soul remains intact... usually. However, when a person undergoes massive trauma during the change, their soul can fracture. They continue through life as the intact piece, but that splintered portion becomes something new. Some*one* new."

Mercy winced as the weight of his words bore down on her. She stared at him, barely processing as his eyes pleaded for understanding. "Absolutely not. No fucking *way*, Levi."

"It's like the Bible said," he whispered. "I'm People of the Book, Mercy. Eve was born of Adam's rib. Made for him, *from* him. But you know what they did? Committed the original sin. We have, too, simply by meeting. We've learned what can happen when an ancient, fractured soul becomes whole again... and it's pure magic. Forbidden knowledge. Unimaginable power."

"I don't believe that one bit, Levi. I'm *not* a piece of your soul. Absolutely not."

He stared at her for a long moment, his eyes wide as he presumably listened to her panicked flight of thought. "Like I said, Mercy, meeting you was like looking in a mirror. You're my rebellious streak, the person fleeing from Spain, the person believing they could protect what is most precious simply by being bold. Vampires can spend millennia without experiencing this innate spiritual reconnection."

Mercy stood numbly, then stumbled into the bathroom. She practically fell into the toilet, dropping to her knees and dipping into the bowl as her stomach emptied its contents. Mostly-digested blood spattered the bowl in thick clumps – it was probably Levi's, she thought with disgust.

He and Mary appeared in the doorway, watching with concern as Mercy fell back weakly. She hadn't thrown up since she was alive. Or, more accurately, since she was dying. She wasn't sure if she was even technically alive at that point.

When Levi's arms came around her, Mercy spun and pushed him away. He thudded against the wall with wide eyes.

"Get the fuck out!" Mercy screamed. She recoiled and curled in on herself, burying her face into her knees. As she bawled, Mary shifted to stand between the vampires.

"You heard her," Mary growled. "I don't know what you did, you creep, but you are to leave my house this instant."

His eyes, a passionate vermilion, flashed toward Mercy helplessly before he muttered, "As you wish. I'm here when you're ready, Mercy."

With that, the front door opened and closed, and Mary dropped the plate she was holding and ran to comfort her sister.

"Hey," Mary said. "I'm here, Mercy. I'm here."

MARY OLIVE WRAPPED her sister in a blanket after she stoked the blaze in the fireplace. She settled on the nearby couch and sipped her tea. "Mercy? Honey? Do you want to tell me what happened?"

Mercy snuggled into the blanket and fought the instinctual urge to hyperventilate. Her lungs, graciously, did not move. "I'm not sure how to explain this, Mary Olive, but I feel like my entire existence has been depleted. Like I, as an individual, do not matter. Like I never did. I think

I understand why Levi's been saying I'm *his*. We're... God, I don't know where to begin."

"Is it a vampire thing?"

Mercy jealously eyed the hot beverage her sister was holding. She wanted something warm to drink... blood, probably, but the thought of hot chocolate did have particular appeal. "I'll be honest, Mary. I don't *know*. I don't think I understand it."

Mary scooted forward. "I'll try to understand, if you'll share with me."

"Do you remember when Mom and Dad made us attend Sunday school?" Mercy asked. When Mary nodded, she continued. "And... you know Adam and Eve."

"God's first people? Sure. Adam was made of dust and Eve was made from his rib."

"He explained it like Adam and Eve. He said when a vampire is made, their soul can fracture, Mary. Like Adam's rib, it breaks away and then you get a whole new being. A new being with its own thoughts, feelings, and *soul*."

Mary blinked, then parted her lips slightly like she was going to say something. She sat in incredulous silence before she pressed, "Okay... so you're implying...?"

"He had a *damn* good explanation for it, Mary. He said his rebellious side was what died – the side running from oppression. So it makes sense that my natural instinct is to run, though I feel drawn to him. I always have, I guess. And I think that's why I've always struggled. I never wanted to be a vampire. I wanted his soul, or whatever, because it's familiar. That's why I asked for immortality... I think the soul *wanted* to be whole. But I, as an individual, don't want that. Eve wasn't part of Adam anymore; she was Eve. I'm Mercy. Jesus, I'm rambling. Am I making sense?"

"Sure," Mary said. "You're that missing piece of the puzzle. His puzzle."

"Right," Mercy agreed. "I'm *not* him. I'm Mercy. I hate my middle name and hometown, I love language and words, I think dark clothes and depressing poetry are cool. I won every race in elementary school. I did ballet in seventh grade and hated it. I'm a conglomerate of all these experiences, uniquely my own, and I want to keep *living for me*. Not him. And yet... I feel like I don't exist anymore. Like knowing this has equated me to a mere thing he lost centuries ago."

Mary tilted her head, and the motion caused a cascade of blonde hair to slip over her shoulder and frame her face. "Perhaps that's why he waited so long to tell you this, sis. Because he clearly doesn't feel that way about the situation. He's smitten with you."

"I wouldn't say I'm smitten with him, but God, Mary, you saw his stained lips. I *need* him, and I desperately don't want to. And, fuck, I just want his voice out of my head."

Mary tilted her head. "Assuming this is real, which I don't wholly believe, you – a new being, spiritually speaking – have tasted life, and you don't want to give that up. That's the situation here, right? He wants you because you make him whole, but you don't want to give up the life you've already built."

"And yet, I did," she said. "For him. Because he was the apple, Mary. The forbidden fruit. Oddly enough, he's also the Tree of Life in the Garden of Eden. Also known as the..."

"Tree of Mercy," Mary finished with wide eyes.

"It's just like the ancient chants foretold. Peace on earth. Mercy Mild. Two separate concepts. I'm doomed to an eternity of restlessness."

"Ancient chants," Mary grumbled. "Okay, let's not be dramatic. So there are some *weird* fucking coincidences here."

She bit her lip and studied her sister, who lifted her mug and held Mercy's gaze as she drank deeply. Mercy finally sighed and looked away. "The worst thing about this, Mary Olive, is I sense that he's right. That's what caused such a visceral reaction earlier. I know nothing about my existence."

Mary rolled her eyes. "Oh no, what a tragedy. Look, sis, nobody knows why they were born, if there's any higher purpose at all. If there's any truth to everything you're saying, you know more than most. But I'll be the first to say, this kinda sounds like bullshit."

"I'm a vampire, Mary Olive. Seriously? This is where you're drawing the line between *too fucking weird* and acceptable reality?"

Mary threw her arms in a wide shrug and bugged her eyes. "*What*? This one just... it kinda sounds nuts, Mercy."

"Don't you get it?" Mercy asked. "Archaeology has shown us that many myths are based in fact. The Great Flood and yada yada. I bet Genesis is a *vampire* tale, sis. One of those odd situations that was twisted by storytellers of the time and written down. It was a common story that just happened to make it into the Bible."

"So... you're saying we might be able to get some more insight right here and now?"

"Well... it's worth a try, right?"

Mary stood. "We have some reading to do!"

MERCY TOUCHED THE BIBLE and withdrew her hand quickly. Like holy water, it burned the callouses on her fingertips when she brushed them over the cover. She shook her hand, then glared at her sister. "I thought you were over the religion crap?"

Mary smiled apologetically. "I mean, I *am*. But this was Grandma's. It's a family heirloom."

Mercy sucked on her burnt fingertips until the pain subsided. Though the pain was fading, a tingling sensation of pins and needles still pricked across her palms, causing them to itch deep between the bones. She shook her hands again. "Okay. Adam and Eve. That's Genesis."

Mary Olive flipped through the book frantically.

"I just realized," Mercy said quietly. "The name of God doesn't burn me, but this book does. Holy water does. It makes me wonder if it's not the religion itself that keeps us repressed, but rather the stories and the power of the words within them."

"Like writing them down was... a way to fight vampires, you mean?" Mary marked the paragraph she was reading and looked up at her sister. "There's definitely *something* to unravel there. God may not be against vampires, but whoever wrote down stories like Genesis may have found a way to weaken you. Perhaps for their own protection, but it could be for something more malicious. Either way, you might be onto something with this story."

"Why's that?" Mercy asked curiously.

Mary cast her eyes toward the book before her and moved her finger as she read. "Therefore, just as sin entered the world through one man, and death through sin, and in this way death came to all men, because all sinned, for before the law was given, sin was in the world."

"Before law, there was vampirism," Mercy said.

Mary nodded, seeming to have reached the same conclusion. "Therefore, just as vampirism entered the world through one man, and death through vampirism, death came to all men." Mary's eyes, framed by dark lashes that looked a bit like hairy spider legs, rose from the page to her sister.

"And if vampirism came into the world from one man," Mercy said. "It might be assumed that Eve was the second vampire to be created. And as Genesis seemingly explores the peopling of the world, perhaps it's actually explaining the spread of vampirism."

"So it may have started with a soul pair, just like you and Levi." Mary closed the Bible, allowing her fingertips to brush the old heirloom cover. "In this way, death came to all men. So... death is the next step after a soul bond is formed? What does that mean, exactly?"

"I don't know, and I can only imagine what banishment from the Garden of Eden means." Mercy groaned. "I hate to say it, but I should probably ask Levi. I'm not ready, though. I still need time to process."

Mary bit her lip. "Are we sure it's okay to wait? This may be pressing."

The vampire huffed and crossed her arms. "Truthfully, I don't know, sis. I feel like I can still hear him calling, so at least I know he's willing to talk when I'm ready."

I'm ready, love.

Come to me, Mercy.

With a sigh, Mercy pulled out her phone. "You're right. I'll text him, maybe try to meet up tomorrow. We'll get some answers."

MERCY KICKED HER FEET as she walked through the Commercial District. Snow shifted around her boots – a fresh layer had fallen last night, keeping the accumulation on the ground light and fluffy rather than compressed and clumpy. To Mercy's amusement, the snowfall had hidden her sister's sign in the yard. Mary hadn't even noticed it was gone.

A small smile danced across her lips as she thought about that. While Levi was right – Mercy had been dangerously close to being *mad with power* – it was a funny situation in retrospect. It would be hilarious when Mary Olive figured out it was gone and, realistically, Mercy did plan to replace the sign when that time came.

But she'd also try to sway Mary into picking something more timeless and elegant. Sweet, clueless Mary just didn't know any better.

A car drove past Mercy and navigated into a parking space – a matte gray Audi sedan, instantly recognizable as Levi's. He got out, clad in a heavy wool coat and bundled into a brown scarf. Paired with the absence of pink-toned pigment in his skin, he looked a bit like a sepia photo amidst a startlingly white landscape, with the edges of snow framing the street in a muddy brown.

The scene would make a pretty painting, Mercy thought. It was mundane. Pedestrian. But there was something beautiful about that mud-encrusted snow. How many people had passed through on their commutes to work, splashing a bit of mud as their car moved forward? With each layer, the story that snowbank had to tell grew. It was a tale of a journey, with each hero heading in the same direction, if only for a moment in time.

Levi's journey was much more slow-paced as he approached.

He locked the car and slipped his hands in his pockets as he walked toward Mercy. She held her chin up, trying her darndest to focus on the colors of his outfit rather than give in to the delicious temptation of wandering thought. It seemed to be working, as Levi's expression was guarded when he came to stand next to her. He didn't know what to expect.

"I'm sorry," Mercy said. "I shouldn't have kicked you out yesterday. I just needed time."

He ran his dark eyes over her face, then exhaled. Had anyone been around, they might have noticed the distinct lack of condensation from his ice-cold breath. "I understand. I didn't intend to tell you like that, Mercy. Admittedly, I kept this to myself because I knew how you'd feel, assuming you believed me at all."

"I believe you," she whispered. "It makes so much sense, Levi. Why I'm drawn to you, but why I want to run. Why I didn't want to die, but I asked you to kill me anyway. It wasn't *you* making me do those things. It was me. These innate, instinctual things..."

"They were mine," Levi finished. "Traits that died when I became a vampire. I was running, wishing I and my family could live forever. Dreaming of endless possibilities – my creativity was always running wild. Now, I'm bland, and I'm aware of that. I'm as sedentary as I can be. I'm more of a collector than a creator. But you... it's nice to have those things back, Mercy, and it's meaningful to receive them in the form of someone so special and unique."

"But I am someone distinct and separate from you, Levi. I understand that whatever I am, you and I were one and the same once, in some cosmic celestial sense. But Mary said it best – I've tasted life, perhaps for the first time as a distinctly individual being, and I don't want to give that up."

"That's why I gave you the space to branch out and the opportunity to move away. You needed that, and you deserved it. But since we've met, we've also needed each other. When we're together, Mercy, we're whole. We're a unit."

"So when you've said you own me," Mercy began, "You meant my soul. Not *me*. I just didn't understand."

"Frankly, love, I don't see any difference. You're mine as I am yours. Our souls fit together in a way two distinctly different entities could never know. It's magical, really, that we're the same at the core. We can love each other wholly and authentically. You literally complete me, and I complete you."

"You see why you scared me, right?"

"In my defense, there was nothing I could say that wouldn't have made you run. And I knew that all too well. After what I went through when I was human, I became flighty. Distrustful. Having not known the evil I did, I can't say I blame you for suspecting it existed in me. I'd suspect you're hardwired to be like that. You can learn to ignore it, you know. I'm here to help."

Mercy cast her eyes away. "I suppose I see now why sires keep their scions close. I do have some things to work through. I'd be lying if I said your guidance hasn't helped keep me sane."

"While your absences drive me insane, Mercy, I feel the same about your presence. I learn a lot from you, too, and you keep me grounded."

They started walking, lazily inching toward a gazebo in the center of what was normally an open grassy area, at least in the warmer months. As they slowly walked up the stairs, he reached out to take her hand.

"When immortal soulmates are together," he began, pulling her closer. "Things *happen*, Mercy. This innate spiritual connection leads to powers the average vampire cannot possibly come into. You can already hear my thoughts, and that's just the tip of the iceberg, from what I understand. There's more to discover, and more that comes with time. The longer you stay, the more we'll see it."

"We get special powers just because we share a soul? I don't understand how that makes sense."

He shrugged. "You and I, in essence, are made from the same stardust. If everyone else in the world was fire, we would be water. We're complementary in every way. I suppose I can see some ancient magic brewing in that sort of environment."

She squeezed his hand. It was cold, of course, but it felt warm to her, being the same not-quite-alive body temperature. "I think I finally understand you, Levi. So, where do we go from here?"

He traced the contours of her face. "I want you to come home, darling. I want it *desperately*, more than anything. I feel incomplete without your presence – empty. Lonely. But I feel it's important for *you* to make that choice completely on your own. After all..." Levi trailed off and smiled slightly. "I used to be just as rebellious and driven as you."

Mercy looked away. "I don't know what I want, Levi. I mean, I want to be with you to a distractingly annoying degree, but I also don't feel that emptiness when I'm away. I *like* being my own person."

Levi's face twisted, clearly pained. "It makes sense. I remember what it felt like to be whole once upon a time. To you, this existence is *already* whole. Simply by existing, you've proven you don't need me. You haven't fractured, not like I did. With that said, the direction we go is still a choice I expect *you* to make. I know you – deeply, intrinsically – and I cannot make it for you. You'll never be happy."

Mercy pulled away and leaned against the railing facing the street. "I need time to think, Levi. And I need to talk to you about something first."

"Okay."

"So, the concept of a soulmate being made from a rib," Mercy said. "The parallel you drew between our fractured soul story and that Biblical tale really stuck with me. So I started thinking, what if it's a *real* story? A story of vampirism that was documented eons ago. And then I realized that the word God doesn't choke me, but Bibles burn me. So it's not the *religion*, but the *stories* and words that hurt us."

Levi shifted to face her. "Well, you *are* Words Girl."

She elbowed him. "Cut it out."

I believe you, Mercy.

At the silent sound of his voice, Mercy smiled fondly. This time, it felt welcome. "Anyway, Mary was reading to me, and we realized that the concept of sin in Genesis may actually be a parallel for vampirism. In addition to preserving ways to hurt us, these stories may also highlight some of our secrets. Ones we don't even know."

Levi studied her, then looked away. "Perhaps. In Judaism, we have this concept of *nephesh*. The breath of life, to provide a translation. *God formed a man from the dust of the ground and breathed into his nostrils* nephesh, *and the man became a living soul.* You know, what's interesting to me is the fact that life and death look similar in the Hebrew alphabet. Depending on the handwriting, *living soul* could be a translation error. I've long suspected that myth holds the secrets of early man... and early vampire."

"The Bible says sin entered the world through one man," Mercy said. "And death through sin. If *sin* refers to vampirism, especially in the context of a being made from a fraction of another..."

Levi didn't respond. He remained as motionless as a statue as Mercy's words hung in the air and faded into oblivion. In the blink of an eye, that instance became a piece of the past. How strange it would be, Mercy thought, to experience this over and over again, with the current present growing ever further away.

"Levi. Is death going to follow us?"

He finally turned his attention to her, then shook his head. "I don't *know*, Mercy. I believe you, of course, but I don't know. I just... the only thing I can think of is the vampire hunters."

"Vampire *hunters*? You're joking, right? No mortal can take us down."

"They're not mortal." His eyes met hers for a long moment. "They're vampires, too, Mercy."

UPON TRYING TO ENTER Mary's house, Levi's foot brushed against an invisible barrier. He winced and kicked at the air, then met Mercy's gaze across the threshold.

Mercy rolled her eyes and pulled out her cell phone. After a few rings, she flipped it to speaker and said, "Mary Olive! I need you to give Levi permission to come into the house."

"Oh, you're on good terms with him again?"

"Mary!"

"Fine. Am I on speaker?"

"Yes, come *on*."

"Alright, Levi, come on in."

Levi brushed his foot across the threshold graciously. Mercy watched his confident strut with exasperation before she took the call off speaker. "Okay, Mary. That was all I needed. Me? Yeah, I'm good. We'll talk later, okay?"

She ended the call, flashed her blue eyes at Levi, and then closed the door. She pulled him upstairs to Mary's guest room. To Mercy's relief, her sister had a spare bed that saved her from sleeping on those disgustingly pastel couches.

Mercy ushered Levi in and closed the door. When she turned to face him, he was already across the room studying knickknacks on a shelf.

"Precious Moments," Mercy commented as she settled on the bed. "Mary collected them when we were kids. So. Now that we're somewhere private and I can appropriately freak out... *vampires* are hunting vampires?"

He looked over his shoulder at her, then picked up one of the ceramic figurines and studied it more closely. "Every single day we live, Mercy, we lay the framework for the person we'll be tomorrow. We'll never be the person we were yesterday because individual experiences alter us with each waking moment. For vampires, the implications of minuscule actions are different. They're much more everlasting, in a way, as we're eternal."

"*Nephesh*."

The corners of his lips twitched ever so slightly. "You could say that, I suppose. Some of us learn at too volatile an age what happens when you drink another vampire's blood."

"Sex?"

"*Lust*, Mercy." He set the figurine down and moved to sit beside her. "You really have to stop taking things so literally. *Lust* happens. In some of us, that results in bloodlust. Bloodlust for *other* vampires, and it only gets stronger with each drop of immortal blood consumed."

Mercy shivered, a surprisingly human response – she didn't feel cold, not like she used to.

"Back in the day, we were more plentiful," Levi said. "Vampirism is a plague, after all. I'm told it impacted a great deal of the human population. Vampires with bloodlust effectively thinned the herd, turning us into more of a rarity. Some of those remaining cannibalistic vampires had matured by that point, and they understood their vulnerability as our numbers dwindled. So they formed a collective front."

"To hunt us?"

"To hunt those of us threatening the stability of our species again," he spat. "Hypocrites, the lot of them. As if they weren't the exclusive reason our dwindling species *needs* protecting. But these vampires are now very, very old. They can control their bloodlust, and they don't feed often. They will wait *decades* for a slip-up."

Mercy bit her lip. "What's a slip-up?"

He tightened his jaw. "Well, it's not like *someone in town learns your dark secret.* That's easily fixable, as long as you know a vampire who can help control the narrative with a bit of suggestion. This is usually a big slip-up. Have you ever seen *Carrie*?"

"I mean, yeah, I know the Stephen King story. Telekinesis, you're saying?"

"Think bigger. I'm talking *massive* displays of telekinetic power, Mercy. But, of course, that's not a power that impacts the average vampire."

"Only those paired in a soul bond," Mercy realized with wide eyes. "Jesus Christ. So we're *food* to these guys? One slip-up, and that's it? They come looking for us and *eat us?*"

He nodded grimly. "And remember what happens when we consume another vampire's blood, Mercy."

"We get their powers," Mercy said. "So what happens when they consume a pair of super-powered soulmates who haven't discovered the extent of their abilities yet?"

When he didn't respond, Mercy stood promptly and moved to the dresser. She emptied her recently purchased collection of clothing and started throwing it on the bed frantically. As she gathered her makeup from the vanity, Levi stood.

In the blink of an eye, he was between Mercy and the pile she'd amassed.

"Absolutely not," he said. "You are *not* running away on New Year's Eve."

"Get out of my way," she growled. "I'm out of here."

He grabbed her makeup bag, but she didn't willingly relinquish it. After a short game of tug-of-war, he successfully pulled it from her grasp and held it out of reach. "First of all, you don't have a car and it's a big drinking night. I'm not putting your safety in the hands of a stranger. Second, it's a big *party* night. A little bit of ruckus could easily go unnoticed. It's not safe."

"Give me my shit back, Levi."

"Mercy Mild Harker, I forbid you from leaving."

She snatched her makeup from him and scooted closer until they were chest to chest. "You are *not* in charge of me right now. Remember? I drank your blood. So fuck you, I'm out. I'm leaving."

As she attempted to sidestep him, he darted in front of her. "Mercy! Listen to me."

"Leave, Levi."

"This isn't your house."

Mercy pulled her cell phone from her hoodie pocket. "Get out, or I'll call Mary. *She'll* make you leave."

He stared at the phone for a long second before he stepped back. "Fine. Good night, Mercy."

She watched in stunned silence as he brushed past her and left the room. As soon as she heard him move through the front door, she started stuffing her suitcase.

Chapter Six

It was storming again, but this time, the lightning was accompanied by heavy snowfall. Mercy marched toward the center of town, huffing in frustration at the bulk of her suitcase. It wasn't heavy – perhaps to a human, but not to her. It was awkwardly shaped, however, and there was no easy way to carry it across the snowy sidewalks. Frustrated, she flipped it behind her as if slinking a jacket over her shoulder. Clutching it against her back, she marched through a curtain of snow.

Little by little, a single pair of headlights permeated the curtain, eventually moving to illuminate the street beside her, then in front of her.

"Mercy!" She stopped marching and turned to stare into the car. The passenger window was down, so she had a clear view of her sister's angry face. "What the *Hell* do you think you're doing?"

"Leaving! I'm sorry, sis. You wouldn't understand."

"Well, let me tell you what I *do* understand," Mary growled. "You're making me miss the *last party night* of the year. Plus, you're making me drive through this shit, Little Miss Weather Control. By the way, maybe don't talk so loud on the phone if you don't want me using shit against you."

Mercy set her suitcase down and crossed her arms. "What do you want from me?"

"I want you to get in the car. God, stop being such an idiot. I don't know what the Hell happened today, but Levi was very clear that you should *not* be traveling tonight."

"Did he call you?"

"What? No way... Yeah, maybe. Just listen to me, Mercy. He's scared. *I'm* scared. You can leave in a few days. Whatever you want. But come on, if he thinks you can get hurt, you shouldn't do this. It'd destroy me if I lost you, sis."

Mercy kicked an icy clump, picked up her suitcase, and waded through the snowdrifts toward the car. She got in without a word, and Mary stared at her before she turned and rolled up the window. She cast her eyes back on the road, then shifted them toward her sister.

"You can turn off the snowstorm now, Elsa."

"I can't control it, Mary Olive," she snapped in a sing-songy voice.

"Fucking fantastic, Mercy." Mary ramped up the heat and side-eyed her sister. "Ugh, I can feel the cold dancing off your undead ass."

Mercy looked out the passenger window in a stewing silence. She was angry for several reasons – that Mary had risked her safety to come after her, that Levi had called and *involved* her in the first place, that she was once again successfully kept in town.

God, the urge to flee was so strong. But she knew, deep down, that she had to resist it. At least for tonight.

"So, you and Levi are friends."

"I mean, yeah," Mary said. "We're friendly. I like him. I guess it makes sense, given that you're low-key the same."

"I like him, too," Mercy admitted, watching the passing landscape with slitted eyes. "Which sucks."

"So do vampires."

Mercy cracked a smile and glanced up at the clouds. The snow was still coming down. She was anxious. Having Mary Olive, someone so fragile and thoroughly mortal, beside her wasn't helping. All Mercy could think about was the fact that ancient vampires wanted to make a meal of her. They were waiting for a slip-up.

Mercy didn't trust herself to not slip. Levi wasn't much more promising – she knew his soul, of course. If she didn't trust herself, she couldn't trust him. She couldn't trust *them* together.

Good God, if Mary was ever in the way...

"I was gonna go to a party," Mary Olive finally said. "You only get to be young once."

"I'll make it up to you."

Her eyes flashed toward Mercy for a second before she returned them to the road and lifted her chin. "Good. Because if you're really going to live forever, you have an eternity to make my New Year's Eves amazing. I expect expensive champagne when you enter your rich lord in a castle era."

Mercy chuckled. "Levi's a few centuries old and still working a day job. I hate to say it, Mary Olive, but you might be waiting a while."

"Hey, if it keeps you around," Mary said with a small smile.

Mercy smiled back, but she gazed out at the falling snow. If Mary Olive worked with Levi, but Levi and Mercy posed a risk of attracting cannibalistic vampires... Mercy wasn't certain she could come around.

She had a lot to think through.

WHILE MARY HAD MANAGED to make her sister laugh a few times on the ride, any ounce of joy faded from Mercy's countenance when they finally arrived at her sister's home. A matte gray sedan sat in the driveway.

"Of course he's waiting," Mercy grumbled.

"I genuinely don't understand the problem," Mary said. "You love him, right? Or am I just dumb?"

Mercy stared at the looming facade of the house, shifting uncomfortably as she realized the snow had started falling harder again. As thick wads of precipitation streaked across her vision, Mercy winced. She closed her eyes. "Ugh, don't make me say that I love him, Mary Olive."

"But you do! All these years, I wondered why you never brought anyone home. Now I understand. You love him, but it's complicated. It's never been easy, has it?"

Mercy opened her eyes to gaze at the house again. The door opened, and Levi stood in the doorway and stared at them. As their eyes met, it was as if she could feel his consciousness brushing hers. There was a thought forming, but he couldn't quite articulate it. "It's more complicated than you can imagine."

With that, Mercy exited the car and pulled her suitcase out. After slamming the door, she met his gaze again. He momentarily lit up, then recoiled when she didn't match his elation.

Mercy marched toward the front porch as thunder rolled behind her. "Really? You had to involve *Mary*? She just drove in this shit!"

"Just come inside," he urged. Mercy loyally followed his direction, but she stopped at the threshold to glare at him. Mary, steps behind her, ushered her in and muttered something about the gas bill.

Before the door was even shut, Levi said, "The first is a historical time of destruction for them, Mercy. The Burning of Norfolk. Operation Bodenplatte. The death of Bach. This is a bad time of year to be traveling alone."

"It's an even more horrible time of year to be with you, then." At that, he recoiled, so Mercy whimpered. "Sorry, I didn't mean it like that. But it's dangerous to be together, Levi. You've made it clear that we're just big game to them."

Mary's eyes flashed between them. "Big game? Who's hunting you?"

"Nobody," Levi said, turning to her. "Thank you for getting Mercy – you're the only one she would have listened to. We're just talking politics."

Mercy glared at him, then sighed. "He's right, Mary. It's a vampire thing. We should..."

She rolled her eyes. "Right, you should go upstairs or something. Interrupt my night and leave me to keep myself company while the Ice Queen over here snows us in. Great."

Mary gave them a chance to protest before she turned her back to the vampires. As Mary made her way toward the living room, Mercy reached out and gently took Levi's hand. She guided him up the stairs.

"I'm very mad at you for involving her," she said.

"I'm very mad at you for *making* me involve her. I wish you'd have listened to me."

"And *stayed*? I'm threatening Mary Olive right now, Levi. You made her follow me... made me choose between risking her safety out in the open during a snowstorm or at home."

Levi ripped his hand from hers to rub his temples. "She's fine, Mercy. As long as we're not digging into this soul bond, things won't change. We won't cause a scene, and we won't discover any new powers."

"But if I stay here as you want me to," Mercy said, "It's a real possibility that we *will* cause a scene. I risk getting us both killed and my sister's safety in the process."

They arrived at the guest room, and Mercy tore the door open and gestured for him to enter. He walked in and sat on the bed while she set her suitcase down and crossed her arms.

"I'm going to be *very* clear with you, Levi. I'm sorry for you – you deserve to have that wholeness you crave. You're a good guy. One day, we'll explore that, maybe. If we want to control this spiritual *whatever*, we have to dig into it eventually. But not while Mary is alive. Not while my parents are alive. I have to leave to protect my family."

A pained look bloomed across his face, but it passed as he averted his eyes.

"I understand." He stood, walked to the vanity, and picked up a hair tie. He raised it to eye level, then strode over to her and gently pulled her hair back. Mercy was too stunned to respond as he tightened the band around her ponytail. "But not tonight. I forbid you from leaving, Mercy, until I say so."

She smacked his hand away from her now-ponytailed hair and glared at him. "You can't control me, Levi."

"I can," he said, gesturing to her hair. "Congratulations, Mercy. You're an estrie. You're getting more of that esoteric vampire knowledge you were craving."

"I'm a *what?*"

"It's a Jewish demon, according to legend. Now that I've bound your hair, you can't leave without permission. It's simply the type of vampire you are, and it's rather convenient in this moment."

Mercy glared at him before she defiantly walked toward the door. When she reached for the knob, her muscles locked. She stood frozen for a moment before she finally stepped back. "You bound me to this *fucking room*, Levi? You couldn't give me the whole *house* to roam around, at least?"

He shrugged apologetically. "Sorry, darling, I'm a bit new to this method. You're the first estrie I've known personally. But... I understand the lengths you'll go to for the sake of protecting your family. When conditions are dangerous, it's not worth risking your safety. Take my word for it."

Mercy was *almost* sympathetic. Levi had mentioned his dearly departed family just days ago, and he had been rather solemn as he spoke about it. Now, however... it felt like he was using that to guilt-trip her.

"Stop it. You know I'd best protect them by staying away."

"I think you'd best protect them by listening to me. Mary Olive wouldn't have had to go out in this weather if you had just stayed put."

Her eyebrows furrowed. "You are going to go downstairs and drink with Mary. Give her the best goddamn New Year's Eve party she's ever had, because you ruined her night. *You* did that, Levi, not me."

He didn't look particularly affected by that accusation. He just ran his eyes over her face curiously. "What are you going to do?"

"Unpack my computer and work on my book. Ann's going to be back in town this week, and I need to give her an update. I'm also going to be cleaning up my neck, because you're going to take my blood and turn this storm off."

Levi's eyes combed over her neck before he took a step back. "No."

"What?"

"It won't work," he said. "Not while you're angry. I won't be able to counteract your rage, no matter how hard I try. This is up to you to work through. Well, I better get downstairs. Looks like I have some partying to do."

AS THEY VENTURED INTO the wild mountain brush just beyond the town, Bernadette looked back at Wager. The wind whipped loose strands around her face as she studied her new business partner. "So how'd a train robber like you become a law-abiding ranch hand?"

"Who said I was a train robber?"

"Nobody," she called, turning her attention back to the barely-visible trail. "I know your type, Wager Watkins."

Mercy's fingers danced across the keyboard, creating a rhythmic clicking sound that almost blended into the barely muffled noise emanating from the living room below.

"Six, five, four..." The combined voices of Mary and Levi floated up to her tauntingly. "Three, two, one! Happy New Year!"

"Fuck me," Mercy muttered. "I wish I could turn off the damn snowstorm and leave."

You can, Mercy. Eventually. This is up to you to work through in the interim, though.

Mercy scooted back, and the friction of the chair against the old floorboards caused a grating sound. She imagined her unwanted roommates pausing and looking up at the ceiling in response to the noise, but she brushed away the thought as she stood and walked to the window.

There was a lot of snow on the ground – a couple feet, at least.

Working through her emotions to control this one wouldn't be easy. She was deeply conflicted. Before Levi revealed their likely fate, she very briefly considered the possibility of staying with him. There may have been a way, she reasoned, to satisfy her wanderlust and his need for companionship. And it wouldn't have been that bad, either – she did have a fondness for him.

And I for you, Mercy.

If you can hear me, she thought. *Come to me, Levi.*

Mercy stood in silence as the stairs creaked, then footsteps came down the hallway. The door opened and closed, and she shrugged off her chiffon cardigan. The approaching footsteps halted when she pulled her cotton turtleneck over her head.

She looked over her shoulder and met Levi's wide red eyes. He was absolutely stupefied, his lips parted slightly to reveal his fangs.

Mercy tilted her head, gracefully elongating her neck. Inviting him wordlessly. He crept forward, his every movement deliberate and filled with anticipation, until he finally enveloped her in his arms. His teeth trailed over her skin, leaving a trail of shivers in their wake before he moved away just enough to allow his cold exhale to brush over her flesh. "Are you sure, Mercy? I can't stop the storm for you."

"It will help me focus," she insisted. "Something tells me that if you help me calm down, I'll be able to focus enough to stop this storm and leave after New Year's Day."

He didn't speak for a moment, but then the brush of his lips against her neck sent shivers down her spine. When he sunk his teeth in, Mercy gasped. It felt *warm*. It was like pure sunshine – she hadn't felt this in ages. She hadn't realized she closed her eyes, but when they fluttered open, she saw that it wasn't snowing anymore.

As her blood thinned, Mercy felt like she was floating in the center of a hot tub. Not a single part of her was touching the ground, and she felt as if she could keep rising. Nonetheless, she broke the mental trance by reaching out to cup his face and pull it toward hers.

Their lips met in a kiss, but Mercy spoke almost as soon as it broke. "What kind of vampire are you, Levi?"

"I'm a dybbuk," he whispered. "I control minds, as you know. It's like possession if misused, hence why it's a distinct subset of vampirism. But you and I share something in common."

"Please don't say we have powers of seduction."

He chuckled. "Only in myth. But I can't imagine a better way to start the New Year."

Mercy kissed him again, pausing only to look out the window at the still landscape. No snow was falling anymore. After a lingering glance, she pulled the curtains closed.

Chapter Seven

Levi lifted Mercy's suitcase into Mary Olive's trunk and closed it. He glanced at the two young women as they trailed out of the house and kept his distance while they giggled and whispered. Eventually, Mercy met his gaze, so he stepped forward expectantly.

Mercy glanced at Mary before she approached Levi. Their eyes locked, but she didn't quite know what to say. He sensed her hesitation and pulled her into an embrace.

"I'll miss you, darling," he whispered. "I hate not knowing when I'll see you next."

Mercy bit her lower lip to stave off the threat of tears. "I'm sorry. I wish there was another way."

He pulled back and gazed down at her with sorrowful eyes. "I'm a call away if you ever need anything. As you figure out what being an estrie means, I'll answer any questions you may have. Obviously, I've never grown into being an estrie myself, but I do know a thing or two about coming into powers you don't understand."

"Thanks. I appreciate you, Levi."

"I love you, Mercy."

Mercy nodded numbly and turned to face her sister. "Ready, Mary Olive?"

Mary lifted her keys and jangled them enthusiastically. "Yes, ma'am! Let's go. Levi, I'll see you at work in a couple days?"

He smiled softly. "See you then. Drive safely, Mary. Take good care of your sister."

The women piled into the car while Levi stepped back and watched them depart. His gaze followed the car as it reversed onto the street, longing evident in his eyes. He lifted his hand to wave goodbye. Mercy waved back.

"So," Mary Olive said softly. "You're not staying with him?"

Mercy raised an eyebrow.

"I'm just saying, he seems pretty heartbroken. And you're like soulmates or whatever. I'd be feeling pretty bad right now if I was you."

Mercy sighed. "Look, Mary, do you want this drive to be pleasant? Or do you want a blizzard to follow us?"

She huffed. "*Fine*, I won't pick at it. How does this weather control thing work, by the way?"

"It's tied with my emotions, I think. I was able to turn off the snowstorm the other night by letting go of my anger. Now, though... I'm honestly a little bit sad, so I'm trying not to think about that. I have no idea what kinds of catastrophes I could cause."

Mary took one hand off the steering wheel to set it on her sister's shoulder, and she shot her a gentle smile. "Well, the good news is that I'm like the Post Office. Wind, rain, and snow won't stop me from having your back, sis."

"I know." Mercy smiled to herself as she looked out at the blanketed yards of the town. Snow plows had been hard at work, so massive piles of muddied snow framed the road. "You know something, Mary? This holiday didn't actually suck. Mom and Dad might have shown me their true colors, but so did you. I won't forget that you gave up your New Year's Eve plans to make sure I was safe."

Mary snorted. "Oh, don't worry. I won't let you forget. But ya know, a week-long getaway in NYC might help ease the pain. That's something I can't really afford on my barista salary."

"You can absolutely come stay with me. Anytime. Just let me know in advance so I can get a blowup mattress or something."

Mary chuckled. "Oddly, I can't imagine a better getaway."

WALKING DOWN THE STREET, Mercy could feel the sidewalk vibrating from the bassline spilling out of the club. Before she was within earshot, she knew it was Bauhaus – *Bela Lugosi's Dead*, probably. The local coven had a sense of humor, and it wasn't hard to find where they were hanging out on any given day.

Mercy flashed her ID at the bouncer as she walked in. The man, a bald character covered in tattoos, glanced at it before nodding with familiarity. She wasn't an unusual sight in this part of town.

She stepped into a massive red and black interior made intimate by the use of low, warm lighting. Her eyes scanned the scene before she spotted a familiar face hovering above a booth in the far corner of the venue.

When she approached, a young man with hazel eyes and long brown hair turned as if he sensed her. "Hey! Harker is here!"

"Mercy?" asked a woman with blue hair. She shooed the men beside her out of the booth and moved to her feet, elbowing the hazel-eyed man out of the way to hug her.

"Hey, Sammi," Mercy said as she fidgeted away from her grasp. The hazel-eyed man playfully punched her shoulder, so she lifted a fist. "You wanna fight, Ivan?"

"Nah," he said. "But I wanna hear how you fought with the family this Christmas. It never goes well with the Harker crew, does it?"

Sammi grabbed Mercy's hand and pulled her toward the booth, then pointed to one of the guys and gestured for him to get up. He rolled his eyes and stood to make room for the newcomer. The man crossed his arms and hovered near Ivan, watching expectantly as Mercy settled and cleared her throat. "Well, I guess we fought. They disowned me... My parents."

The man Sammi had evicted leaned closer. "I'm sorry, Mercy. That's what we have covens for. We can't trust humans."

Mercy thought of Mary Olive for a moment, but she knew better than to argue with Dave. He was one of the oldest members of the coven – he'd been a vampire for three decades or so – and was fairly respected among her peers in New York. Among vampires like Levi, he was barely mature. "Yeah, I guess it worked out, Dave."

He ran his eyes over her face, then snapped at Ivan. "Have our guy behind the bar get her a drink, man." As one of the palest members of their gang slinked away, Dave watched for a moment before he turned back to Mercy. "And did you bump into your sire?"

Mercy had to fight the urge to fidget under Dave's gaze. While he was a mature, fully-fledged vampire, most of Mercy's peers were fledglings. Only a handful, including herself, still had sires. The others had been forcibly freed – abandoned before they were ready, in one way or another – or had lost their sires. Some young vampires made fledglings while they were still too young to protect themselves, let alone a full bloodline. It was a sad fate that caused many of her contemporaries to crave companionship, especially alongside a few mature vampires. The coven gave them stability and protection.

Mercy was there for companionship and free blood. But at times, she also felt like an outsider. An oddity. While she previously rebelled against listening to the vampire who made her, she could feel their envy at her situation. *Having* a sire made her an outsider.

She cleared her throat. "Yes, I saw my sire, too. Briefly."

Ivan returned and shoved a glass into her hand, so Mercy nodded gratefully. Dave sympathetically gazed at her before softening his expression. "Are you okay? I know you've mentioned that he's controlling."

Mercy glanced at the vampires around her, then took a sip from her wine glass. "It went fine, actually. I learned quite a bit about him, including the type of vampire he is."

"Type?" Sammi shifted to scoot closer. "What do you mean by *type*?"

Mercy met Sammi's gaze, trying to think of a way to explain this new concept without revealing her own powers... and vulnerabilities, assuming any of the vampires were thinking about biting her. "Well, I've mentioned that he's controlling in the past. He's a dybbuk vampire – control is actually something innate to him. It's a special ability he and other dybbuks have, and I didn't realize it before."

Sammi squirmed. "I thought sires could just *do* that. Control us."

Mercy studied her sympathetically. Sammi had been made and abandoned – perhaps by accident, but likely on purpose. "I think it might be innate to some sires, yes. But Levi has a special sort of hypnotism that extends beyond his scions. He can get into anyone's head."

"A dybbuk," Dave echoed. "He's Jewish, then?"

"Sephardic," Mercy said.

"Didn't know there were different kinds," said the man to Sammi's right in the booth.

Mercy shrugged ambiguously.

"I told y'all," Ivan said. "A scion killed Kennedy. His sire told him to. Musta been a sire with enhanced powers, like Mercy's describing."

Dave nodded with consideration. "That's very possible... I've heard that story a few times. If what you're saying is true, Mercy, you have to stay away from this guy."

Mercy laughed coldly – she had already emotionally disconnected from the hurt of realizing she couldn't be near him, lest she risk her family's safety. "Oh, believe me, I will. Between my parents and everything that happened with him, I'm never going back to Connecticut."

The man at Sammi's side shifted. Mercy knew him, but she could never remember his name – he was the most mundane, vanilla person she'd ever met. "So... if there are types of vampires, what are we?"

Dave scoffed, but Mercy tilted her head sympathetically. If Levi hadn't been so forthcoming with information, she'd be just as in the dark as these young vampires. And Dave, a fully-fledged vampire who grew more woefully immature each time Mercy encountered him.

"We aren't anything special," Dave said. "Powers aren't common, and *types* aren't common. Most of us are vampyrs – v-a-m-p-y-r. We rise after death, feast on blood, and avoid the sun. Those *are* our powers, Joe."

His name is Joe, Mercy reminded herself. *Average Joe. That should be easy to remember.*

"And your sire didn't say what you were, right, Mercy?" Joe asked curiously.

Mercy chuckled. "Like Dave said, Joe, I haven't found any ability to control minds or turn into a bat."

Sammi reached into her pocket and fished out cigarettes, which she loudly packed against her open palm. She hip-checked Mercy and scooted out of the booth. "I'm gonna have a smoke to stave off the depressing reality that I'm startlingly average by Dave's standards. Harker, you coming?"

Mercy stared down at the pack of cigarettes. "Those menthol?"

"You know it!"

"Why not." Mercy downed the rest of her blood and set the glass on the table, then waved to her peers before she trailed after Sammi. They wound their way through the crowded club on the trek to the door, dodging uncoordinated dancers and drunk patrons spilling drinks almost every step of the way.

As they pushed outside, Sammi fumbled with the plastic on the pack. She triumphantly ripped it away, slipped out a cigarette, and offered it to Mercy. When she fished one out for herself, Sammi stared down at it for a second before she brushed her blue hair behind an ear and placed it between her lips.

She stared at the sidewalk for a long moment. Completely silent, she lifted a finger to the tip of her cigarette. When she pulled it away, the cigarette was lit. She exhaled a puff of smoke.

Mercy stared in amazement. When Sammi caught her gaze, she looked away and fished a lighter out of her pocket. She offered it to Mercy before she lifted her smoke to her lips again.

"I think my sire was like yours," she said as Mercy lit her cigarette. "She might not have been a dybbuk, but she could control minds. It was like her voice could hypnotize you, and you'd have to do what she said."

"I'm sorry, Sammi."

"So I lied to you guys – I wasn't abandoned after I was made. I ran as soon as I realized I could do this." She gestured down at the lit cigarette in her hands. "It was subtle at first. I was still warm, like I was alive. It was weird, but I didn't think it meant anything. Then, I was on the phone arguing one day when it suddenly melted in my hands. I realized my sire could do a lot of damage with my powers. So I ran. *Anyone* could do damage with my powers, so I've kept them hidden. I couldn't tell you what my sire was or what I am; I didn't stay long enough to get that information."

Mercy took a hit and ashed her cigarette. Her eyes followed the gray particles down to the concrete, where they danced for just a moment before blowing away.

"Don't tell them," Sammi said. "The coven doesn't need to know. But I thought you'd benefit from knowing that you're not alone. I know what it's like to be a powerful scion hiding in plain sight."

Mercy tilted her chin. "You think I have powers?"

Sammi shrugged. "I don't know what they are, but I see myself in you right now. You don't have to tell me, Mercy. I just wanted you to know you're not alone."

Mercy studied Sammi for a long moment before she ashed her cigarette again and took another hit. "Did you love her?"

"Who?"

"Your sire, Sammi."

Sammi scoffed. "I hated her. Why?" When Mercy didn't immediately answer, she flicked her eyes away and took a long drag. "Oh. You love him. I'm sorry you feel like you need to run from someone you love."

"I didn't say I *loved* him."

Sammi gave her a sad smile. "Okay, *fine*. I'm sorry you like him romantically but have to run. That sounds even lonelier than I am. Can I ask...?"

Mercy chuckled. "Yeah. Like your melting phone situation, I'm triggered by emotion. And I'm a danger to the people I love at home. It sucks, but I have a life here to look forward to, at least."

"Yeah, just two powerful, lonely scions hiding in plain sight," Sammi said again. "It's a joy, especially when the oldest vampire we can look to for guidance is a dumbass."

Mercy grinned. "Yeah, Dave's the worst. But their connections get us free blood – you really can't beat that."

Sammi dropped her cigarette butt and stomped it out. "I say we go take advantage of that. You'll need the energy for that big meeting with your agent tomorrow!"

MERCY'S FINGERS DANCED across the keyboard, humming to herself as her Andrews Sisters record spun on a turntable just across the room. As she finished the scene – a sorrowful reflection on her main character's childhood under the guardianship of his grandmother, who died while he was still young – she couldn't help but glance out the window. Snow was falling in heavy clumps.

She was certain she was behind the bad weather. She was hurting after admitting the truth of her situation to Sammi. While she had been able to separate her feelings from the experience when she first arrived home, talking about everything made it fresh again.

Writing her feelings into her story hurt worse.

Mercy drew a long, steadying, and unnecessary breath before reaching for her phone. Glancing at the locked screen, she made her way to the window, where she fixed her gaze on the snow clumps drifting gently to the ground. Finally, she unlocked the screen, navigated to her contacts, and lifted the phone to her ear.

After a minute, a quiet voice answered. "*Hey, Mercy.*"

"Hi, Levi."

There was a long silence as he waited for her to say something more. Eventually, he cleared his throat. "*I miss you, love.*"

"I miss you, too. It started snowing again."

He chuckled. "*Try thinking of the other night – that experience stopped it. Maybe it can stop it again.*"

"That's why I'm calling, I think. I *was* thinking about that. It made me sad. To think that we risk attracting vampire hunters just by being together... It's not fair, really. I wouldn't mind your company right now."

He was quiet. Mercy heard something that sounded vaguely like the clinking of ice cubes against glass.

"Are you drinking, Levi?"

"*I'm drinking a little, yes. Like I said, I miss you.*"

Mercy leaned against the window frame. Her eyes followed one particularly fat clump of snow as it gracefully danced through the air down to the street below. Something else caught her attention there – a man almost as white as the falling snow stood on the sidewalk. He was staring up at her.

Though there was a decent distance between them, Mercy swore the stranger saw her eyes widen, because he seemed to smirk. He stared for a few seconds before jamming his hands in his leather jacket pockets and walking away.

A chill crept down Mercy's spine.

"*You still there, darling?*"

"Yes, sorry, I..." Mercy trailed off as she gazed at the empty street. "I'm just making myself paranoid. What are you drinking?"

"*Cheap whiskey on the rocks. What are you doing?*"

"Writing. Well, I was. I just wanted to hear your voice. I saw the coven tonight."

Mercy could hear the patient smile in his voice when he spoke. "*I know. A coven is no stand-in for the closeness we share. I remember what it was like way back in the day. Good enough to learn from, but not a long-term solution for creatures like you and me.*"

"So... you found them because you were abandoned, right?"

He took a drink, his ice clanking softly into the speaker. "*Abandoned in the carnage of my loved ones, which broke me. I suppose the latter part of that worked out. But I wandered aimlessly for a while, unaware that I was a dybbuk. I eventually found a mature vampire who was sympathetic enough to invite me to their coven. It was like a shanty town – we lived in a makeshift home in the tunnels under the city. The mature vampires taught us a lot.*"

Mercy smiled to herself. "Very nice, Anne Rice. Where was this? Paris?"

"*Bohemia.*" He fumbled with something and thudded a cabinet door closed. "*Like I said, I've lived in many places.*"

"What brought you out here?"

"*To America? Instinct, perhaps. Boredom, in actuality. I'd traveled Europe many times over, and the idea of seeing a burgeoning culture unfold before me seemed fascinating. It's been a good few centuries here. It'll be a pleasant few more once we can finally be together."*

Mercy drew a heart in the condensation on the window. "One day, maybe. We're not there yet, Levi, and I won't put my life on hold waiting for it."

"I know you're not, Mercy. And I'm not asking you to."

"But you're expecting me to, eventually."

"Well, yes, I am. And you know why. I've been incomplete all day, Mercy. Then you call, and I'm whole. Being whole makes life worth living. You make life worth living."

A smile danced across her lips as she reached out and traced the heart in the condensation again. "I'm talking to my agent tomorrow, Levi."

"Are you? Tell me about it, love. I want to hear all about your big plans."

MERCY SAT DOWN AWKWARDLY, shuffling her briefcase beside her. She crossed her ankles and folded her hands in her lap.

Ann gestured to the stack of papers on her desk. "Well, Harker, you've done it again. Only six chapters in, and I'm hooked. We need to think of a better title, though."

Mercy was surprised, and it must have shown on her face. Ann's sharply arched eyebrow rose a little higher in expectation. She tucked her hair behind her ear and cleared her throat. "Oh, thank you, Ann. I can work through some title ideas."

"I've got a few interested editors." Ann picked up another stack of papers – this one thin enough to be paperclipped together – and licked her fingers to flip through the pages. "We've got Frank, Thomas, Ginger, and Stephanie. Read their profiles and see which feels like the best fit for you. I'll make it happen."

Mercy took the pages gratefully and flipped through the stack, then slipped it into her briefcase. Ann swiveled in her chair and motioned toward the television mounted on the wall. Intrigued, Mercy directed her focus to the screen.

"We've got a few different creative treatments we could pursue for its branding." Ann turned the television screen on, revealing a brown-toned doodle that was almost Art Deco. "My team suggested a sepia palette, though perhaps with splashes of sage and rust – those were colors I saw you mention in your manuscript. But we can go for something artsy, like this slide, or we can seek out models, like this."

Mercy stared at the screen. It showed a couple embracing before a frontier – the exact type of book she, as a reader, would avoid. "It's not a love story, Ann. You know that, right?"

"Well, I know you don't typically write romance, but cowboy romance is so *in* right now. I thought it might have been a subplot. You're telling me Wager and Bernie *aren't* in love?"

"Not that it matters," Mercy said, "But no, they're not. And they won't be falling in love. They're just my co-leads."

Ann puckered her lips and stared at the ceiling. "Would you consider adding in a romance subplot?"

"Absolutely not," Mercy said. "Aside from not being a romance writer, I really, really hate love at the moment."

Ann's eyes found Mercy's face again. She smirked slightly. "Ah. Someone didn't get a kiss under the mistletoe this season, eh?"

Mercy tilted her chin and glared at her agent. "Actually, Ann, I did."

Ann studied her impatiently, her eyes lingering for a long moment before she rolled them and shook her head in exasperation. "Alright, then we'll probably want to skip over the buff cowboy suggestions, too. So, Harker, where *does* this story end?"

"Bernadette is revealed to be a trick rider," Mercy explained. "And she creates a new economic booster in her first performance: tourism. She becomes a legend, so their business naturally starts providing all sorts of oddball entertainment, from frog jump races to sideshow attractions. It ends with Mark Twain coming to town and hearing about the frog jumps, which you know supposedly inspired his first acclaimed story. Essentially, it ends with my characters making literary history without realizing it."

Ann scratched her chin, then flipped through a couple slides. "What do you think about this type of visual treatment?"

Mercy carefully observed the picturesque scenery, which included a striking silhouette of two people riding on horseback and a sample font treatment. She nodded approvingly. "I like it. If we can do a silhouette of a trick rider closer to the foreground, that might be cool."

Ann scribbled that down and turned the television off. "Great. I'll leave you with my stack of suggestions, then –

tweak the story at these parts, keep building her out, and keep me updated. We'll get things rolling soon."

"Thanks." Mercy accepted the bigger stack of paperwork. This one was held together with a fat rubber band. "This was a fast meeting."

"Thanks for coming out," Ann said. "I value this face-to-face time. A shame it started snowing last night. Just when we thought this blizzard was clearing up."

Mercy's stomach churned as she forced a smile. She stood with her briefcase in hand. "Yeah, weird timing. Thanks, Ann. I'll keep you in the loop on progress here."

The women parted ways with a curt wave, and Mercy flashed a few smiles at passersby as she headed toward the elevator. She hit the button, and a mechanical whir instantly responded as the elevator came to her floor.

She spent the ride to the lobby praying the snow would let up. She also wished she could enjoy this small victory – impressing Ann was no easy feat – but there was a heaviness resting in the base of her tummy.

She wanted to celebrate with Levi.

When the elevator reached the lobby, Mercy pulled her jacket close despite the cold not bothering her. Something else was bugging her... she wasn't sure what it was, but she was uneasy.

I must be missing Levi worse than I imagined I would, Mercy thought as she moved through the revolving door onto the street. *How dreadfully embarrassing. Note to self – resist the urge to call him tonight.*

Guardedly, she walked to the curb and waited until a taxi came into view. She waved to flag it down, and it graciously slowed and eased its way to the sidewalk. She opened the door and scooted into the backseat. "India Street in Brooklyn, please."

"Just across the tunnel," the driver noted as she buckled in. That was all he said before he took off. Truthfully, Mercy was grateful for his silence. She wasn't feeling particularly conversational.

She leaned back and closed her eyes. She was relieved that Ann had received her story pitch well, but something still felt off. When she opened her eyes again, they were passing the Chrysler Building.

"Oh, you're heading toward Midtown," she said. "Greenpoint is across the river."

"This is a different route," the driver said, meeting her eyes in the rearview mirror.

That was a lie, she thought. There was no alternate route – the most direct way home was a mere fifteen-minute drive. As she held the driver's gaze, she saw his eyes shift from brown to vermilion.

Mercy gasped and grabbed the door's handle. It didn't budge. Panicking, she shoved her weight into the door as the driver turned onto First Street and navigated onto the shoulder of the road. When he turned to face her, he was holding a stake. She screamed as he dove into the backseat.

Chapter Eight

Mercy's eyes fluttered open. Wherever she was, it was dark. Massive concrete-supported metal beams stared back down at her from a ceiling that was maybe thirty feet up.

She was in an abandoned warehouse, it seemed. There was no shortage of those in New York City. She could feel dust and debris on the floor beneath her, but she couldn't move to pull herself away from the detritus.

It took her a long moment to realize that a stake was jammed into her mouth. It left her paralyzed. Her eyes darted around the space in a panic as two figures approached.

She recognized one instantly as the taxi driver – he had dark skin, though he was still pale, and long dreadlocks. The man beside him, by contrast, was short-haired and roughly the same hue as a marshmallow.

As white as snow.

It was the man she'd seen on the street, she realized. She'd been tracked, and she could guess why they'd set their sights on her. These must have been the vampire hunters Levi had warned her about.

The men approached her as she whimpered helplessly. Each moved to a different side, then kneeled beside her. She winced as she felt them toying with the hem of her pants down by her ankles. Just barely out of her line of vision, they stretched the fabric and drove a pin into it, firmly locking it into place. Slowly, they moved up her legs, pinning fabric as they moved, then repeated the ritual with her shirt. She could see now that they were pinning her clothing to the debris on the ground with thumbtacks.

As they finished securing the fabric around her shoulders, they stood and looked down at her.

"Her mate will come," the marshmallow man said. "If he's really a dybbuk, he'll know. He should be able to hear her thoughts, or at least sense her fear."

Mercy stared at the ceiling. Totally frozen, there was no way for her to move. She wanted to throw punches at these strangers, but even if she could, she was certain she couldn't fight them. Something told her that these vampires were far older than Levi.

And they were absolutely the very cannibals she'd been warned about. Since she was turned, she'd never been scared by another vampire. But these men? They were terrifying. She could sense how dangerous they were, and she realized that she'd been feeling uneasy since last night. Since she saw the marshmallow man on the sidewalk.

Mercy had been sensing their predatory gazes for hours.

The darker vampire moved to linger over her face. As he leaned forward, his dreads cascaded framed his face. "I'm going to remove that stake from your mouth. If you scream,

I'll drive it through your heart instead. Blink if you understand me."

Mercy blinked frantically.

He smiled, revealing two ridiculously long fangs. Mercy had never seen a vampire with teeth like that. "Good. Now, we've been keeping a pulse on the local enclave for years, and we started noticing that *someone* in that circle seemed to be able to control the weather. We're watching over the holiday, and nothing changes weather-wise, so we naturally suspect our vampire of interest left the area. Suddenly, you return to town as an absolutely unpredictable blizzard blows in. We just want to know where you went and who you saw."

"Wait," the pale man said. When his lips parted, Mercy noted that he also had two massive pearly daggers where normal vampire-sized fangs should have been. "Don't move the stake yet. The man said her sire is a dybbuk. She could be something we've seen in the Miqra, too. She could be a rahab, with control of *water* rather than weather, or even a mazzikin, simply enacting the direction of her sire. We should pin her hair, too."

The vampire directly above her leaned down to release Mercy's ponytail. She gasped when her hair fell loosely around her shoulders. Like a few nights ago, Mercy suddenly felt warm and weightless. Floaty. She was rising from the ground before she knew it, like that game they play at sleepovers – light as a feather, stiff as a board. Though she felt the world around her growing lighter, the experience felt surreal, and it took her a moment to process everything.

Holy shit, she finally thought. *I am* not *on the ground.*

While her ascent at first felt slow, Mercy was violently jerked through the air after mere seconds of suspension. Despite her shock, she twisted her neck around to gaze down at her attackers, who were staring up into the air with absolute stupefaction. The stake rested on the ground beside them, surrounded by a person-shaped outline of multicolored thumbtacks. When she looked up again, she was approaching a cloud.

She hadn't recalled leaving the building.

Mercy shrieked as she moved into the cloud. It wrapped around her gradually, but then her velocity changed, sending her soaring over the cityscape as fast as an airplane. Faster, maybe. The wintery brown of the Hudson River shimmered below her as it sped past and faded into the horizon.

As Mercy continued her unsolicited journey, she began to accept that whatever was happening, it was out of her control. Like a passenger on an airliner, she started focusing on the landscape. It felt like she was suspended for an eternity before she saw a massive body of water, like a lake, break through the endless stretch of trees and roads.

That can't be the Kensico Reservoir, she thought. *I'd be close to home.*

Mercy realized with horror that it very likely *was.* In actuality, she was probably zipping her way toward Connecticut. She clawed at the empty air in confusion, but it didn't change her direction or the fact that the ground felt miles away.

Below her, something not quite like a lake, but not quite a river flashed past alongside tiny snow-covered communities. Mercy started nearing the ground when another creek came into view, but she knew she wasn't going to crash. Innately, she somehow understood she wouldn't fall. Another body of water flashed past, and she was sure this one was the Housatonic River. She was, without a doubt, back in Connecticut. As she inched closer to the ground, she tore through sleepy communities near the speed of light.

She finally knew where she was going.

Eventually, her route left her rushing toward a historic white Colonial. She braced for impact by stretching her hands in front of her, but they instinctively caught the handle when she should have collided with the front door. The force of her collision pushed the door open.

Mercy tumbled, rolling across hard wooden floors and skidding into a hutch with a painful thud. Wind violently whipped around her, knocking over snow boots and umbrellas while unleashing pure chaos in the enclosed space.

Levi was picking Mercy up before she could even process what had just happened.

He wrapped his arms around her, then moved to close the front door and cut off the draft. Supporting her weight, he looked down at her with concern. "How did you get here? Where did you come from?"

"I... I flew, I think." Mercy gulped and rubbed her head where she'd bumped it. Then, a hand numbly snaked up to feel her jaw. There had been a stake in her mouth, but something tore her away from it *and* the thumbtacks. It was almost like she'd *passed through* them.

"You manifested out of thin air," Levi said slowly. His eyebrows raised as if he had just come to a great realization.

"So my suspicions are confirmed, then. You *are* a shapeshifter."

Mercy shook her head. "I didn't change, Levi. I just... Flew here, I guess. Or something."

"You did shift," he said with certainty. "You became *wind*, Mercy. You're an elemental. *Very* powerful. What brings you here?"

Mercy met his eyes and tried her jaw. She shook her head weakly.

"Very well," he said. "I'll get some blood heated on the stove. We'll talk after you have a bit of sustenance in you."

LEVI WATCHED AS MERCY hungrily chugged the entire serving of blood, and he dutifully refilled the chalice a second time.

"According to legend," he said. "It's your hair. Tying it back binds you to the ground, possibly to a place if your sire commands it. Estries love to feel the wind in their hair, so your abilities make sense. I'd heard stories of estries many years ago... I always suspected you might have this ability."

"I can fly," Mercy said in disbelief.

"You understand me here, right? You became *wind*, Mercy. Some estries can shapeshift. Not all, by any means, but it's a common enough experience to be preserved in legend. What triggered it?"

"These two men," Mercy said, which caused Levi's eyebrows to lift with concern. "I got in a taxi outside my agent's office, and this man attacked me. He staked me through the mouth."

"Oh my God." Levi leaned against the countertop.

"Then I woke up in a warehouse or something, and they were pinning my clothing down with thumbtacks."

He nodded. "Staking you in place. A modern twist on a very old ritual. Slavic in origin, I think. Did they hurt you, Mercy?"

Mercy took a sip and shook her head. "No, I, uh, turned into wind. They took my hair down and it just *happened*."

"Do you know why they targeted you?"

She lifted a shoulder in a half-shrug. "I can make an educated guess. They were looking for my sire, Levi. They mentioned knowing you're a dybbuk vampire."

"*How?*"

"They blamed it on the New York enclave," she said. "The local vamps I pal around with. They knew my sire could command me to do things – a few scions had mentioned their sires could. It wasn't anything I hid."

"And it need not be hidden," he said. "*Usually*. There's so much to explain with so little time, but vampires like me can create different types of fledglings. You were likely to become what you are based on the time of day you went through the change. Knowing what I am allowed them to narrow in on what *you* might be. They must not have guessed you were an *estrie*, given that they let your hair down. But now that they know, they just need to search for signs of a dybbuk and an estrie. They'll find us easily."

Mercy chugged the rest of her drink and carelessly tossed the chalice in the sink. She washed her hands and shook them dry as Levi picked up a towel and offered it to her.

After accepting it, she glanced down at her feet, nervous as she twisted her hands beneath the towel.

"So they're absolutely hunting us. We're their next meal."

"Yeah, I would say they're hunting us. That was a massive blizzard you conjured... they must know a soul bond was fueling it. But *we* haven't done anything together, so they don't know who or where I am yet. However, we should be worried that they know who *you* are, Mercy. They're likely to come looking."

"Here?"

He shook his head. "If I had to guess, they'd trace former addresses."

"*Fuck*. We've got to get to my parents' place."

"I'll call Mary Olive. She'll get there sooner than us."

WHEN THEY PULLED INTO the driveway, Mercy's eyes landed on her sister's Honda. She rushed to the doorstep and knocked.

When the door creaked open, Mary's eyes lit up with relief and joy. She hugged her sister. "Oh my God, I'm so glad you're okay. Get in here."

Mercy lifted her foot, but it thudded against an invisible barrier. Her eyes lifted from the threshold and darted past her sister, staring at where her parents had walked up behind Mary. She lifted her chin. "They uninvited me, Mary."

Mary turned to her parents. "Jesus Christ, guys. Let your daughter in the house."

"That *thing* is not my daughter," Dad spat. "Get thee behind me, Satan!"

"I'd *love* to," Mercy said sarcastically. "But I can't even enter. Mom, *please*. Don't listen to him. I'm still your daughter. I've been staying with Mary. Let her vouch for me."

Mary nodded. "She hasn't bitten me *once*. Although she *did* do something with my *Live, Laugh, Love* sign."

"Mary Olive!"

"Ugh, *fine*. Missing sign aside, she's still Mercy. If anything, that *proves* she's Mercy."

Mercy didn't take her eyes off her parents, but her father wouldn't look at her. Her mother, on the other hand, was staring at her with tears in her eyes. "Mom, *please*. I'm begging you to listen. Whatever he's said, you need to ignore it. I'm not here to hurt you."

A tear slipped down her cheek. "I know, baby. Get in here."

"Beth!"

"Can it, Steve!" she exclaimed. "You kicked her out on *Christmas*. That was heartless. She needs help and she's asking to come home."

Gratefully, Mercy stepped over the threshold and embraced her sister. Beth eagerly accepted a hug when she turned to her next. However, when her gaze settled on her father, he turned his back to her. Stung, Mercy let go of her mother and took a step back. "He needs to come in, too, Mom."

Her eyes flicked past Mary to the stranger at the door. Levi waved.

"The guy from the coffee shop?" she asked with recognition. "Sure, he can come in, I guess."

Levi smiled wickedly as he stepped over the entryway. He slipped past Mary and Mercy, then moved to take their mother's hand. He kissed it. "A pleasure to meet you, Beth. Now, Steve."

At the hypnotic tone in his voice, the girls watched as their father's head snapped in Levi's direction. His eyes widened.

"Pack a bag and get in your daughter's car."

Obediently, almost in a trance, he walked off. Levi turned back to their mother. "Beth, you must do the same. You're both going to be staying with me for a while."

"We have a cat," she said helplessly.

Levi winced. Mercy knew he hated cats. "Very well – pack it up. You're going on an all-expense paid vacation."

After she brushed past him and wandered upstairs, Levi turned his attention to Mary Olive.

"Thank you for your help, dear," he said. "And I'm sorry to say I'll be uprooting you, too. I'll explain everything at my house."

Mary ran her eyes over him and Mercy before she nodded. "Okay. This feels impulsive, but I trust you guys."

"IT USED TO BE AN INN," Levi explained. "There are nine rooms – not enough private bathrooms to be a modern inn, I'm afraid, but spacious enough that none of us will step on each other's toes."

"Your house is beautiful," Beth mustered politely.

"Thank you," Levi said with a flourished bow. "I decorated it myself. Make yourselves at home for the time being."

"So you're not going to tell us why you uprooted us?" demanded Steve.

Levi lifted his chin. "Sure, but you cannot tell *anyone*. And that was a command, not a request. Try and you'll choke. Some much meaner vampires are hunting your daughter. We've brought you here for your protection, as we figure they'll go looking for her family members when they can't find her."

The family cat – a Persian named Schnitzel – meowed, seemingly in concern. Mary scooped him up from where he was perched on the arm of the couch, but Schnitzel squirmed away. He slinked into Beth's lap just in time to be scooped up with a concerned gasp. "They'll come for *us*?"

"Let me be clear," Levi said, leaning forward. "I don't care about either of you. Mary Olive, you're near and dear to me, of course. After all, I need someone to open on Tuesdays. But Mercy loves all of you. I'm doing this for her, so you better be kind to her during your stay. You think you can handle that, Steve?"

He grumbled under his breath, but he couldn't physically argue. Levi had prevented that. Mercy thought it was kind of funny. Her father was religious to the point of being brainwashed, and he must have thought this was actual Hell. After suffering through a childhood of living under his rules, that made her chuckle a little.

"This will be like an even bigger sleepover!" Mary exclaimed as she turned to face her mother. "It'll be so *fun.*

We can order pizza, watch movies on that massive television, snuggle up with Schnitz on this humongous couch..."

"You'll definitely need to order food," Mercy said. "Levi doesn't... well, his kitchen isn't stocked."

"Is he the reason you're like this?" Steve finally asked. Mercy tightened her fists and narrowed her eyes, but she didn't feel the need to respond to his question. Fortunately, she didn't have to.

"That's *not* your business, Dad," Mary snapped. "Look, you don't know how long she's been like this. You couldn't draw a clear line between loving her unconditionally and hating what she's become if I asked you to. You've loved her while she's been like this – your *religion* told you not to."

"Vampires are the descendants of Lilith," he said. "They're soulless demons."

Mercy shifted to meet her father's gaze. "Jesus Christ, Dad, me having a soul is the *explicit problem* here. That's what got us into this situation. I'm not a demon. I'm not a hellspawn. I was built from the framework of a very dumb girl who made bad decisions. Someone out there wants to kill me, and they'd happily make a snack of you along the way. Excuse me for stepping in to prevent that."

She spun on her heel and marched into the kitchen, trailed by the sound of Mary berating their parents. Levi didn't follow immediately, and by the time he stepped into the room, she was leaning in the fridge.

"Why are you moving the blood supply to the drawer?"

She closed what might have been used as a vegetable drawer and straightened her back. "I don't know. I guess to prevent drama while they're here. I mean, that nasty remark about being a soulless demon was bad enough."

"I won't allow drama here. We're going to protect your emotional state, Mercy. And remember that this is only temporary until we figure out what to do with them. We really shouldn't stay in Connecticut now that they're looking for you."

"Where else could we go?"

He shrugged. "I have a few properties – I alternate every ten years or so. I'm thinking Cleveland."

Mercy moved to the stovetop to stir the blood she'd poured before he came in. "I'd rather die than go to Cleveland."

"Oh, come on. It's not that bad." He tilted his head as she produced a wine glass. "You're not going to use the chalice?"

"No, it's stupid."

"Okay, ouch." He stepped closer to her. "Look, Mercy, I know you're scared. It's okay. We haven't slipped up. With any luck, we won't, and this is all just an extreme precaution. If we lay low and stay cautious, they won't find us. Nothing is going to happen to you."

"And if we *do* fuck up?"

He shrugged as she ladled liquid into her glass. "Then we can assume they're looking for signs of you or your family about a forty-minute drive away from here. You'll all have to stay put for now. You, your parents. Mary Olive. Shit, I'll have to find someone to open on Tuesdays."

While Levi dug his phone out of his pocket, Mary Olive walked in. "Ooh, are we drinking wine?"

When Mercy cocked an eyebrow, she smiled apologetically.

"Wine's in the tall cabinet," Levi said dismissively as he typed. He didn't even look up as Mary flitted across the kitchen and claimed a bottle of red wine.

Mercy grabbed a glass for her sister while she wrestled the cork. Mercy watched her struggle for a moment before she reached out, took the bottle, and popped the cork with almost no effort.

"Those soulless demon powers are pretty handy." Mary Olive accepted the bottle and poured a deep red liquid into her glass. "You're stronger than you look."

"And I make a mean coffee, too."

Mary chuckled. "For what it's worth, sis, I'm grateful you chose to protect us, though I'm not sure I fully understand the situation. I mean, yeah, this sucks, being cooped up with them again after we *just* did this shit over the holidays. But we'll get through this. Cheers."

Mercy clinked her glass against Mary's with amusement, then took a drink. The blood was a bit bland and tasteless – it was clearly going stale. They'd have to finish that bag soon, she thought.

We have our choice of fresh blood now.

At the sound of Levi's voice in her mind, Mercy promptly turned and shook her head. Levi smirked, filled a chalice, and disappeared.

"Just saying," Mary said. "You guys were *loud* the other night before you left. New Year's Eve, was it? Remember that Mom and Dad are in the house now."

Mercy pushed her playfully. "Ugh. I could have gone my entire eternal life without knowing you heard that."

"I could have lived my entire ephemeral life not having heard that," Mary said. "And now that your love affair has trapped me in a house with Mom and Dad and left me unable to leave for work or groceries, I'm going to be on hall monitor duty. No way am I going through that again. I *will* pound on the door."

"I know who to go to when my blood bags run out, then."

"Don't make me tell Dad."

"Oh no, he might kick me out on Christmas again. What a travesty."

The girls chuckled, and for a moment, everything seemed like it might be okay.

Of course, Mercy couldn't shake the chill that had settled over her. Her mind kept replaying the scene in New York – from the thumbtacks pinning her to dusty debris to the shock of suddenly rising toward the atmosphere.

Life's a funny thing, she thought. *It's as unpredictable as wind. Forces outside your control may cause it to shift in a rather destructive way. But that unpredictable gale can be so welcome on a pleasant summer day.*

She thought of the sensation of sunshine that came over her before she realized she was rising. One day, summer would return.

Goddamn did this feel like winter, though.

Chapter Nine

Mercy pulled away and sat down at the window seat. Levi wiped his mouth on his sleeve before he settled beside her. He side-eyed her, leaned forward, and touched a single fingertip to the bay window's glass. Seemingly stretching from his fingertip, a tendril of ice extended across the outer window pane and settled into the shape of half a heart. He gestured to it expectantly.

Mercy leaned forward and breathed on the glass, then outlined the other half of the heart in the condensation.

"Mercy," he scolded. "You didn't even try."

She sighed. "I'm sorry. I'm not in the headspace." She glanced toward the stairs, where she could hear the muffled echo of her bickering parents. They hadn't stopped yelling since they'd arrived. Mercy was used to noise, as New York was a loud and restless city, but this was unsettling.

Levi caught her chin and turned it toward him. "Hey. Life is going to put you in many positions where you're *not in the headspace*. We're predators, darling. Being distracted is a death sentence."

"I learned that the hard way in New York. Look, Levi, I'm sorry. I just don't feel a connection with the weather. This isn't easy for me. It doesn't feel natural."

He smiled gently and reached out to pull her ponytail down. His fingers danced through her hair, fluffing it out. A deep crease caused it to wave in that feminine way Golden Age actresses often wore their hair. "Well, not when you're grounded, I'd suspect. Now that your hair is down, try again. When you inhale, feel the absence of warmth in your breath. Focus on that."

Mercy frowned at him, but she turned and touched a fingertip to the glass. She inhaled, feeling the cool air dance through her nostrils and fill her oxygen-deprived lungs. When she exhaled, she felt the chill of death dance along with her breath. She focused on harnessing that cold and directing it through her fingertips.

Long, vein-like lines of frost stretched from her fingers, tracing and icing over the condensation. Her brow furrowed with focus as the chill connected her frost-encrusted art to Levi's solid shape. He reached out and covered her hand with his, and something magical happened: the ice kept climbing. It began to branch out, filling the area around the heart with stained glass-like fractals.

Mercy drew her hand back and watched in amazement as the ice continued crawling. She crinkled her brow with focus, watching as the veins of ice followed the design in her head and became more complex, coiling into a complicated frame of swirls. When she looked away from her handiwork, Levi was grinning at her.

"What?" When he didn't respond, she nudged him. "I *told* you I could do it."

"Right," he said sarcastically. *You told me.*

Mercy, intrigued, mentally reached toward the soundless whisper of his voice. Her consciousness brushed his – cautiously at first, then more confidently – as she wondered, *what more can we do?*

Before she could press forward, someone walked in and jumped. Mercy realized that she and Levi were face to face, mere inches apart. Locked in a lover's gaze full of wonder and yearning.

How dreadfully embarrassing.

"I'm so sorry, Mercy. I didn't know you were in here."

"It's fine, Mom." Mercy waved her into the room and gestured to the window. "Look what I did."

Beth slinked forward and eyed the window timidly at first, then with awe. "You did this? How?"

Mercy grinned. "I'm learning I have an affinity for the elements, as Levi put it. There are things I can do, and I'm just now scratching the surface of what that means. Isn't this pretty?"

She admired her daughter's handiwork as her eyes combed over the window pane with genuine admiration. "It is. It's amazing that you can do this, sweetie. Levi, right? I don't think we got much of a proper introduction today."

He shook her hand and politely smiled. "It's good to get to spend time with you, Beth. Mercy has told me much about you over the years."

She settled in a chair, offering a smile that felt forced. Levi cocked his head, which Mercy interpreted as a sign that he was listening to her mother's thoughts. Beth stared at her daughter for a long moment before she finally cleared her throat. "How long has it been like this, Mercy?"

"Around nine years now. I was twenty."

"Yes," Levi said when Beth's eyes impulsively darted in his direction. "I changed her."

Beth opened and closed her mouth, struggling to articulate her thoughts. She cleared her throat before ultimately giving up and casting her gaze downward.

"I asked for it," Mercy explained. "Levi and I crossed paths and... well, I found out what he was. I asked for it."

Beth bit her lip and stared at her daughter for a long moment. "I still love you, honey, and I'm so sorry we kicked you out on Christmas. But... I'll be honest, I have difficulty wrapping my mind around this. I'm trying to be supportive, but I don't know what to do. I don't know what to think about you two."

"If it's any consolation," Mercy ventured. "Levi is my soulmate, Mom. We're built of the same stardust. I only asked for it because of that – it was this innate awareness that I was meant to be at his side. For what it's worth, though, I'm not romantically involved with him or anything. I've genuinely been living in New York and publishing books while I try to figure out what life looks like for me."

She shifted, clearly uncomfortable. That knowledge wasn't the comfort Mercy had hoped it would be.

"She wasn't referring to us as a couple," Levi said quietly. "She meant us as vampires."

If Mercy's heart was beating, her cheeks might have flamed. In this moment, the lack of heat in her cheeks made her hyper-aware that she was dead. It might have been odd, but she didn't frequently find herself reflecting on her vampirism. Although, in fairness, she also hadn't spent a ton of time reflecting on her humanity when she was alive.

"Have you killed people, Mercy?"

"Of course not," Mercy said. "Maybe from boredom because, I mean, some of my first books were rough. But boring a reader to death is probably worlds better than what you're thinking."

She chuckled. "I've read all your books, you know. I've been cheering for you this whole time. I always knew that imagination would serve you well. You're very talented."

"I've read them all, too," Levi said. "I've found that they really capture the essence of the human condition. Remarkable coming from a soulless demon."

Beth recoiled.

"Levi!" Mercy scolded. "Don't antagonize my mother. She wasn't the one who said it."

"But I'm sorry I didn't defend you," she said quietly. Her eyes darted to Levi, and she lifted her chin. "Steve is lost. Since he retired, he's thrown himself into volunteering at the church. Truthfully, I don't even think I believe anymore. But it's his whole life right now."

"It has been for a long time," Levi said knowingly. "He had an encounter with a vampire when he was a young man, and he threw himself into religion as a result. It scarred him. I, ahem, got that impression during his hostile outburst earlier."

Beth tilted her head curiously and was quiet for a prolonged moment. Finally, she cleared her voice and clasped her hands in her lap. "He might have mentioned it to me in passing, yes. I don't really know the details. When we were young, it just sounded like a monster in the closet. Something he imagined as a child. When the girls were growing up, though, he found comfort in religion. I always thought therapy would have done the trick, but his faith calmed him down. Or so I thought."

"And you're okay with that?" Levi asked. "You're okay with him using religion to bandage his wounds and hurt your daughter?"

"No," she admitted. "But just like he thinks *you're* lost, Mercy, I know he's lost. We'll get him back. It'll just take breaking down his walls. He'll come around."

"I've seen a lot in my life, so I'll give you that," Levi said before Mercy could say something regrettable. "If I've learned anything, hatred comes from fear. And we can unlearn fear."

In the silence that followed that statement, Mercy tilted her head, waiting for him to elaborate. When he didn't, she shifted to face her mother. "Levi was running from persecution when he was turned."

"Oh," Beth said in surprise. "Can I ask...?"

Levi chuckled, then glanced at the complicated icework on the window. The chilly surface was catching falling snowflakes, adding softness to the design. "Sure, you can. I'm Jewish. I've seen centuries of hatred and racism toward my people, but I've also seen a shift toward acceptance. Ironic to be a personification of all that."

"What do you mean?" Mercy asked.

He shifted his attention to her and frowned. "*Oh*. You genuinely don't know. Well, Mercy, the literary vampire is a metaphor for antisemitism."

Mercy, taken aback, shifted forward. "What? *How?*"

"The outsider with the funny accent who hoards ancient wealth and plots to defile innocent Christians," he said. "I mean, look at Dracula – he had curly hair, bushy eyebrows, a hook nose, *and* he moved to London at a time when an influx of Jews were arriving. People understood the parallel, and they understood that this literary monster came to their home not for protection, but to bring ruin."

Mercy blinked. "I'm an author... how have I never heard this?"

He shrugged. "It's not knowledge that's particularly accessible – we still have work to do as a collective world and society. But it all goes back to the blood libels. In the Middle Ages, Jews were often accused of using Christian blood in their rituals and recipes. Ironically, by making us social outcasts and scapegoats, they made us likely victims, too. I'm not the only Jew who was expelled from my own land just to have to live to see the Holocaust."

"Levi..." Mercy put her hand on his knee to comfort him, but he didn't even react.

"So, in short," he said to her mother. "No, Mercy isn't a killer. And many of us are not. You'll be safe in my home, but the monsters out there who are looking for you... *they're* the killers. We should all be very afraid of them."

"Thank you for welcoming us," Beth said. "And for keeping our family safe and together."

LEVI WALKED INTO THE kitchen, his shoulders already slumped. "I know you're lurking in here, Mercy. I can hear you."

She set her book down. "I wasn't lurking. I was reading *Dracula*. Found it in your library."

When he turned to face her, she huffed.

"*Fine*. I was waiting for you. This book is honestly not my favorite."

"You'll like it, darling. It's a bit slow at first, but it picks up." He leaned against the counter. "Yes, I hear your thoughts right now. You don't have to ask me. I did hear Steve's thoughts, and yes, he genuinely knew a vampire back in the day. In the Biblical sense."

"Ew." Mercy covered her ears. "I'm *not* listening."

He chuckled and studied the floor. "I ought to mop. You know, I think spring is the worst season after you die. When you're alive, watching the flowers awaken to greet the warm sunshine is such a treat. When you're undead, all you can see is an eternity of mud. You'd think wintertime would be something of a mud off-season. I'd really like to spend less of my eternity cleaning."

Mercy lowered her hands and rolled her eyes. "For the record, I hate when you do that."

"What? When I entertain your childlike avoidance?" He turned his back to her to fumble through a broom closet for a mop and bucket. As he moved to the sink, he glanced over his shoulder to briefly meet her gaze. "But if you really want to know, love, it sounds like Steve had... well, what we have."

"What do you mean?"

With his back still turned to her, Levi dropped to his knees to dig under the sink for tile polish. He stood and added it to the bucket before he turned the water on. "There was a woman who seemed to care a great deal for him. He thought about her earlier."

"He had a soul bond?" Mercy asked, leaning forward. "That's what you're saying, Levi?"

He turned off the water and turned to face her, crossing his arms over his chest as if to comfort himself. "*Had*, yes. He saw her die. Another vampire took her life right in front of him. He has a deeply rooted hatred... Both from the pain of losing that kind of love and seeing the destruction our species can cause."

Mercy looked down at the weathered book on the table before her and bit her lip. Like the titular Count in the story, she wasn't human. But, goddamn, did she feel a human response at that moment. Her heart ached for her father's lost love and subsequent trauma. From Levi's body language, she could tell the lingering shock of *imagine if* was clinging to him, too.

"Hate can be unlearned," Levi said again.

She propped her elbows on the table and intertwined her fingers to make a shelf for her chin. As she settled into her new position, she said, "I believe you. It's just... who killed her? And why?"

"I don't know. His thought was fleeting. Truthfully, darling, I don't think it really matters. It's a moment in your father's journey that's now a monumental piece of his past. It shaped him, but it's long gone. Lost to the ages."

"So that's why he had suspicions about me," Mercy said quietly. "And probably why the holy water came out. He wasn't going to let a vampire hurt him again. He's fragile and protecting himself the only way he knows how."

Levi moved the bucket to the floor and gently dipped the mop in it. "Don't be too sympathetic here. He still hurt you. Nonetheless, I think we're doing the right thing by keeping them out of the hunters' sight."

"Me, too."

As he started cleaning, he glanced over his shoulder at her. "Why don't you go relax, dear? Take your book and take it easy. You deserve a break from this stress as much as I deserve a break from this mud."

MERCY, WHO WAS RECLINED on a couch in the library, sat up when Levi flitted past with a feather duster. She raised her eyebrows as he grumbled under his breath. "Did I just hear that right? You *hate* this?"

He stopped to scowl at her. "Why, yes, I do. I don't like forming relationships with humans – they die so quickly."

"You're still feeling bad about the Steve thing, huh?"

"Yes, perhaps I'm a bit haunted by the thought of losing a soulmate. Excuse me for being anxious. Plus, while I've opened hotels over the years, I'm not quite accustomed to having company now. You could say I'm a bit flustrated. Ah, see? I just mixed flustered and flustrated. *Frustrated!* Dammit."

"It's okay, Levi." Mercy pulled her knees toward her chest and wrapped her arms around them. "It's not that bad. At least you have me here. You've been wanting me to stay for years."

He sighed. "While I'm grateful for your presence, Mercy, I wish it was just us. We never had a chance to explore what our abilities look like. And now we've got an audience and people hunting us, waiting for a mistake. It's *frustrating.*"

"Hey, look on the bright side. At least our audience can't run off and tell anyone what we're doing."

Levi took a few steps toward her. "Speaking of running off, Mercy, why did you feel the need to reassure your mother that we're not romantically involved? That you've spent all this time away from me?"

Mercy huffed and shrugged. Her eyes landed on the window across the room – it had been snowing all day, and it wasn't letting up now. Each snowflake was as delicate and complex as this very situation, and the metaphor – perhaps appropriately – chilled her a bit. "I don't know, Levi. Maybe because she walked in on her daughter and her kidnapper mere inches apart, exchanging visual sweet nothings?"

He crossed his arms and followed her gaze to the window. His lips pursed as he watched the subtle dance of movement that the falling snow lent to the landscape. "I'm sorry – I'm still defensive. You're right... that would be jarring. Sometimes you need to offset the tension of the situation, I suppose."

Mercy studied him sympathetically. Since he could read minds, he doubtlessly knew what she was actually thinking. Even if there *was* some mild mutual interest, they couldn't be together. That was a recipe for disaster.

But now... while they were hiding out, literally plotting together to escape the risk of hunters finding them...

"Fuck it. Let's just *do it*, Levi. Let's see what we can do. Push the limits of our powers."

Speechless, he fumbled with the duster before setting it down on the edge of a bookshelf. "What if we cause a disturbance and they come for us?"

"What if they've already narrowed in on us and we have the ability to stop them? We'll never know unless we try."

He pursed his lips and tore his gaze back to the window. As he scanned the frozen landscape, he himself was as still as ice. Eventually, he dropped a shoulder. "If we have any chance of being successful, we need fresh blood. The packaged stuff is keeping us alive, but it's not the best for our diet. We're not as sharp as we could be."

Mercy was silent for a moment before she incredulously declared, "We are *not* feeding on my family. No."

Nonetheless, the pair found themselves knocking on Mary's door. She opened it and ran her eyes over them. "Um, hey guys. What's up?"

When they didn't immediately respond, Mary started closing the door. Mercy stuck her foot out to stop it from latching. "Hey, sis. We have a tiny favor to ask."

She crossed her arms. "I can guess what it is. No."

"We won't hurt you," Levi promised. "We just... we need to see what we can do, and fresh blood makes that discovery possible. I can't take Mercy out to hunt, Mary Olive. We need help right here, right now."

She huffed, blowing her blonde curtain bangs away from her face. "I don't want to do this."

"Neither do we," said Mercy. "Believe me, I *really* don't want to do this. But I'm asking you from a place of pure humanity and humility, Mary. *Please* help us put an end to this so we can all go home."

She glanced at Levi. "So is Plan B to allow the count here to control my mind if I say no?"

Mercy shrugged, so Mary sighed and opened the door. "Fine, as long as you don't kill or turn me."

As the vampires glided into the room, Mary was caught off guard, unable to react when they reached out to brush her hair back and leaned close in tandem. She came to her senses and pulled away.

"*Whoa*. At the same time? *Really?*"

"Don't you want it to be over fast?" Levi asked, his vermilion irises sparkling.

Mary sighed. "Fine. Get it over with."

Once again, the vampires stepped forward. *Just a little bit*, Levi's voice reminded. Before she could even pierce the skin, Mercy's tongue snaked out and tasted the air. It tasted like *life*. She closed her eyes before her fangs met Mary's skin, but when her sister whimpered, Mercy was caught off guard. Her eyes fluttered open, and she nearly pulled away.

Relax, Levi reminded. Mercy willed herself to close her eyes – it might make the experience go by faster, she reasoned.

When she emotionally disconnected from the experience and focused on the syrupy texture of the blood, that strange warmth once again flooded over her. Levi seemed to feel the shift in temperature, too. Rather than hearing his thoughts, Mercy could suddenly *feel* his spacial awareness as nourishment finally strengthened her body. His arm slinked around their reluctant donor, and once his hand settled on her shoulder, a sense of weightlessness overtook them.

Mercy didn't realize at first that she had lost her footing with the ground, but Mary's expression of shock made her understand. In the blink of an eye, Mary couldn't see them. Her hair violently whipped about, moved by a wind Mercy couldn't feel.

She let go of Levi's hand and felt her feet make contact with the ground again. Once she was steady, Levi's eyes locked on her as he pulled away from Mary, his lips parted in an expression of shock.

"*Wow*," he said. "So that's what it feels like."

"Can you wrap this up?" Mary nagged. "This is uncomfortable enough for me – the glitching in and out of existence thing is a new level of weird that I'm not ready to unpack."

"Right." Levi raised his right hand to his mouth and pricked a finger against his fang. He lowered it to Mary's wound. Mercy stretched her neck curiously and watched as Mary's skin healed before her eyes.

Almost skeptically, Mercy mimicked Levi's actions. She was almost entranced as she pricked her finger and lowered it to Mary's skin. Fibers of dermal tissue stretched across each tiny puncture, engulfing it until a brand new patch of skin covered the injury.

Mercy stared on in amazement. *There's still so much to learn.*

"Levi," she said in awe. "If we were meant to kill people, we wouldn't have the ability to heal them. Isn't that true?"

He smiled slowly. "I wasn't lying when I told your mother I'm not a senseless killer. I made mistakes when I was a sireless scion, but I learned this from my coven shortly thereafter. Life is sacred, and feeding on it is something we all do. Humans often pray before meals... I suppose this is my version of that. Instead of praying for a dead thing's soul, I prefer to invest in the longevity of its life."

There was something beautiful in that sentiment. Life, Mercy had long thought, was a bit like a religion – something full of greater purpose and blind hope. You're thrust into existence from a void of nothingness, with an entire blank canvas stretching before you. You can't see the end of it when you start painting – the furthest edge that determines where your artwork will stop and the void begins again – but you must blindly trust that your work will be a masterpiece, and that your vision will perfectly fill the space you've been given. If every brushstroke isn't perfect, that's okay... You just have to hope the rest of your art overshadows those few flaws.

Life is art. Levi, a dead person, could see that more clearly than most humans could. That was a shame, really.

"Thank you, Mary," Mercy said. "We'll leave you alone now."

"Oh, no you won't," she stated. "You *fed* on me, and you better have a damn good use for my blood. So I *will* be watching."

Levi stood, and Mercy followed his lead. She looked to her sister expectantly, but as Mary Olive attempted to rise, she stumbled.

Mercy caught her. "Take it easy, sis. You just went to a blood drive. Drink water and eat a granola bar."

She glared at Levi. "See, I would, but our gracious host hasn't stocked his prison with food."

"*So* whiny," he chided. "I'll bring home food from the cafe when I go in tomorrow, and like Mercy said before, you can have things delivered in the interim."

"It's inconvenient for us but *awfully* convenient for you two."

He stopped walking and turned to face her. "How *dare* you think even for a second that I'd keep you here as livestock? Mercy loves you. This was a one-off where you just did her a *very* big favor. I understand your frustration, Mary Olive, but you don't understand how precarious our situation is."

Mercy, hoping to offset the blooming tension between the two, reached out to take her sister's hand. "You helped us more than you know, sis. Back there, I turned into *wind*."

Mary nodded. "I saw. That was weird as *shit*."

"I didn't know I could do that until yesterday," Mercy explained. "After all these years, I'm still discovering things."

Mary's expression softened for a moment before that same uncharacteristic coldness returned. "Me too, truthfully. See, I've had this barista gig for years, and I never would have guessed my boss was a vampire. I mean, I knew he sucked, but you truly do learn something new every day."

"There's *so much* to learn," Mercy gushed while Levi attempted to protest behind her. "And after facing my mortality head-on, I'm finally eager to learn. It took me long enough to come around."

"Facing your mortality?" Mary asked, suddenly serious and empathetic. "Mercy, what happened yesterday? Is this experience why you think other vampires are hunting you?"

"Well, sis..."

Don't you dare, Mercy. Levi's voice floated into her mind.

Mercy cleared her throat. "Shut up, Levi. I'm telling her. Yeah, Mary Olive, this experience is why I *know* those vampires are hunting me. They tried to kill me, and they would have succeeded if I hadn't turned into wind. Levi figures they probably know who I am, which means they know where I live and where I've *lived*. That's why we had to get you out of town. I couldn't bear knowing you guys might be caught in the crossfire."

"Jesus Christ," Mary Olive muttered. "That's *terrifying*. But why did they try to kill you?"

Mercy, warned Levi. *Don't give a human more information about us than she needs. This is one of those lessons in self-preservation.*

"Levi, you better shut it, or so help me God." Mercy's voice caused him to tense for a second as her sister's eyebrows lifted in confusion. "So... you know how Levi and I are soulmates? Long story short, that's why he *won't get out of my head* and why I have this wind thing going on. For some reason, our state of being gives us unique powers. And if these guys eat us, it makes them extra powerful."

"It does make them extra powerful," Levi added. "But, to clarify, the wind thing is simply a side effect of being an estrie. We don't know what abilities our bond gives us, but... these hunters certainly might."

Mary stared at them with wide eyes before she crossed her arms and shivered. "Damn, yeah, that certainly paints some added color. I'm so glad you're okay. And I'm grateful you and Levi reacted fast and brought us here. So you don't think they know who Levi is?"

The group started walking again, the historic floorboards groaning under each step. Levi, at the front of the group, tilted his head slightly in the direction of their footfall. "They intended to lure me to them. They don't know who or where I am. Not yet, at least."

Levi led them into his library and pulled an easel with a massive sketch pad toward the sitting area. He opened to a clean page while Mary Olive spun around and took the room in with awe. Mercy glanced at her before she claimed a corner of the couch.

"Mercy," he said, doing his best to ignore Mary as she buzzed toward a bookshelf and started examining his collection. "Let's talk about what death looks like. I know you're a visual rather than conceptual learner, so I'll draw it out for you."

"Really? You didn't tell me when I *asked*, but you're willing to tell *Mary* how to kill us? What happened to not giving humans too much information?"

"You were intending to kill me when you asked. Mary has *never* tried to kill anyone, and I can hear her thoughts. There is not a single ill intention in there."

"Nope, I'm a good guy through and through." Mary walked toward the couch and took a seat on its other end. "That's an extremely invasive skill, by the way."

"Believe me, I'd never listen to your thought stream again if I could help it." Levi uncapped a marker and turned his back to them. He scribbled, then stepped back to reveal a smiley face with a rectangular cube protruding from where its mouth should be. "We'll start with incapacitation. Dislocating the jaw can put us down temporarily... don't ask me why, Mercy. I don't know. Stakes through the mouth or even a brick can keep a vampire down longer, or at least until the item is removed."

"Or until the vampire turns to wind."

"Bingo," he said, tapping his temple.

"Question!" Mary interjected. "Is it *only* wooden stakes and bricks, or will other things work?"

"Possibly other things," Levi said. "But the moral of the story is to break a vampire's jaw and get away."

"Noted," Mary said, which made Mercy chuckle. Other than her present company, Mary hadn't met any vampires. With any luck, she wouldn't meet another ever again.

"And pinning clothing to the ground," he said, drawing a stick person and then a line of spikes around it. "That's another way to prevent us from *rising*... That used to mean rising from the grave. For those of us who *did* rise and become vampires, it means we can't get up. As you know now, Mercy, neither method stops us from using our powers. Abilities triggered by emotion or thought can still be very dangerous, even if the vampire is restrained."

"Like me," Mercy realized. "I'm dangerous, but you're..."

"Not," he said with a guilty smile. "If I can't speak a command, I can't control anything. I'm not terribly difficult to hurt."

"And I know holy water and holy items can hurt us, too," Mercy said knowingly. "Come on, Levi. I want to know how to *kill* a vampire."

MARY EXCUSED HERSELF to retrieve a DoorDash order, so Levi waited until she stepped out before he started drawing again. "A stake through the heart, as you know, is the most common method of offing us."

"And only those made of acacia wood," Mercy said.

"Yes, very good. The other method..." He turned to the board and drew again. When he stepped aside, Mercy was sure she knew what he was going to say. "Is decapitation. Doesn't matter what does the trick – axes, swords, conveniently low branches on a popular horse riding path. But if our head comes off, our life is over."

"What else?"

He tilted his head. "Well, according to legend, angelic weapons like the swords carried by Uriel or Jophiel would do the trick. I haven't seen any angels myself, but some vampires claim to have encountered holy weapons. Fire in general can get the job done if it burns us to dust, but we can usually recover from the standard burn."

After he finished his thought, Levi turned his back and drew a kindergarten-quality angel with a flaming sword.

"Levi." Mercy leaned forward and folded her arms in her lap. "You're saying it takes *Biblical weapons* to kill us?"

He crossed his arms, then looked down with frustration when he realized the marker had brushed against the brown fabric of his shirt. He stretched his arm, brushed at the stain on his sleeve, and sighed. "I can hear your thoughts, Mercy. We're not angels."

"But what if we're *fallen* angels. Or their children."

He shrugged. "Could be. I don't know, Mercy, and I candidly don't care. I've never met a fucking angel. Our curse is absolutely Biblical in some way, but that's not the mystery we're here to solve."

Mercy laughed and shook her head. "It *could* be, Levi. If Genesis is a story on the birth of vampirism, then perhaps there's more to uncover there."

Levi finally capped the marker and set it on the easel tray. "There are no soulmates in the Bible, Mercy. You know that."

"Behold, I know your thoughts and the schemes by which you would wrong me." Mercy shifted. "Come *on*, Levi. Is that *not* where this all started? You knowing my intentions to kill you but tolerating me nonetheless because you *know me?*"

"We can cherry-pick verses all night, Mercy. I've literally watched the evolution of Abrahamic religions for five hundred fifty years. I'm telling you, we're focusing on the wrong thing. There may be some truth in there, sure, but it's not going to give us the answers you're looking for."

"Then why did you bring up flaming swords?" she asked. "I can *sense* it. Levi. I can..."

Though she wasn't initially aware of what she was doing, Mercy found herself reaching for his subconscious again. This time, Levi reached for her, too. As their psyches intertwined, the last thing Mercy saw was Levi's eyes rolling back in his head before they both hit the ground.

MERCY SAT UP. SHE WAS on bare dirt, and it took her just a second to realize she was on a road. A piece of a carriage wheel was beside her, its dry wood splintering in the hot midday sun. She looked behind her at the destruction – an entire buggy was scattered across the road. Maybe *buggy* wasn't the right word for it, though. It was more of a farm wagon, a simple piece of wood pulled by a single horse, loaded with personal items that had been torn and scattered. Its horse was lying motionless in a pool of blood.

When she turned her head, she saw three more bodies. These ones were human.

She crawled toward them in horror. It was a woman and two small children. Their throats were torn out. She broke down crying despite not knowing them – it was like she was enacting someone else's life. As she leaned over the woman's body and bawled, something caused her spine to prickle. Her head started to pound, and the roof of her mouth suddenly burned as two retractable fangs ripped through the flesh and set in place behind her teeth.

She threw her head back and screamed. The sun was nearly directly overhead, and it burned her eyes. She whimpered and cowered over the fallen woman again. This time, however, she didn't feel the pain of loss. As she slowly moved toward the woman's mostly-drained throat, she ached with bloodlust.

She was about to do something regrettable. Unfathomable.

"Mercy."

She looked up. Levi was standing above her, his face twisted with unbridled sorrow. Slowly, she stood and curled into his embrace. He held her tightly.

"This was it," he whispered. "My first moment as the Levi you know now. This is what broke me."

Mercy turned her head enough to glance at the bodies. The children had curly hair, like Levi. She hugged him tighter as she looked away.

"So we're in your memories?"

"I don't rightly know." Levi let go of her and stepped back. "Perhaps we're in some sort of space beyond our plane – somewhere where our souls are bared, where our memories are laid out."

"Purgatory?" Mercy asked as she scanned the landscape. Far down the road, dust from an approaching wagon was rising above the horizon.

"Beats me," he said. "Soul bonds do weird things."

"Well, we did say we wanted to test our abilities." Mercy stepped back and intertwined hands with him. "Should we see what we can do here?"

He studied her skeptically, "Well... it's worth a try, I suppose."

Mercy was operating off pure instinct when she closed her eyes and focused. She envisioned the warmth of sunshine, a shimmering sea of grass blowing in the wind, and a deep mountain valley perfectly poised to create a wind tunnel. She could feel herself growing lighter until she was suddenly sure her feet were not on the ground. Guarded and slow, she opened her eyes.

To her surprise, she was now standing a few feet away, beside Levi rather than in front of him. He stared straight ahead at a small tornado that swirled out from his fingertips. It had two tails – one grounded on each hand – but one funnel that stretched far above him. His eyes were still wide when he slowly turned to meet Mercy's gaze.

"This is *you*." He gestured to the tornado with his chin. The funnel was loud, but his voice was clear and distinct from the din. "My God. You can't control your power, but I can control *you*."

"How would that be me?" Mercy challenged. "I can't be in two places at once."

"You're not," he said knowingly. "I can see through you. *That's* your consciousness. *This* is your body."

Levi turned his attention back to the tornado. He lifted his chin as he followed its funnel up to where it towered above him.

"*Give me full control, Mercy.*"

Her back bristled at that tone – almost helplessly, she blurted, "Okay. I give you full control, Levi."

Cautiously, he shifted both of the tornado's tails to one hand, watching with fascination as they intertwined and became one. His free hand lifted to trace the length of the tornado as far as he could reach, and then he guided it to stretch before him. The funnel followed the flow of his hand, almost magnetically pulled forward and pushed backward as he familiarized himself with its motion.

The scene around them shifted, and they were suddenly in a grassy field like the one Mercy had envisioned. Levi, without so much as flinching, lowered the funnel of the tornado to the ground. He spun in a circle, watching in amazement as it flattened the grass in a massive ring around him. Mercy – or her consciousness, rather – was standing in the flattened path, but she hadn't even felt the wind pass through her.

Levi lifted the wind funnel again, almost tender in his motion as he allowed it to stretch toward the sky above. He watched it reach toward the heavens before he closed his eyes and commanded, "*Come back to me, Mercy.*"

In a fraction of a second, Mercy blinked and was in front of Levi. When she looked down, both hands were stacked atop his, resting where the tornado had been grounded. She pulled away and shook them anxiously. "Oh my God."

"This place," he said with realization. "It's a safe space to test our potential – perhaps it's in our minds, perhaps it's somewhere else. It's not real, but these are our real abilities. And wherever we are, it gave you the ability to see what you can become from the outside looking on."

"I'm not just wind, then," she said. "I'm a force of *nature*. Jesus Christ."

"And if you draw me back into that state with you," he said, his words hanging in the air, "Like you did when we were with Mary... I wonder what we'll become."

"Only one way to find out."

Chapter Ten

Mercy felt the familiar jolt of impact as she collided with the unforgiving floor yet again. She winced and massaged her aching head as she struggled to sit up. Beside her, Levi also shifted into a seated position. He stretched and rubbed his shoulder.

"Welcome back." They turned their heads in response to the third presence in the room. Mary had a coffee pressed against her lips, but she waved with the three fingers that weren't wholly supporting its weight. After she loudly gulped, she cleared her throat. "You two were like, I don't know, ten feet in the air. And totally unresponsive, by the way."

Levi looked up at the vaulted ceiling, then returned his gaze to her with consideration. "And... you're drinking a coffee from Thanks-a-Latte?"

She widened her eyes and shrugged. "*What?* Competition is healthy. I like their mochas."

He shook his head disapprovingly as Mercy affectionately nudged him. "You're not threatened by *human* business owners, are you?"

"Of course I am. I only have a decade or so in each area before I have to move on to the next. Those guys can run their shops for a lifetime; some even pass them on to children. Humans are the worst part of the economy."

"Amen to that." Mary Olive lifted her cup in cheers. "So... are you guys going to tell me what that was? Just a casual evening astral projection? Or is that how vampires actually sleep?"

"We weren't doing either, sis. Or, at least, I don't think we were. We were, um..."

When she turned to Levi for help, he shrugged. "Whatever that was, it supersedes words. Mary, you said we were airborne?"

"Levitating," she said as she bit into a bear claw. "Spooky, but also uneventful until you two fell."

Levi looked up at the ceiling again and nodded. "Okay. And nothing moved here? No mass display of telekinesis?"

Mary shook her head. "No flying objects beyond your pale asses. Speaking of which, Mercy, are those my jeans?"

Mercy lifted her chin defiantly.

"I want them back," Mary declared, which elicited a huff from her sister.

Levi nudged her with his elbow. "Mercy, we've got to try these things in the real world, you know. If we can control this like we did in there, we won't have to run. The hunters seek out vampires who *can't* control their soul bonds for a reason... We're more powerful than them if we can keep it in check."

Mercy blinked. "You really think we can control this shit, Levi? We just passed out and apparently levitated. That sounds pretty freaking close to *not having control* if you ask me."

"You saw the same things as me in our personal purgatory. If we can manage this, there's *nothing* that can stand in our way."

"Sure, maybe in like a century or so. But we *don't* have the ability to control this yet, Levi."

"A century?" Mary asked, perking up. "Oh, *Hell* no. I'm not spending the best years of my life cooped up with my parents, their cat, and a not-a-couple-maybe-a-couple vampire duo my sister is half of."

"We're a couple," Levi said confidently as Mercy scoffed and declared, "We are *not* a couple, Mary."

"I'm with Levi," Mary stated. She leaned forward to meet her sister's gaze. "You two better figure this shit out. I'll be honest, Mercy, that while it's been great having you back in town, this will go down as the worst holiday season *ever* if it's the beginning of me being stuck with you and Count Dorkula."

"Aligned," Mercy said. "But Levi, I have to ask... Does this feel oddly political to you? If a pair of soulmates can control abilities the average vampire can barely imagine, I'd think that would translate into social power. Political power. I mean, think about it. These guys knew what to look for, so they found me. They didn't even give us a chance to explore our combined powers... and if I wasn't running away and forcing some distance between us, we would have presumably reached this point much sooner. I would have mentioned hearing your voice, or our proximity might have inevitably caused any other unpredictable side effect."

"And, were you here, it likely would have happened before I even knew you were an estrie," Levi said grimly.

"And being fairly defenseless myself, we wouldn't have stood a chance. Like the others they've hunted, I suppose. I don't think it sounds political, necessarily, but I do think you're onto something. They're hunting us down when our partnerships are young. You and I are lucky to have had this time to mature into our soul bond. We're likely not what they're used to."

Mary took an offensively loud glug from her coffee and wiped her mouth on her sleeve. "I mean, sure, but it doesn't exactly *not* sound political. Does the vampire world have any sort of government or order?"

Levi scoffed. "Don't be ridiculous. Outside of covens and the strange cult those hunters are in, we're all fairly solitary creatures. The only exception being when we have a scion."

Mary shrugged. "Okay. So maybe it's something else."

"Something else?" he asked, slowly cocking an eyebrow.

"Pfft, I don't know. Fairies. Unicorns. Aliens. I can't say those are on my list of things I believe in, but once upon a time, vampires were also not on that list."

Mercy looked around, suddenly realizing she and Levi were still on the floor. She slowly pulled herself to her feet, grumbling at the stiffness from her most recent fall. "I believe there are wild Tasmanian tigers out there, I think. But secret alien governors on unicorns kinda sounds far-fetched. I meant... I don't know. Maybe there are some super powerful counts out there who are challenged by our existence."

She offered a hand to Levi, and he accepted it gratefully. He brushed a wrinkle out of his shirt when he was on his feet again. "Again, Mercy, I don't think it matters if there are. I just want to see that we're strong enough to stop these guys. What do you say we head outside and see what we can do?"

"Okay," Mercy said. "Let's do this. But, I don't know, Levi. I can't stop thinking about how they knew what to look for. How did they know to look for someone who can control the weather?"

"It's probably just a more observable power," he assured her. "Compared to, say, psychometry, it was easy to spot. Let's get it under control, though. What do you say, love?"

AS THEY WANDERED AWAY from the house and approached the forest near the edge of Levi's property, Mercy glanced back. Schnitzel was sitting in a windowsill, watching them longingly. Being longhaired, he didn't mind spending time outside in the snow. Despite his longing look, Mercy knew he wouldn't want to accompany them. Risk aside, he didn't like Levi, and Levi didn't like him.

"We're not a couple?" Levi asked, breaking the blissful stillness of the wintry day. In the silence following his question, the soft brush of crystallized snowflakes over the compacted snow on the ground was the only sound.

"What?"

"You told Mary Olive we're not a couple."

Mercy sighed. It was a habit she hadn't broken since she died – she didn't need to breathe, but she also couldn't unlearn two decades of autosomatic instinct. "You know we're not. We never have been, and a temporary cohabitation doesn't change that."

"Perhaps not," he said. "I guess I assumed that mutually acknowledging our shared experience as soulmates was confirmation enough, especially given that you came back to me."

Mercy stopped, and Levi paced a few steps ahead before he halted and turned to face her. "Look, Levi. My presence here is still temporary."

He tightened his jaw, his eyes darting away. "Okay."

With that, Levi spun on his heel and kept walking. Mercy followed him wordlessly. Once they'd walked a considerable distance from the house, he stopped and turned to face her again.

"I was thinking about your father again, and that vampire from his thoughts. It was like a wall of sound, very confusing, but... I almost think she chose to kill herself. I think they figured out what they were, and she sacrificed herself so he wouldn't die. Like she saw being hunted as an inevitability if they stayed together. From the way Steve was processing it, he seemed to believe she hired the person who killed her. I think he tried to stop it. Truthfully, I think he's a bit mentally broken after that."

Mercy bit her lip. "And had I stayed initially, that could have happened to us. One or both of us would have died years ago."

"I suppose I should be grateful for your flightiness, at least in that regard."

Levi offered his hands, so Mercy intertwined her fingers with his. She smiled at him, but he didn't return the expression. Despite his coldness, Mercy closed her eyes and reached out with her mind.

Levi's consciousness didn't reach for her.

"Levi! Focus, dude."

He frowned. "I'm *trying*. I can't find you."

"You're reaching out with your mental arm thingy?"

"*Yes*, Mercy. I feel like I'm fumbling in the dark. Like you're not there."

She let go of his hands and stepped back. "So you're mad at me, then."

He pursed his lips. "I'm not mad, Mercy."

"Remember how easy it was in that strange purgatory place? Before there was this shift in your attitude?"

He averted his dark eyes. "Fine. I suppose I'm disappointed. Hurt, I guess. I relived a horrifically painful memory earlier, but it didn't sting as bad with you there. I think the comfort of your presence has made me... I don't know. Complacent? I know I'll be stung when you leave again. Each time you go, it gets more painful. And it kills me to know you'll be leaving again as soon as you can."

"I'm not rejecting you, Levi. With most people, a no from Mercy is a firm *no*. With you, it means *not right now*. Situation aside, you know why. I'm focusing on my career. Let me live a little before I consider committing to you for the rest of forever."

"I've *been* letting you. And I will keep letting you. But for the love of God, I need *something* this time. Tell me you love me. Tell me you hate me. I don't even care. Just *please* tell me *something*."

In that moment, Mercy desperately wanted to turn into wind and fly away. New York would be nice, but that was also where two people tried to literally eat her. Other than her apartment, she couldn't think of anywhere that felt safe. "You know that's not a fair request while I'm your scion. I'll answer you after I get my freedom."

He studied her for a long moment, carefully chewing over his words. "It's not safe for me to give you that yet. You know that."

Mercy crossed her arms. "So we're at an impasse."

"We're not," he said. "I admit that it wasn't a fair question – as a scion, you're stuck with me. That skews things. But I just need to hear it from you, Mercy. Do you love me? At least a little?"

An unexpected gust of wind ruffled Mercy's hair as her tummy churned. She quickly tucked a loose strand behind her ear and looked away. "I mean, yeah, Levi. I do. But it's complicated, and you know why."

"That's enough for me," he said quietly. "I just needed to know, Mercy, that *not right now* means we'll circle back when you're ready, rather than you're just avoiding the discussion. Because you've spent ten years avoiding it so far."

She lifted her chin. "Well, yeah, I have. I was *running* from you, remember?"

"Yeah," he said with a small smile. "But I understand why. I used to think running away was a viable solution, too, once upon a time. At least you bought us more time than I bought my family."

Mercy smiled sympathetically. "When I'm free, Levi, we'll talk more definitively. I promise you. Because I *do* love you."

"I love you, too, Mercy." He leaned forward and kissed her. "I'll wait another ten years if I have to – as long as I know that love is shared, it's enough for me. If anything does happen... I just needed to hear it. Upon reflection, I don't want to spend the rest of forever wondering."

She smiled and took his hands in hers. "Let's try this again."

Levi ran his eyes over her face before he smiled. This time, when Mercy reached out with her mind, she felt his spiritual presence beckoning.

MARY POURED A GLASS of wine and sat beside her sister. She looked out the window. "Damn, there's a *lot* of damage out there. A lot of trees down. What happened?"

Mercy drank from her chalice and shrugged. "We, uh, practiced a thing we thought might work. It did, I guess. Sort of. I wouldn't say it went *well*."

Mary lowered her glass from her lips and cocked one perfectly plucked eyebrow. "So we're still stuck. That's what you're telling me?"

"Well, *yeah*, Mary. We weren't going to magically learn how to control my skills enough to fend off vampire-hunting vampires. Practice makes perfect." When her sister huffed, Mercy leaned forward to meet her gaze. "I do have some news, though. Like, girl-to-girl, you're-gonna-freak news."

"Ooh," Mary said. "Do tell."

"I told Levi I love him."

Mary squealed and clapped her hands, then grabbed her sister and shook her by the shoulders. "Yes! I knew it!"

"I mean, I didn't *commit* to him." Mercy brushed Mary Olive's hands off her. "Forever is a long time, you know. But he needed to hear it, so I told him the truth. Told myself the truth, I guess."

Mary playfully kicked her under the table. "That's amazing, Merce. I stan you guys."

"Don't call me that, Bloody Mary."

Mary kicked her again, this time a little more forceful. "*Bloody* Mary? Look who's talking – I know that ain't wine in there."

"Or holy water." The girls' father entered the kitchen. He glanced at them in passing as he walked to the fridge, now stocked with actual human food like apples and pot pies.

Mercy side-eyed her sister before she said, "I don't know what more you want me to say, Dad."

When he turned to face them, he was holding a pudding cup. Despite his coldness, he approached the table and sat down. He peeled the cover off the pudding. "Truthfully, the only thing that can make a difference is if you can *convince* me you're not demonic."

Mercy rolled her eyes. "You mean that your judgment is the exclusive deciding factor. I have to convince *you*."

"You can't touch *holy water*, Mercy. Honestly, I'm amazed the rest of the family is okay with that."

"Whatever this is, Dad, it's Biblical," Mercy said. "But it's not demonic. That I can guarantee."

"Why does holy water burn you, then?"

His daughter defiantly lifted her chin. "You didn't ask your girlfriend back in the day?"

"I don't know what you're talking about."

"Girlfriend?" Mary asked. "Dad... is that why you suspected Mercy was a vampire? You *knew* a vampire?"

"I don't associate with demons, Mary Olive."

Mercy took a sip from her chalice, trying her best to prevent the smile from reaching her eyes when she saw him fidgeting uncomfortably. He knew its contents, which made her smirk a little behind the rim of the glass. Smugly, she said, "Truthfully, I think we're descended from angels. During the War in Heaven, they were able to cross into whatever plane earth is on. I mean, we saw Satan infiltrate Eden. But I think angels made us, and Biblical weapons hurt us because it ensured we could be kept in control. They couldn't have invulnerable immortals walking around all willy-nilly. Satan himself taught them what that kind of power can do to a person."

"Wait, you think angels made vampires as a second line of defense?" Mary asked. "A set of soldiers to fight for their cause if they failed... and a group that was fairly immortal, at that. But not wholly godly, like them. And also not made by God. That would mean you're not unholy, but you're also not a part of His realm. You're spiritually neutral, then?"

"You're revisionists."

"Shut it, Steve," Mercy said. "The Bible was *written* by revisionists. Please, for the love of God, Google that."

"Dad," Mary said gently. "If anything, the existence of Levi and Mercy *attest* to the stories in the Bible. Mercy and I have uncovered things that are absolutely *wild*. I won't tell you out of respect for their privacy, but you should seriously think about it. At the very least, they attest to the existence of life after death. They have proven to me that a soul exists."

He frowned, but that was quickly blocked by the appearance of his spoon as he lifted a mouthful of pudding. "And how did you meet this Levi character, Mercy?"

"Actually," Mary said, "I'm not sure if I know this story."

Mercy looked down at her drink and chugged it. Once finished, she slammed the chalice against the table. "It doesn't matter anymore."

"It matters to me. I'd like to know where I caused your faith to falter."

Mercy stood so quickly that Schnitzel, who had silently wandered into the kitchen, jumped and ran away. As she narrowed her eyes at her father, she was certain her irises were blood red. "Stop playing the victim, Dad. You ruined Christmas, not me. Your life may have been ruined by a brush with vampirism, but it wasn't because of me, so I don't deserve to be treated like this. I'm sorry your life isn't perfect. I'm sorry that the real world conflicts with the one you want to live in and that it's made you bitter."

"Really? Not only did you uproot us, but you *kidnapped* us, and you're holding us captive in some stranger's home!" Steve's voice was loud, rising over the noise outside. "That is *actually* insane, Mercy. We're hostages. *That's* the real world! Perfect isn't even on my fucking radar right now."

"Uh, Mercy..." Mary interjected.

Ignoring her sister, Mercy pressed, "You have the *audacity* to accuse me of holding you hostage? Would you rather I leave you unprotected so these monsters can kill you? I know all about what happened to your girlfriend and how she was trying to protect you from this fate. They tried to *kill me,* Dad. For good."

Mercy! Levi's silent pleadings didn't even register in Mercy's mind.

"Maybe that would be for the best!"

Mercy's temper flared, but Levi tore into the room before she could explode. He looked panicked, and he pointed to Mary. "Get under the table! Cover your head!"

Mercy watched in confusion as her sister and father darted under the table. Levi was holding her shoulders before she could even blink.

"Relinquish control, Mercy!"

Confused, Mercy said, "It's yours, Levi!"

The windows shattered, but Levi didn't even flinch as glass flew past and sliced their flesh. Mercy, by scion intuition or some stroke of pure luck, followed his lead and remained rooted in place. As quickly as it started, the incident ended with the puttering of glass shards against the tile floor. When Levi's hands slid off Mercy's shoulders, she collapsed into her chair. She winced and shifted, lifting up a massive piece of glass.

Levi watched her, but then he knelt and peeked under the table. "Everyone okay?"

Mary popped up like a whack-a-mole, but Mercy swallowed her comment when she saw her sister's wide eyes. It suddenly dawned on her that she wasn't comprehending whatever had just happened. Mary, on the other hand, fully understood, and she looked terrified.

Across the table, Steve stood. He looked at his shirt distastefully – the contents of his pudding cup were smeared down his front. Despite the mess, neither he nor Mary were hurt. When Mercy's eyes moved back to Levi, she realized he was beaten up. A long cut ran down the right side of his face, and the tip of his nose was bleeding. Mercy looked down at her hands in shock – there was blood on them, but she wasn't sure where she was bleeding from.

"Was that what I think it was?" Mary asked in shock.

"Mercy's having an emotionally intense day," Levi said. He eased around the table until he was toe-to-toe with her father. He met the man's eyes, then dropped his voice into a familiar cadence. "You will not disrespect her like that moving forward. If anyone shows up to investigate, you were not near the windows when the incident happened, you're happy everyone is okay, and you're *not* being held here against your will. Understand me?"

Hypnotized but still stubborn, Steve's lip ticked slightly higher on the right side of his mouth. "I understand."

Levi held his gaze threateningly before he turned to Mercy. She stared at him with wide eyes before she asked, "Levi? What happened?"

"There, uh... There was a tornado, Mercy. F1, I'd guess. A little one. We stopped it."

Mercy looked at the wind-torn windowpanes and tried her jaw. For a moment, no words came out. "*You* stopped it. I lost control and couldn't reel it back in. Jesus, that could have been bad."

He pursed his lips and looked up at the shattered windowpane. "Unfortunately, I fear it has already gotten bad, and there's nothing we can do now."

Chapter Eleven

❝In tonight's report — a twist on New Year's you wouldn't expect. A twister in January! The F1 tornado is estimated to have reached speeds of up to 92 miles an hour, and it's our first wintertime twister in recorded history."

The shot changed to a male anchor. *"January tornadoes have hit the East Coast before, though primarily in the Carolinas. This is the first wintertime tornado in Connecticut, and meteorologists are nodding to climate change as the culprit. The incident in Roxbury caused significant damage to an historic residence and took down several trees. There were no reported injuries, but damage includes missing siding and roof tiles, plus a few broken windows. The twister turned from south to north before dissipating, fortunately missing the home."*

Levi turned the television off and rubbed his brow. "You do understand what this means, right?"

Despite the dead silence in the room, Mercy leaned forward. "I should immediately call Ann and pitch *Vampnado*? I mean, it's like Peter Parker with the Spider-Man pics, right? Nobody can resist the authenticity of a first-hand experience."

"Jesus, Mercy," Levi said. "The hunters knew who you were. They likely knew where you were from, and *this hit the news*. They're looking for signs of an estrie in this area. They'll be here soon."

"We're in danger, then?" Beth asked with wide eyes. She clutched Steve's hand, but his face had been set in a scowl since the window shattered. He didn't even react.

Schnitzel, on the other hand, looked absolutely astonished by the unfolding situation. He was loafing on the arm of the couch beside Steve, but his eyes were wide. He looked uneasy.

"We all are," Levi said. "You three should run. Find a hotel out of state. Hunker down for a few days. They'll be gone after they finish their business, so you can return home then."

"*Business?*" Mary demanded. "Killing you two, you mean? No way in Hell, Levi. I'm not leaving."

"We are," Steve said. "Beth, pack your bags. Get Schnitzel in his crate."

"Mary," Mercy said slowly. "These guys aren't fucking around. You can't stay, sis. You'll be hurt. There's always a chance Levi and I won't be."

She crossed her arms. "Yes, you will. You don't have control over your weather shit, Mercy. Levi might be able to stop it when it gets bad, but you certainly can't use it to protect yourselves. I'm not leaving you to face that alone."

Levi looked at Mercy desperately, and she nodded a silent affirmation. He stepped forward and met Mary's gaze. "Mary Olive, you will leave with your parents and stay away until you have reason to believe it's safe to return."

Mary's blue eyes widened, and then she blinked. She pouted a lip and looked away. "Fine, I'll pack. But I'm disappointed in you both."

"Me, too," Mercy said. "Sorry we didn't learn to fully control it, Mary. I wish we did."

"I don't," Steve said as he stood. "I'm happy to finally leave. Beth, Mary, let's go."

When the women stood, Mary scooped up Schnitzel and kissed his head. She glared at Mercy as they passed, but their mother stared straight ahead as she moved to the staircase.

Mercy pulled her lower legs under her, tucking them between her thighs and the cushion. There was a chill in the house, despite Levi covering the broken windows with a tarp. "So what does this mean for us, Levi?"

"It means confrontation is inevitable." He moved to the cushion next to her, then took her hands in his. "And we'll do the best we can, Mercy, but this might be it. We don't have time to run. We'd best stay put. Give your family a chance to get away."

Mercy sat straight up. "Oh, *Hell* no. I can't die, Levi! Ann will resurrect my ass all over again if I don't get *Water Wars* to market."

He smiled slowly. "Yeah, and the cafe staff might riot if I'm not here to sign their paychecks."

"So what do we do?"

"You said it yourself, Mercy. You're a force of nature. If they come, get *mad*. Destroy them. We have to fight back."

"But I'm more scared than mad, Levi."

"Yeah, me too."

THE VAMPIRES SAT INTERTWINED on the couch, holding each other closely. While Mercy had been reluctant to let Levi in, the thought of losing him and everything else all at once terrified her. In this moment, she wanted nothing more than the comforting embrace of his arms.

Immortality is a funny thing, Mercy thought. Vampires are colloquially known as immortal, but in actuality, they're *biologically* immortal. They could still die, it just wouldn't be old age that took them down.

Facing one's mortality is never easy, but to a degree, it's easier to grasp when age is the culprit. When you're young and facing the possibility of death, the fragility of the world around you is suddenly that much more potent. Holding Levi, Mercy couldn't help but think that he felt frail. Here was this immortal being, fortified by five centuries of sustenance, who was just as extinguishable as the glass knickknacks on his display case.

And then there was Mercy, a woman young enough to be considered immature by humans and a fledgling by vampires. Her death would be particularly tragic.

Levi must have been listening to her thoughts, because he shifted uncomfortably when Mercy began imagining what death as a vampire might look like. "You'll give me control, right?"

Mercy snuggled into his chest. "Of course. I saw what happens when I don't. It gets bad. Are you sure you'll be able to guide my wind? It didn't go well when we practiced."

"No," he admitted. "But I believe in learning on the job. Maybe it didn't come naturally because the stakes weren't high enough."

"Learning on the job? Isn't that why your first cafe failed?"

"Like I said, darling, the stakes likely just weren't high enough." Levi began gently stroking her hair. "There's no skin off anyone's back if my patrons hate my cappuccinos. If anyone ever hurts you, though, I will unleash the fury of hellfire upon them. You're more precious to me than all the riches in the world. My love for you is vaster than empires."

Mercy closed her eyes and leaned into his hand as he caressed her raven-black hair. It sent trickles of electricity down her spine, easing the tension in her muscles. That was good, Mercy thought. Levi had said they shouldn't waste energy.

"Tell me about the night we met, Levi. What was it like for you?"

His hand paused for a moment. He was clearly startled by her question. When the motion picked back up, the reverberations of his voice echoed in the hollow of his chest. With such a warm timbre engulfing her, she could have easily dozed off to the sweet sound of his voice. "I was hunting. Masked by the shadows like any practiced predator, I scanned the room for my prey. Then, suddenly, it was as if the whole world slowed down and was bathed in a golden hue. When my eyes found you, I felt complete for the first time in centuries."

"And then you approached me."

"And I was speechless for the first time in my life. You made me realize I never believed in this Christian idea of Heaven – we Jews never worry too much about what afterlife may come, but I always heard these people around me spouting off about a paradise awaiting us. And while I never believed in such a place myself, when I met you, I knew it didn't exist. There is no paradise more perfect than how I feel when I'm with you."

Just as paradise was once lost by man, their moment of solace was interrupted. It was subtle at first – the distant scraping of ice – and then the front door opened and closed.

The vampires froze.

Let me use your power, Mercy. Give me control.

Mercy was about to silently respond, but she realized something about this visitor – she could hear their heartbeat. She sat up and peered over the back of the couch, locking eyes with her sister. Mary, bundled up in a purple knit hat and oversized infinity scarf, had a fine layer of snow frosting her outerwear. She defiantly lifted her chin as she brushed the snow off. There was a smugness about her as she held her sister's gaze.

Mary Olive must be the most witless, stubborn person on earth, Mercy thought. It was all she could do – she was too stunned to speak.

Levi instantly responded to Mercy's thoughts. Before he even sat up, he exclaimed, "*Mary Olive?* How did you break my compulsion?"

She flipped her hair. "I didn't. You told me to leave until I believed it was safe to return. I believe it's safe, so here I am. It's a legal loophole."

Mercy and Levi were on their feet in an instant, marching toward Mary while shouting a slew of insults. She shouted back a few times, but she finally broke through the chatter with, "*Hey!* Shut the fuck up, both of you. I get it – you think I'm dumb. But I *know* I'll be okay. It's this unshakable certainty, I can't explain it, but I just *know* it."

"Your woo-woo crystal-charging ass might have just signed your death certificate, Mary."

"I didn't, Mercy. You'll see."

Levi stepped between the women. "Mary Olive, you are underestimating how dangerous this situation is. Truly, sincerely, you should not have come back."

"But it's too late for me to get away, isn't it?" Mary removed her knit hat with a flourish. Her eyes sparkled as she held Levi's gaze, challenging him with eyes as vibrant as a stormy sea. She took a confident step forward. "They're close now, right? I'm safest with you two."

Frustrated, Mercy turned her back and started walking to the couch. She only took a step or two before everything suddenly seemed to move in slow motion. Levi turned after her and reached out. His hand brushed the tie out of her hair before tightly clamping on her shoulder. When she turned toward him, he was pulling her with wide eyes. Silently *pleading* with her to follow his lead, to not look over her shoulder. In that split second, she decided to trust him over satiating her curiosity.

Mercy tumbled forward, and she and Levi hit the ground and slid as the entire house vibrated. She coughed and lifted her head, absolutely stupefied to see half a car sitting where the bay window used to be. She stared at it in shock before she realized it was *Levi's* car.

She coughed and swiped at the debris particles dancing through the frosty air. The world was absolutely still as they trickled to the ground. A few pieces of debris – siding, perhaps – swung over the gaping hole, but outside, not a bird chirped. It seemed as if traffic had halted, too, as not even the lazy *thunk* of wheels passing over uneven pavement trickled over the landscape.

Mercy shifted, and Levi slowly let her go. She hadn't realized he'd wrapped her in an embrace as they tumbled. In tandem, the vampires sat up. Mercy spit out some dust – if she had human functions, breathing in so much dust would have been painful. That fleeting thought gave her the clarity of mind to scan the space for her sister.

"Levi!" she exclaimed, rising to her feet. "Where's Mary?"

He rose, too, and grabbed her wrist. "Focus, Mercy! We don't have time to panic."

With a thunderous *bang*, the front door was kicked open. Two silhouettes marched in, dark against the blindingly bright snow. Mercy squinted – being young, her eyes were still sensitive to light. She didn't need to see the features of the intruders to know that they were the vampires who had harmed her in New York.

As they sauntered forward, Mercy's eyes adjusted enough to see their unusually large fangs glinting in the excessive natural light. Their eyes were absolutely predatory. There was a particular triumph in their motion, too. They'd finally found their prey.

"Hey, Tweedledum and Tweedledee!" Mary was standing to the side, clutching her fists tightly. Mercy realized that one hand was holding something – a long, skinny piece of wood, seemingly a leg from a side table. "Don't you dare touch them."

"A human," the paler man hissed. He sounded genuinely surprised. "Get her, Ozymandias."

The darker vampire stepped forward, his eyes locked on Mary. While she had previously worn a look of confidence, her expression faded into pure panic as she stared at the man approaching her. Mercy's temper flared, but Levi's hand slid into hers before she could react. She felt herself growing lighter, less tethered to the ground.

Give me control, Mercy.

It's yours, Levi. End this.

Mercy finally felt the pure warmth of sunlight as weightlessness overtook her. Though she could still feel Levi's hand grounding her, she only caught flashes of the world as she seemed to hang suspended in mid-air. The front wall came crashing down with a deafening roar, sending dust and debris flying in all directions. Ozymandias used that moment as a distraction to attack Mary. Before he could land a blow, he was abruptly swept off his feet and hurled violently against the far wall, carried by a ferocious wind.

The next thing Mercy knew, she was standing next to Levi, and the marshmallow-hued vampire was dead, staked through the chest. His eyes grew more sunken by the second, and a darkness unhurriedly crawled over the valleys of his face.

"What happened?" Mercy asked, desperately curious to gaze at the wreckage around the room but unable to tear her eyes away from the corpse.

"Ozymandias got away, but your sister staked Valefar."

"Acacia wood," Mary said. "I heard you mention it the other day, so I Googled what it looked like. Levi had a side table made of it in the hallway, either knowingly for situations like this or accidentally in the oversight of the century."

"Knowingly," he said. "But even so, I'm impressed at the initiative you took, Slayer. I wish you showed half so much enthusiasm at work."

"So it's over?" Mercy asked. "We showed enough control to kill one and chase the other off. They wouldn't be dumb enough to come back, right?"

"Usually. But we have another situation on our hands now, love. We have a human who broke my compulsion and effortlessly killed a very dangerous, very ancient vampire."

Mary shrugged. "Maybe I'm just a badass."

"Or maybe there's something going on here."

"Levi," Mercy said, stepping between him and her sister. "There's nothing going on with Mary. We *both* know her."

"You're right – we both know Mary Olive. She would never take that much initiative under normal circumstances."

Mercy winced. He wasn't wrong, but admitting that felt like a betrayal to her sister.

"Mary," Levi said, stepping around his scion to come face-to-face with her. Her eyes widened. "Do you suspect Ozymandias will return?"

She bit her lip, but he clearly heard whatever she was thinking. He huffed and turned away.

Mercy looked between them in confusion. "What?"

"When the wall came down," Mary said quietly. "He pushed me out of the way, Mercy. The ceiling should have come down on me, but look – it's curved *around* where I fell. He protected me. He went out of his way to do so."

"Why the Hell would a one-thousand-year-old vampire protect you?"

Mary tried her jaw, but her eyes darted helplessly to Levi. He cleared his throat. "Mercy, your sister didn't break my compulsion. She knew, deeply, intrinsically, that she'd be okay. Because she sensed that he'd be here."

"But what does that mean?"

"Do you remember when we met? How we were drawn together?"

Mercy felt her throat go dry. "Yes, but... you're not saying..."

"I'm not," Levi said. "But I think Mary is."

Mercy shook her head. "Oh my God. Mary. *No*. You can't choose this life, sis. You know better. Changing *hurts*. Giving up your life *hurts*. And this guy is trying to *eat us*."

Mary blinked a few tears away, but she ultimately gave in to the wave of emotion and started bawling. She turned and walked toward the kitchen as Levi fished his phone out of his pocket. "Be nice to your sister, Mercy. She didn't choose this. I better file an insurance claim. Well, two. The car is going to need some love, too."

⸻ ❧ ⸻

MERCY LOADED HER SUITCASE and the cooler into the trunk of Mary's car, then came to stand next to her sister to watch as a tow truck lifted Levi's Audi. He stood nearby, watching sadly as the driver leaned out the window and waved. He lifted his hand but stayed rooted in place as his car was towed away.

"He loved that thing," Mercy said. "I hope it gets a different paint job, at least, if it's not scrapped. You okay, Mary Olive?"

Mary side-eyed her. "I... I understand how you've been feeling, Mercy. This is scary. And, my God, what a *horrible* individual to feel this with."

"I know. I felt the same way. You don't have to pursue it, you know. If I hadn't let Levi turn me, I could have walked away. We're whole without them, Mary. They're the ones whose souls are incomplete. Don't let this stranger suck you in."

"I don't want to be like you," Mary whispered. "I know you hate it, Mercy. I like who I am. I don't want to *not* like me. And I could never give any piece of my heart to a man who wanted to kill you. But, God, it's so tempting to know him."

"Absolutely not. No way."

When Levi approached, Mary glanced past her sister and asked, "Did you know anything about those vampires, Levi?"

He nodded. "Valefar and Ozymandias. They've been around a thousand and a half years, perhaps more. They're brothers, at least through their vampire lineage. Roman soldiers, purportedly. Valefar is not a dybbuk, but he's like me – he can command vampires, sometimes without so much as a word. His powers of control are legendary, and he has swayed many mature vampires into carrying out atrocities like a helpless scion.

"Ozymandias is a nosferat, meaning he encompasses most of the traditional vampire stereotypes – telekinesis, control over select animals, the ability to shapeshift."

"Into a bat?" Mercy asked jokingly. When Levi didn't respond, she rolled her eyes. "That's a dumb power."

"Wait, brothers through vampire lineage?" Mary asked. "What does that make you guys?"

"Sire and scion," Mercy said definitively as Levi sarcastically joked, "She calls me daddy."

"You guys are fucking weird."

"He was *kidding*, Mary. I call him annoying more than anything."

"Uh-huh. So there's different kinds of vampires, then? You're a dybbuk, you said. What's Mercy? Is she that *estrie* thing you were talking about?"

"Yes," Mercy said. "I'm an elemental vampire. Tied to the wind."

"Speaking of which." Levi dug in his pocket and produced a hair tie. "Here, keep your hair restrained for now. We don't need another incident."

While Mercy tied her hair back, Mary kicked a clump of snow. "Can you choose what you become?"

"No," Levi said. "It's circumstantial. I became a dybbuk because I had a strong attachment that was broken at my time of death. The word literally means 'to cling' in Hebrew. I can attach to and command anyone."

"And Mercy? How'd she become an estrie?"

"Mercy became an estrie due to circumstance, too. Estries can only be made by dybbuk vampires, and only at sunset. And the human turning has to be a night owl by nature. To a degree, a sire can control the outcome of what their scion becomes. If I'd turned Mercy at any other time of day, she wouldn't be an estrie. But there are *great* perks that come with the type of vampire she is, so I would imagine that some sires have absolutely set out to create a specific type of scion."

Mary nodded. "That makes sense. Can we get in the car now? It's cold."

The vampires conceded, and Mary gratefully settled into the driver's seat. "What hotel are we going to?"

"Let's go to the Marietta Inn over in Winchester," Levi suggested. "It's close enough to the cafe for us to easily head into work."

Mercy, who was in the front passenger seat, turned to face him. "You want to go back into public?"

He shrugged. "We've proven we can fight back, and these hunters aren't interested in making a scene. They're always going to corner their prey or remove them from a public situation. They wouldn't come for us there. We do have to be careful, though."

"Careful is a Harker specialty," Mary declared.

BY SOME MIRACLE, MARY Olive convinced Mercy and Levi to let her stay in her own room. They didn't want to leave her alone, but she was insistent that she didn't want to hear them loudly "reading the Bible" again. (She'd naturally made her declaration with great enough emphasis that the woman at the check-in desk averted her eyes and covered her mouth.) Embarrassed, they didn't press the subject. Mary's focus on that had allowed her real intentions to go unnoticed, a feat she was proud of given Levi's special abilities.

To add credence to her presumed desire to stay put, she'd offered him her car keys so he could drive to the cafe in the morning.

Now, as night was falling, she was bundling up in layers and praying she wouldn't encounter either of them as she snuck out of the hotel. Her thoughts were racing as she wound down the hallway, and her heart started pounding when she stood alone in the elevator. When the cold night air pricked her skin one floor down, she relaxed, moved her scarf over her mouth, and pulled up her hood.

Mary walked down the sidewalk, venturing just until the hotel was out of sight before veering off the snow-cleared path and entering a thicket of pine trees. She marched into the woods, turning her head at the sound of every snapping branch and falling clump of snow.

Eventually, she made her way into a clearing. At its far end, a single bat hung upside down from a low-hanging branch. It opened its eyes, drinking her in with a gaze that shimmered like moonlit rubies.

It dropped from the branch, and by the time it reached the ground, it was seemingly human. The man marched toward her, his eyes wide and sparkling. "You freed me. He was controlling me, you know. It's been centuries. Longer, maybe."

Mary's eyes widened as he came to a stop a few feet away from her, but she didn't move otherwise.

"I'm Ozzy. What's your name?"

"Ozzy? Like Osbourne?"

"Absolutely not. Given the whole bat thing, I find that offensive."

Mary cracked a smile and pulled her scarf from her face. "Handsome *and* culturally literate. I'm Mary Olive. I think you were trying to eat my sister."

Ozzy threw his head back and laughed. Mary couldn't stop her eyes from locking on his fangs. "Maybe at first, but hunting was Valefar's deal, not mine. Besides, as soon as we met her, we knew we couldn't eat her."

"Why's that?"

He reached out and gently tilted her chin toward him. "Isn't my meeting and saving you reason enough?"

Mary stepped back. "No, but I wish it was. She said she met you before."

He nodded. "She did. We restrained her rather than harmed her. And when she turned into wind, we realized she was exactly what we're looking for."

"What's that? And *who* has you searching?"

Ozzy turned his red eyes toward the moon. "I will send rain on the earth forty days and forty nights, and I will blot out from the face of the land every living thing that I have made."

"Genesis?"

"The story of how vampirism first truly spread. They echo it quite a bit, Mary Olive. Your sister can carry out the very will of God, unless she chooses to serve a different master."

"Who would that be?"

"Lilith. The first vampire. She's not an elemental, but she needs one to help her prepare for the end of days. She had us ancients searching for vampires with Biblical abilities. We naturally looked for signs from Genesis, given its prominence in our folklore, and that line had us looking for someone with weather abilities. Candidly, we've never seen an estrie with control... or, rather, one whose sire can control their direction. Lilith will try to tempt your sister into a fall, Mary Olive."

Mary parted her lips, but she was speechless. She stared at the vampire before her for a lingering moment before she turned and exhaled. The cloud that rose from her warm breath temporarily obscured her view of him.

"You're beautiful."

Her eyes wandered back to him. "So are you."

He smiled and inched toward her. "You know what this is, don't you?"

She nodded. "It's what Mercy and Levi have. Something about a splintered soul."

"I remember the moment it happened. It was in the midst of the *Sabīnae raptae.* I saw horrible atrocities committed by men against men, and it broke me to be a part of it. When I awoke, I found I had the power to gather the pieces... I could move mountains, I always suspected. But I was never whole after that."

Mary tilted her chin. "But I'm whole. This soul is entirely mine."

"Nevertheless, you're drawn to me," he said with a smile. "Or else you wouldn't have sought me out. You know I'm dangerous."

"You wouldn't hurt me. You saved me when the wall came down."

His smile grew. "You're right. But perhaps it was a temporary lapse in judgment."

"It wasn't," Mary said with certainty. "You want to know me, just like I want to know you. I've sensed you for days now. There's been this weird, irritating sense of waiting. I knew something would happen. You did, too, didn't you?"

Ozzy approached her and took her hands in his. "I did. I never would have expected it was you, Mary Olive. But how fortunate we are to have met."

"Levi will know," Mary stated. "He reads minds."

"I can help you block him out," Ozzy offered. "Let me show you what I can do."

Chapter Twelve

The sound of a ringing phone ripped Mary from her slumber. She sat straight up and gasped, then looked at the digital clock. It was half past ten. Clutching the blanket to her chest, she answered the phone, graciously ending the onslaught of digital sound. "Shit, Mercy, I'm sorry. I *way* overslept. Yeah, I'm fine. Um, yeah, tell Levi I don't feel like going into the cafe this morning. Yeah, I think all the drafts in his tornado-strewn house gave me a cold."

She faked a cough, then listened to her sister for a moment. "Oh, um, maybe around dinnertime? I'd like to get some more sleep first. Thanks, sis. Love you."

Mary hung up and fell back on the bed with a sigh. Ozzy's arm snaked around her waist as he pulled her closer and playfully nibbled at her neck. Mary giggled as she rolled onto her side and scooted back into his embrace.

"Stop," she muttered lazily. "I hardly got any sleep last night."

His fangs briefly brushed over her flesh before he started trailing kisses down to her shoulder. "We can sleep when we're dead."

"Well, if Mercy and Levi find out about this, I will be." She looked over her shoulder at him. "I mean, don't get me wrong, that was the best sex I've ever had. But the whole *trying to eat my sister or give her to Lilith* thing isn't cool. I'm struggling with that."

"Eating other vampires is not something I wanted to do," he reminded. "Not anymore, at least. I'm grateful to be free of that obligation. But Lilith is going to come to town if I don't take Mercy to her. She knows about her now."

"I guess she's coming to town, then. You're *not* taking my sister."

"Then I better help you three form a front against her. And I better prepare to walk away. Because she *will* come, Mary Olive. And she's the embodiment of earthly evil. I hope, when it's time to leave, you'll come with me."

"I'm not walking away from Mercy. You're so sweet and adorable, Ozzy, but I'm not doing that. What can we do to stop her?"

"Precious little, I'd say. But a little bit of preparation doesn't hurt. Maybe your sister can, at the very least, fend her off. She's quite powerful."

"Now I have to figure out how I'm going to tell Mercy and Levi about this. Because something tells me they won't want you around."

"And something tells me they'll have no choice," he said, grinning. "Now that I've found you, Mary Olive, I'm not leaving without getting to know you first."

"Let me talk to them before they meet you," she begged. "Teach me how to block Levi from my mind."

"Focus on your breathing when you look at him," he explained plainly. "Feel each and every breath, think about it deeply. Women can think about multiple things at once,

I've heard, so it doesn't matter that your mind is running wild with other thoughts. Focus on your breathing first and foremost, and that's all he'll hear."

Mary kissed the tip of his nose. "Where have you been all my life?"

"Traveling all over the world. Indulging in the delicacies that eternity offers. Wishing I was with you all the while, though. I'm so grateful for you securing my freedom and giving me the choice to pursue this."

Mary laughed. "And I've been wishing I was with *you*. No wonder I could never find a boyfriend. I thought I was either annoying, a hopeless romantic, or both."

He chuckled. "Me too. Eternity is lonely, you know. You wonder how long it will last every time you form a bond. Human life is fleeting, and I've seen many vampires cease to exist in my time, too."

"Because you ate some of them?"

He smiled guiltily, and her eyes landed on his fangs. They were larger than Mercy's or Levi's – these looked undeniably predatory. "After I changed, I was angry at the world. After war showed me the worst of humanity, I wanted desperately to see good. To feel good. And I liked the power that came with feeding on vampires. I felt like I was protecting humans by helping bring the plague to its conclusion. But it just caught the attention of Lilith, and she forced me to stay on that path.

"I had to hunt down vampires who risked exposing or hurting our species, effectively providing protection to vampires instead of humans. I took a lot of very sick people down. It's ironic now that I've found a soul bond of my own.

If I change you, Mary Olive, we could be in the very same boat as my prey. And there are others like me still hunting."

"I don't want to be changed," she said confidently. "Not yet, at least. What do you mean there are others, though?"

"Ten hunting pairs – nine now, I guess. Ancient, powerful vampires scouring the world for their next meal. That's why my fangs are like this, candidly. After so much vampire blood, it was like we each adapted to hunt tougher prey."

Mary pulled the blankets up. "And they didn't know your soul fractured? Your hunter peers?"

He shook his head. "They'd had to have known me as a human to observe the change. I was always acutely aware of the lapse, but they weren't. Lilith might know, though, if I had to guess. She's not like the rest of us. God made her, you know."

"Like, Yahweh?"

"Yeah, way. Purportedly, she was made before God made modern man. She was His trial run. Legend maintains that she was too fiery, too rebellious, so He made future humans more subservient and less supernaturally powered. Some supernatural control has slipped through – some humans are psychic, some have extrasensory perception. Some are descended from the broken souls of vampires."

"So God is real?"

He laughed. "Of course He's real. And He made vampirism when He made her. Lilith had children, once upon a time, but God's other earthly creatures destroyed them. So she set out to make more children. She targeted the humans. Vampirism happened. Then it spread."

"Have you met Him?"

"No. But I've met Lilith and her partner, Samael. You know... Satan?"

"Oh my God." Mary covered her eyes. "So you're saying *Satan* could come to Connecticut?"

"Well, sure. He's spent a lot of time in the American South. The East Coast might be new territory for him, but it's also new territory for tornadoes, right?"

MERCY TOSSED THE WHITE rag into the laundry bin and washed her hands. Levi walked into the backroom carrying a few boxes. He glanced at her when he passed but didn't say anything.

"You know, any color other than white wouldn't show stains," she called.

"Any color other than white doesn't bleach well," he returned as he settled the boxes in the corner and straightened his back.

"Well, someone's not using enough bleach to clean them, then. There are stains all over your clean towels."

He cocked an eyebrow, then walked past her and examined the folded towels. "Dammit, you're right. I'll talk to Joe, he has been handling this chore. It's so hard to find good help nowadays. You know, Mercy..."

"I'm not abandoning my career in favor of helping you run a subpar cafe with bad décor."

"Okay, ouch." Levi moved to stand behind Mercy, and he pecked her cheek and rubbed her shoulders. "You can relax, darling. We've shown them that we can control it. They're not likely to come for us, and if they do, they won't go after us in public."

"I'm just on edge," Mercy said as she pulled away from his hands. "I have to be literally attached at the hip with you until we're certain they're not coming back for Mary. How *dare* she have a soul bond with one of those monsters?"

"Be nice," Levi said. "She didn't choose it, like we didn't. I do find it odd, however, that two soul fractures came into the human world around the same time in the same household. And from a man who *also* had a soul bond, though fate robbed him of the opportunity to explore it. That seems quite a bit like intelligent design, don't you think?"

"Maybe," Mercy said as she pushed out the swing doors and headed toward the register. "I've been saying this whole damn time that I think the Bible holds our answers, but you've been telling me it didn't matter."

"It's a Biblical curse, Mercy. We know that much. I just... I wonder what the intention of putting you two together was. I wonder why Steve matters here. There has to be *something* there, right?"

"Maybe it's happenstance," Mercy suggested as she leaned against the corner. "Maybe your fractures go into a black hole that only farts us back into the world on a particular cadence that just happened to align with my parents' and paternal grandparents' fornication."

"As much as I enjoy your books, I really hate what your mouth does with words. I cannot emphasize that enough."

Mercy smiled as a customer approached the register. "What can I do for you?"

"I'll get a warm cinnamon roll and a large americano for here."

"That'll be $7.57." Mercy took his card, processed the transaction, and returned it to the customer. "Thanks so much. Settle in, we'll bring it to your table."

She moved to the display case and grabbed a cinnamon roll with tongs, then guided it into the toaster oven while Levi was preparing the man's coffee.

"What if he *does* come for her, Levi? I mean, you pursued me."

"I might have to change her before he does," he said slowly. "Those guys are pure evil. They could do real harm with a scion, especially if she turned out to be as powerful as you. Of course, I don't want that, Mary doesn't want that, and something tells me you two would bicker a *lot*."

"And she would probably call you daddy, now that you've planted that idea in her empty head." Mercy picked up a plate and grabbed the tongs again to ease the cinnamon roll out of the oven. "What if I turn her?"

"You can't. You're still a fledgling. You'd kill her if you tried."

Mercy grabbed a wooden tray and placed the cinnamon roll on it with a napkin and a set of silverware. She reached for the coffee Levi had just prepared and side-eyed him. "You're lucky I'm responsible. It's *really* late to tell me that information. I could have killed people, Levi."

He smirked. "Yeah, I'm lucky you're responsible."

Mercy rolled her eyes before she smiled and walked the tray to the customer. He had long hair and a beard, obscured only slightly by an oversized beanie. He beamed when Mercy approached. "Thank you! This looks amazing. That man up there – he's the owner, right? The Levi from the cafe name?"

Mercy chuckled. "Yep, that's Levi."

"How long have you worked with him?"

"Oh, I don't work here. Not really. Think of me like a substitute teacher for baristas. I'm just filling in since our regular cashier is out sick. Er, *his*. His regular cashier. Like I said, I'm a fill-in."

"That's compassionate of him," the man said. "To not overwork staff. That's a very human approach that more cafe owners need to adopt."

Mercy nodded. "Yeah, Levi's a good guy, deep down. Annoying, but his heart has always been in the right place. Let me know if you need anything else."

"I'm a food critic, so I'm sure I'll be up to talk with Levi after I'm done."

Mercy froze and forced a smile. "Oh, excellent! Well, thanks for stopping in – we can't wait to hear what you think."

She flitted back up to the register and whispered, "See the hipster with the Amish beard? He's a food critic."

Levi's eyes widened. "*Great*. Just what I needed today. Do me a favor and tie your hair back, Mercy. We don't need another incident, especially not in front of a member of the press."

MARY GLANCED UP AT the jingling bells when she opened the door to Café au Levi. When her eyes fell back on the cafe storefront, she was surprised to see that it was busy.

It closed in half an hour, so things should have been winding down.

Behind the counter, Mercy and Levi were staring at her with pure horror. She approached them. "Hey, guys! Turns out it was just allergies – my hotel room is dusty, and Zyrtec did the trick."

"*Good*," Levi hissed. "There's a food critic here, so I can't have sick employees wandering around. Also, what the *Hell* were you thinking?"

"I was thinking I was hungry and knew where to find a good soup."

"*Mary Olive*," Mercy whispered. "You can't walk around on your own right now. *He* might be looking for you."

She lifted her chin. "I'm *fine*, Mercy. He's not going to hurt me. Why can't you trust me on this?"

"Because he didn't hesitate to drive a stake into my throat, Mary."

Mary's mouth parted, but she didn't say anything. Levi raised his eyebrows. "Weird time to suddenly start thinking about your breathing and how much you hate your knees."

Her eyes widened. "I didn't just start thinking about those things. I've been thinking them all day."

"You've never had to remind yourself to breathe before." Levi leaned forward to lock eyes with her. "*Tell me what you're hiding, Mary.*"

"I'm hiding so much from you that I don't even know where to start," she blurted. She lifted her hand to cover her mouth as it continued sputtering verbal diarrhea. The rest of what she said came out muffled, but Levi's eyebrows rose as he presumably read her thoughts.

"Mercy," he said. "Go turn off the neon sign and flip the one on the door to closed."

Mercy obeyed his command, then returned to his side. Mary ordered a soup and disappeared into the back while Levi cherry-picked which of her thoughts he'd share with Mercy. He told her that her sister met up with the remaining vampire hunter and that he'd warned her that Samael and Lilith may be coming to town to seek them out.

"Samael?" Mercy looked at him wide-eyed and whispered, "I thought you didn't buy the angel stories with the flaming swords and stuff!"

"I don't," he said, glancing across the store as another group of customers finished their meals and left. "So I'm *very* curious to see what figures these people actually are. I don't believe we'll like our answer."

He and Mercy moved to clean up the empty table, and the food critic eyed them thoughtfully. Levi removed the dishes while Mercy wiped down the table. When she was done, she headed to the backroom to wave at her sister and place the dirty rag in the hamper. Upon returning to the storefront, the only customer besides the food critic was spilling out the door.

The bearded man stood and purposefully approached her, so Mercy forced a smile. *Levi, get out here*, she thought desperately.

"Mercy Mild Harker," the man stated knowingly. "I've come for you and your sire."

Mercy reached up to let her ponytail down, but the man's hand caught her wrist in the blink of an eye.

"No." He lifted his hand, and the shades fell down over the windows. The lock on the door clicked into place. "Don't cause an incident. I'm just here to talk. Negotiate, if you'll hear me out. Maybe you can make me another cup of coffee?"

Levi pushed out of the backroom and came to stand beside Mercy. He crossed his arms as he gazed at the food critic.

"Levi Romero," he said. "I appreciated the hospitality – I'll be giving your cafe a glowing review. This was truly an excellent display of *hachnasat orchim*. Can I please request a moment of your time and another cup?"

"Did you just threaten my scion?"

The stranger shook his head. "I issued no threat. But I'll warn you that turning me away *will* put you in a dangerous situation. It's best to hear me out, Levi."

He's fast, and he closed the blinds with his mind, Mercy thought, hoping Levi was listening. *Hear him out, but stay close to me.*

"Yes," Levi said. "Sure, let me make you a coffee. Can we get you another pastry?"

"Sure. I thought those sugar plum tarts looked pretty inviting."

Chapter Thirteen

The stranger sipped his coffee, then nodded to the vampires sitting across from him with satisfaction. "Excellent. You sure you don't want to charge me for this round?"

"It's on the house," Levi offered. "Who *are* you?"

"Michael," the man said, his hazel eyes scanning Levi's face.

"Jesus Christ," Mercy muttered.

"No," he corrected. "Saint Michael the Archangel. I'm the Protector of the Jewish people and the Guardian of the Catholic Church. I believe you both, by extension, have earned my guidance in matters of Heaven and Hell."

Levi, unconvinced, crossed his arms. "Prove it."

The hipster nodded, then leaned down to his backpack. He shifted a laptop forward, moved a water bottle, and slowly extracted a sheathed sword. He had to rise to lift its incredible length from the bag. He held it fondly, then unsheathed it. The metal, seemingly made of gold, burst into flame.

Mercy and Levi sprang to their feet, but Michael let out a low chuckle and smoothly returned the sword to its sheath. "Don't worry – you can sit down. I haven't used it in millennia. But that is why I'm here, I'm afraid. You see, I'm on this plane to keep an eye on an angel I rather dislike. Samael. We've been warring on and off since time began. When God cast him down from Heaven, Samael grabbed me and tried to take me with him."

"Satan," Mercy said knowingly.

"You might call him that." Michael slipped the impossible length of his sword back into the backpack and sipped his coffee. "Oh, Lord, that's heavenly. You have a gift, Levi."

Levi leaned back and crossed his arms. "Thank you. I have to ask – why masquerade as a food critic?"

"Masquerade? This isn't an act. I'm a bit of a secret rebel. We don't have sinfully delicious foods in Heaven, so... When in Rome..." Michael shifted. "Ah, I see I'm making you grow impatient. I'll give you the stage. Tell me how I can assist you two."

"You don't already know?" Mercy asked skeptically. "Something must have made you think we need your guidance."

Michael slowly smirked. "Perhaps. But like I said, I'll give you two the chance to elaborate."

"Very well. Mercy's sister believes Samael and Lilith will come looking for us. She believes Lilith was the first vampire and that she and her partner have recruited some of the oldest vampires to hunt down soulmate pairs. They say it protects our species."

"So it has," Michael noted. "While many of His creations have ceased to exist, your species has continued quietly thriving across the ages. Squashing threats doesn't exactly seem to have a downside here. And who better to oversee that process than the Angel of Death himself?"

"Sure," Levi said. "I'll follow that for the sake of conversation, though I naturally disagree as one of those suspected threats. So, Michael, here's the thing – Mercy and I, with a little help from her human sister, took down one of our pursuant hunters. And yet, the other is still pursuing us at the request of Lilith... she and Samael will be coming to town if we are not hand-delivered, from what I've heard."

"That's what I've heard, too," Michael stated. "There are many ancient members of your race, and I have kept in contact with some over the years. I've heard rumors that Lilith and Samael would like to take Heaven. She has an entire legion of near-immortals at her disposal – she just needs her weapon now."

"An entire legion of *what*? Vampires?" Mercy asked.

"Naturally. You're her children. And though she's a demon, she was created by the head honcho Himself. That means you're children of God, too. The entirety of your species, like the angels before you, will be forced to pick sides if this plane falls victim to another Heavenly War."

"Why are you here with us, then? I'd think you have bigger fish to fry."

Michael beamed. "Fish to fry! I get it, because I'm a food critic. Clever, Levi. Well, I'm here because it appears that your scion just may be their weapon of choice. While she's a fledgling, you're a package deal, but it's really *Mercy* that they want. And Mercy, your powers are a true force of nature."

Mercy leaned back in her chair and focused on Levi. *Am I being asked to take sides in a Heavenly War?*

It sounds like it, Levi thought in response. *Do what you must, Mercy. I'll stand by your side whatever you decide. But I don't like this. I don't trust this guy.*

"So," Mercy said slowly. "What do you want, Michael?"

The angel lifted his cup, took a drink, and smacked his lips. "I want to keep working as a food critic and acting as an earthly watchdog. It sounds leagues better than another Heavenly War."

"Pardon me for being forward," Levi said. "Why don't you do something?"

Michael set his coffee mug down. "Because intervening would inevitably start the very war I'm hoping to prevent. But what I can do is invite you to join me in protecting Heaven, Mercy. And Levi, I'll need your help, too, of course."

Mercy pursed her lips. "You're asking me to act as your weapon rather than becoming Satan's. Is that what I'm hearing?"

"I am not asking. I am inviting you to do so, Mercy. It is wholly your choice, but yes. I would like your powers on my side."

"There's one problem," Mercy said. "We can't *control* it, Michael. I certainly can't create wind or anything on demand, and Levi has precious little control over me unless it's absolutely dire."

"Good thing you have me, then. Come and train with me. Both of you."

Mercy cocked an eyebrow. "Or else...?"

"Or else Lilith will come for you, and you can face her without the knowledge I'll provide to you. I can't force you to make a choice here, Mercy, but I will encourage you to think really hard about what she and Samael are capable of. Ask yourself if your morals align with theirs, and if not, question how you'll be able to stand your ground when they come. This situation has already become dire, my friends, and you are not currently in any position to protect yourselves."

Mercy and Levi exchanged a look, and then he slowly nodded. Mercy confidently met the archangel's eyes. "We'll train with you, but only if my sister can come, too. We need to keep her away from this Ozymandias character."

FROM MARY'S PERSPECTIVE, the car ride was full of silence. Mercy and Levi, however, were engaged in a conversation she couldn't hear.

I was running from religious persecution, Mercy. So, no, I don't feel any loyalty to a God who allowed my family to be slaughtered by antisemitic assholes while I had to live with the consequences of that. He's abandoned my people time and time again.

But you're Jewish.

Yes, because I was born Jewish and like the customs. It's not about God. I don't trust this angel.

Mercy met her partner's gaze in the passenger mirror. *I haven't committed to anyone, Levi. Just to train with the biggest badass in Heaven. Let's give him a chance, at least. It would be silly not to.*

He tore his eyes away from her gaze and took in the passing landscape. Mercy still studied his reflection in the mirror as he tightened his jaw. *I do think we should study under the archangel's tutelage, but we should reserve our judgment until we hear from Samael, too. Life on earth has been cruel, and a cruel God is not one I'm inclined to serve.*

And you think Satan is a more viable option here? Mercy returned.

Likely not, but I can understand his dissatisfaction with Him.

Truthfully, I can, too. So, what are the chances that Jesus is chill with an ally rather than a worshiper?

"So," Mary Olive said, breaking a stillness that must have seemed uncomfortable to her. "We're going to stay at a house owned by a guy you *just met* who claims he can help you control your powers?"

"That's the gist of it." Before Mercy could say anything more, Levi leaned into the front seat between them.

"Mary, tell me he *isn't* in your hotel room right now."

Mary glanced at her sister with wide eyes and smiled guiltily as she drummed her fingers against the steering wheel. "I mean, maybe. I don't know."

"Why would he be in your hotel room?" Mercy asked in horror. "Oh my God, Mary Olive, tell me you didn't..."

"I didn't," Mary said quickly. *Too* quickly. Her sister's eyebrows rode up, so she sighed. "Okay. Maybe I did. Like, a little."

Mercy rubbed her temples. "Jesus, Mary, you're sleeping with a guy who wanted to eat me."

"*Wanted.* I freed him from someone's control, Mercy. He doesn't want to eat you anymore."

"Oh, that makes it better," Mercy said sarcastically. "Thank you for correcting me."

Mary sighed. "I know, Mercy. It doesn't make it right. I wish I was strong enough to ignore the soul bond. But if I'm being honest, I'd cross oceans for him. It's scary. I can see why you were running, sis. No offense, Levi."

"None taken. I guess this makes a case for my intelligent design point, eh, Mercy?"

She grumbled, but Mary perked up. "What do you mean by that?"

Levi, Mercy warned silently. *Don't say a word to her about the archangel.*

"Steve, Mercy, *you*," he said. "God seems to have a plan with so many soul bonds clustered together. But it is hard, though, Mary. I feel for you. I've been watching Mercy deal with the shock for a decade. Still, even. It's not an easy thing to process."

"I'm perfectly adjusted, thank you," Mercy snapped.

"*Right*," Levi said sarcastically. "We'll support him for now, Mary, but you truly need to tread cautiously. Don't let a stranger sway you into accepting the allure of vampirism."

"Like you did with me?"

"Mercy," he hissed.

"It's true," she told her sister. "This guy, he's going to promise you a lot of grandeur. A lot of freedom. And while you'll get that one day, maybe, you'll be a possession until then. I'm not a vampire, Mary - I'm a *fledgling*. Until I'm a mature vampire, Levi owns me."

"Don't be dramatic," he said. "You're a city, and I'm the state. You're a sovereign entity. You just have to act within my rules."

Mercy rolled her eyes. "Rules that I have no say in. Mary, you don't know this guy. You don't know what he'd do with you as his scion. If he's coming with us, you have to *promise* me you'll heed my warning. Tell me you won't even consider taking this path. Not right now, at least."

"I promise," Mary said. "I'm so, so sorry it's him, sis. I wish it was anyone else in the world. He hurt you, and I know that's not okay. I'm sorry I can't stay away from him."

"Mercy understands," Levi said. Mercy just looked out the window and grumbled.

You're encouraging her to suffer a life like your father's, he thought. *Steve is miserable and broken. Would you really condemn Mary Olive to that?*

Of course not, Mercy snapped. *I'm reminding her that we have a choice. If we don't buy into the allure, we can ignore it. My soul is whole, I came into this world as one distinct piece and I've remained such. The same is true for Mary Olive.*

And I pursued you. Ozymandias won't leave her alone. You know that.

Maybe Michael can help Mary find a way to stand her ground, too.

MARY PLACED HER CLOTHING in a suitcase and sighed. "This must be how Mercy has felt lately, getting shoved from one couch to the next."

Ozzy rolled to face her. "My presence won't stop Lilith from coming, Mary Olive."

"I know. But you and I, we're going to support Mercy in getting a fighting chance. And you can tell her everything you know."

"I will," he said. "But, truthfully, I doubt it will be of any use. *She'll* still win. I might as well change you now; that way, you'll at least be immortal. Lilith is not gentle in her interactions."

Mary stood completely still with her back turned to him. Then, she absent-mindedly fussed with a folded shirt. "I'm not interested in being turned, Ozzy."

He sat up straight. "But Mary, that's the only way we can stay together. How would this work if you keep aging?"

"We just met. What if we don't last?"

"We're soulmates," he said confidently. "The moment I first met your gaze, I knew you were meant to be at my side. I saw it on your face – you knew it, too. Love at first sight."

Mary moved to the bathroom to fetch her toothbrush and comb, and when she returned, he was standing next to her suitcase, awaiting her. He spread his arms open, and she curled into his embrace as she plopped the items in the suitcase.

"Thank you for coming with us," she said. "I know this is weird. It's not really a situation I want to be in, but they feel like they need to protect me from you."

He chuckled. "I understand – I'd feel the same way if I was in that position. But I'll travel to the ends of the earth for you. Hell, I'd argue that I have. So I'm sure you understand why the idea of watching you grow old and die terrifies me."

Still encircled in his arms, Mary smiled to herself. "But I grew up expecting that course of events, as I'm sure you did, too." She pulled back just enough to boop his nose, which made him scowl and swat at her hand. "And you just met me, big guy."

He tucked a strand of hair behind her ear. "I've known you for a thousand years, Mary Olive."

She pulled away from him and closed her suitcase. "Well, Ozzy, *I* just met *you*. You're lucky Mercy's situation gave me the knowledge to make sense of this experience. I probably would have been too terrified to even speak to you otherwise."

He studied her for a moment before he smirked, his eyes drinking in her presence with absolute admiration. "I'm lucky for Mercy's situation in more ways than one. I wonder how many lives you've lived before we found each other."

Mary Olive crossed her arms and sank down onto the edge of the mattress, her body stiff with contemplation. Her eyes bore a distant and thoughtful look for a moment before she turned her full attention back to the vampire. "You think I've lived before, Ozzy?"

"I don't see why not. You're worldly. Smart. Cautious and contemplative. You were a part of my soul once, but I feel like you've more than matured into your own being. Mercy, she... She's a young soul, don't you think? Flighty and distrustful, that one. I suspect she still carries a lot of her sire's past trauma. You are so pure that I have to assume you're already long unburdened, fully separated from it."

When he sat down beside her, she smiled coyly. "Maybe you're right. Either way, though, I have a lot to learn from you. I don't even know where to start with all the questions

I have. Feeling like I've always known you, yet not knowing you at all is so strange."

"Well, ask away. When I'm with you, I have all the time in the world."

Mary nervously bit her lower lip, a grim expression on her face. "Well, it appears we don't have as much time as we'd like. Do you want to tell me about Lilith and Satan?"

"Samael," Ozzy corrected. "The Angel of Death."

"They're bad guys, right?"

"Well, they're not kind."

"So they're not going to be happy that you stopped wanting to serve them?"

He placed his hands on her cheeks, drawing her near and savoring every precious millisecond that passed as he held her and leaned to tenderly press his lips to her forehead. "I can't do that, Mary Olive. There's no backing down from a contract with them. We have to convince your sister to willingly meet Lilith. She can decide then if she wants to serve her. But I have to complete my mission before I can walk away."

"But what if we run instead?"

"We can't. Samael is Death incarnate. You can't run from Death, not even as a vampire. But she *will* be given a choice. I wish I had been granted the same leniency."

"So you're *certain* she'll be given a choice? Lilith won't hurt her?"

"She won't hurt her before then," he said. "But I can't guarantee she won't lash out if she doesn't like Mercy's answer. I suppose that's why she wants to get her power under control."

Mary Olive shifted uncomfortably. "What was it like, Ozzy? Being under what's-his-name's control?"

"Valefar," he said almost distantly. "It was the strangest thing... Like a time slip. I can't recall entire stretches of my life. I felt like a zombie under his command, and while I had thoughts of my own, acting on them was hard. I cannot even explain what it's like having someone in your head."

She winced.

"What's wrong, Mary Olive?"

"I think I owe Mercy an apology. Her sire, Levi, is one of those mind-control vampires. She complained to me about him always being in her head, and I really shrugged it off."

He smiled reassuringly. "You didn't know, honey. And I imagine it's a much different experience for her, being a splinter of his soul."

She beamed. "You're right. Thank you for lifting some weight off my shoulders. I'm still planning to apologize, though. I guess I'm kind of a shitty sister for having to hear it from a second vampire to wholly believe it."

There was a knock at the door, so Mary reluctantly rose and moved to open it. "Mercy! Hey. Come on in."

"Is he here?" Mercy asked before she rounded the corner. She froze when she spotted Ozymandias. "Ah. He is."

He waved. "Hi. I'm Ozzy."

"I'm aware. We've met."

"Right." He brushed his hair back, tucking his locs behind an ear. "I'm sorry about that, Mercy. I know it doesn't make it better, but my hunting partner forced my compliance. I didn't want to hurt you. I mean, that's why I only staked your jaw."

"Yeah, that still hurt," Mercy stated. She crossed her arms as if comforting herself.

"I see you're wearing black again," he said, grasping at straws to make conversation. "Your favorite color?"

"Yeah, what of it?"

"Mercy always wears black," Mary, ever the peacemaker, explained helpfully. "It's how she feels comfortable. Anyway, Mercy, Ozzy was just saying how *grateful* he is to have the opportunity to make things right with you."

"Ah, yes," he said. "I'd like to tell you and your sire what I know. It might help you as you, ya know..."

"Navigate the situation you brought to us?" Mercy asked with narrowed blue eyes.

"If it wasn't me, it could have been any of the nine other hunting pairs. If anything, you're *lucky* it was me. I stopped as soon as I was freed from Valefar's control. The others aren't operating under such constraints. They *want* to see you suffer, Mercy. I genuinely do not want that."

She pursed her lips and nodded. "Heartwarming, what a way to start the New Year. Alright, Ozzy, you do have a fair point. When we get to my friend's place, I'll talk with you more. Levi and I are going to ride there with him, so you two can follow us."

"Okay," Mary said. "Thanks for giving us a chance, Mercy. Have I ever told you that you're the best sister ever?"

"You could stand to mention it more," she said with a smirk. "Meet you downstairs in fifteen?"

"Sounds good," said Mary. "We're just wrapping the packing up. Well, *I* am. Ozzy didn't really bring anything."

"Okay." Mercy forced a smile. "See you soon."

As she left, she couldn't help but think, *If my hair wasn't tied, I'd be tearing this place apart. I hate him.*

Relax, Mercy, came the sound of Levi's voice in the back of her mind. *It will get better.*

It fucking better, Levi. I don't trust him one bit.

"WELCOME TO MY HOME!" Michael announced as Mary and Ozymandias stepped out of their car. "My, what a handsome couple you two are."

Mary Olive brushed a strand of wavy hair behind her ear and blushed. "Aw, thank you. I'm Mary Olive. This is Ozzy."

Mercy crossed her arms. Levi side-eyed her and thought, *Be nice.*

"Michael." The angel reached up to tuck a few stray strands behind his ear. With a patient expression, he turned to Mercy and Levi. "It is such a pleasure to have you as my guests. The rooms are upstairs. Make yourselves at home, and then, Mercy, I would like to talk to you."

Ozzy stepped forward cautiously. "What are you?"

"Quite a bit like you, I'd say, but much older. I hope you like discussing ancient politics, because I'm curious to pick your brain. Tell me, what was your favorite food when you were alive?"

Ozzy blinked, evidently not expecting that question. "Bread, I suppose. It was the bulk of my diet as a soldier. I liked berries quite a bit, too."

"Fascinating," Michael said. "I work as a food critic, so a modern approach to ancient Roman staples might be an interesting topic to explore."

Ozzy turned to Mary Olive, seemingly stupefied. "Is this guy for real?"

"Mercy and I have day jobs, too," Levi added. "It's not uncommon for immortals to still have to earn a living."

"Ugh," Mary said. "An eternity of job hopping sounds horrific. It's hard enough in this day and age."

Levi raised his eyebrows. "How would *you* know what the current job market looks like?"

Mary smiled guiltily and shrugged as he sighed and shook his head. Michael, meanwhile, was moving to the bright blue front door to open it. He gestured grandly. "Please, come in."

Finally able to enter, the vampires slowly filed in. Mercy made a point to enter last, never taking her eyes off her sister and Ozymandias. That wasn't an easy feat to accomplish, as she desperately wanted to examine the new space. Mary certainly was.

Michael gestured to the stairs. "Go get settled, and feel free to explore. I'm so grateful to have you all as my guests."

MERCY GLANCED AT LEVI. "They're on the other side of the house, right?"

He tilted his head, listening to what seemed like silence to Mercy. "They are. I'm ready to alert you two if they approach."

"I hate him," Mercy said, finally putting emotion to the thought that had been brewing all day. "I don't know how but he's pulling one on Mary. *Nothing* he's peddling is real."

"Hatred stirs up conflict, but love covers over all wrongs."

"Look, Michael." Mercy turned to face the lanky hipster. "I like you, dude, but you're really starting to remind me why I don't go to church."

He chuckled. "I don't go myself, and I've been here a long time. Religion is a strange thing, and I say that as the defender of Heaven. We Heavenly beings either seek to restore or disrupt order – our job is about balance. No amount of prayer or pleading will change the fact that God is simply trying to keep order."

"Really?" Mercy asked. "Prayer doesn't matter, then?"

"Not for most things. God isn't listening to every damn individual. Sure, He might perform a miracle every here or there if He's bored, but it's not the norm. He has bigger fish to fry. Fortunately for you, Mercy, you're a fucking whale."

"That's no way to talk to a lady," Levi chided.

"You're the *biggest* fish, Mercy."

"I think whales are mammals, not fish," Mercy said. "But I get it. God sent His baddest, hispteriest angel for my biggest battle."

Michael studied her, then looked past her at Levi. "Has she always been mean...?"

"Oh, yes," Levi said. "She's got a sharp tongue. I hope that's not a sin."

"It might be," Michael said. "I've never been a math guy."

"Math?" Levi asked. "Are you saying that sins exist on a spectrum and that actions are evaluated as such based on an *equation*?"

"I've said too much. The mysteries of Heaven will be revealed to you when you stand alongside us in the War to End All Wars. Until then..."

The archangel drew his sword. When it burst into flame, it cast yellow highlights and dark shadows across the dunes and valleys of his face. His smile grew wicked and intentional before he suddenly charged Mercy.

Her eyes widened.

She darted to Levi. Despite her almost mechanical reaction, Michael caught up *fast*. He reached for her hair, and though his fingers sliced through the air, he wasn't quite close enough to grab it. While Mercy cowered before Levi, Michael scowled and swiped his sword. It took a chunk of her hair out before she even realized she was being pulled out of his reach.

She hadn't even felt Levi's hands on her shoulders, but the unexpected motion of his reactive yank sent her gracelessly tumbling into him. They should have collapsed into the snow, but when their bodies collided, something unexpected happened: they became intangible and perfectly in sync.

They were rising into the air weightlessly, moving away from Michael's blade and gliding in a way that felt as natural as wind itself. Mercy, in perfect time with Levi at a level that must have been molecular or spiritual, had a moment of clarity in her suspended state: this must have been a test of some sort. Michael's behavior, though, was deeply unexpected. His eyes followed their ascent as if he could see their bodies stretched amidst the particles of the moving air. With the grace of a cat, he hopped up and hooked Mercy's foot with the blade of his sword.

While the fire didn't burn her, its flame encircled her ankle like a shackle and halted her ascent. With a flick of his wrist, Michael brought the vampires crashing to earth.

Mercy collided with Levi – this time, feeling the painful thump of bone against bone as they were suddenly corporeal again – and skidded across the snow. The force of the impact caused it to pile around her, obscuring her view of the bloodthirsty archangel. She popped her head up and glared at him. "What the *fuck*, Michael?"

Michael moved his head from side to side, cracking his neck with two loud *pop*s. When the angel blinked, his eyes were suddenly replaced by two flickering flames. He readied his sword again and charged them.

Panicked, Mercy threw her hands out in front of her. A massive gust of wind knocked Michael's balance off, causing him to slip and skitter over the snow as he fought it. The golden flames emanating from his sword swooned and waved in the gale but never faltered. Though she held her ground, Mercy had to fight the instinctual curiosity that left her wanting to break the onslaught of wind to stare down at her palms in shock. She knew she wasn't particularly skilled in controlling her power and dared not break her position, lest she potentially lose her advantage.

"*Mercy*," Levi pleaded. "Let me take over! You're not focusing!"

Upon hearing that, Michael broke away from the wind tunnel and rushed them head-on, stealing their opportunity to establish a connection and causing them to scatter in opposite directions. Michael skidded to a stop between them, smiling virulently as he straightened his back and rose to his full height.

He looked over his shoulder at Mercy, then turned to face Levi. His arms rose, clutching his sword high above his head. It was ready to strike.

Michael was about to slice into Levi.

"*No!*" Mercy shrieked.

Before she could react, the world around her dipped into a stark state of inky blackness. It took her a moment to realize that a thick layer of clouds had seemingly materialized out of thin air. A storm brewed overhead, and a massive bolt of lightning tore through the stratosphere and met Michael's raised sword. The entire bolt of lightning burst into blue flame as it crawled back, and its presence was replaced almost immediately by a descending funnel cloud.

Michael looked up at it, then lowered his gaze to meet Mercy's. He lifted a single finger, touched the base of the funnel, and pushed it back toward the heavens. It folded into the cloud, then seemed to suck the blackness of the sky into it. A normal, wintry shade of gray gloom replaced it.

The angel sheathed his sword and blinked the flames in his eyes away. "Very good, Mercy. I knew you could do it. Seems like Levi is your soft spot."

Her cheeks flamed. "He totally is *not* my weakness, if that's what you're implying. Also, what the fuck was that, dude? Are you on our side or not?"

"I had to see what your powers could do. That was impressive, but a single bolt of lightning won't stop Death. We're going to have to figure out ways to spur more intentional displays of power... Something tells me you won't buy it if I pretend to flip a switch again. You okay, Levi?"

Levi, who was planted firmly on his back in the snow, sat up and forced a smile. He brushed a bit of accumulation off his shoulder and shook his hair. "Oh, absolutely. Just saw my entire long-ass life flash before my eyes, but it's fine. I had no idea Mercy could generate lightning."

"She can probably do even more. Anything weather-related may be probable, though she clearly has an affinity for wind. Thanks for playing along, buddy."

"Playing, *right*," Levi said. "That wasn't *genuine* terror."

"And that *also* wasn't genuine compassion for Levi," Mercy added. "I was, uh, just protecting a... person."

"A person?" Levi asked. "Come *on,* Mercy. Michael said it: love covers over all wrongs. You're allowed to let yourself be vulnerable with me."

Mercy scoffed. "I'm literally training with an angelic warrior right now, Levi. Vulnerability is the last thing I should be striving for."

"Actually," Michael interjected. "Seeing your power blossom when you thought Levi was about to be hurt, I think you could use a bit of vulnerability. Why don't you two cozy up inside and bond for a while? I'll prepare dinner."

"Um, we don't really eat human food," Mercy said slowly.

Michael winked. "I know. Just *wait* until you see what I have in store!"

Chapter Fourteen

Mercy gathered her hair in a ponytail, then picked up the scissors that were sitting on the sink. Carefully, she evened out the length of her hair to disguise the chunk Michael had taken out. As she let her hair down and fluffed it, the door opened. She turned in frustration.

"Dude, *knock*."

Levi shrugged. "I heard your thoughts. I knew you were just trimming your hair."

She sighed and moved to sweep the loose hair into a pile. As she wiped it up and disposed of it, she muttered, "Great, two violations of privacy there."

"The angel told us to bond. You closed me out, as usual. Look, Mercy, just like when I first told you I suspected you had this power, you won't be able to control it until you acknowledge it. You know, the state of being vulnerable. You're allowed to let your walls down with me. Michael made it sound like you should."

Mercy moved back in front of the mirror and examined her handiwork. Her hair looked mostly even now. Satisfied, she fluffed it and admired its raven-black sheen before picking up the hairbrush and styling it in a ponytail again. "The last week – more than a week now – has been *nothing* but an exercise in vulnerability, Levi. Maybe *you* need to be vulnerable with me."

"More vulnerable than letting you in my memories?" Levi raised an eyebrow as he searched for a reaction in the reflection of her features. "More vulnerable than *begging* you to stay home this time? I don't know what more I can do to open up."

"Do you want to talk about the *Decreto*?"

"About how my people were executed and exiled? About how my very last memory as a human was seeing my family slaughtered?"

Mercy pursed her lips. "About how God betrayed you, maybe?"

His shoulders slumped. "Yes, that I am struggling with. Especially after I watched an archangel swipe at me with a flaming sword."

Mercy leaned against the sink and crossed her arms. "That was scary for me, too, Levi. I thought I'd see you die, and that was genuinely terrifying. I don't want to lose you. But I keep thinking... you mentioned how curious it was that Dad, Mary, and I, all soul fragments, came into the world with the same family. What if... what if that's *why* you were made immortal back then? Maybe I was *meant* to be created, like, in that moment. Maybe this is all intelligent design."

He cracked a smile. "That sounds like main character syndrome, dear."

"Fine, that's fair. But what if it's true, and I was made to be a backup plan in case Steve and his soulmate took the path they did? What if I was made to be this heavenly weapon? And what if you and I... what if we're meant to carry this skepticism toward Heaven?"

Levi crossed his arms, either mirroring her body language or comforting himself. "What if it wasn't God who made us?"

Mercy let her gaze wander down to the floor. Black and white granite tiles sparkled back at her, sprinkled with little glimmering specks of metal or mineral. "I guess we won't know. But we'll be forced to pick sides when the angelic infighting begins if our loyalty isn't secured before then."

"And I do hope it's *not* secured yet, love. I'm still not sold on this Michael character. Flaming eyes do not seem to be a particularly *good guy* trait."

"We're just here to learn, Levi. And like Michael said, maybe love is a weapon. Maybe we're meant to tap into that energy, to use it to oppose Lilith. But... if love is the earthly equivalent of whatever we're fighting for, what the Hell does Lilith represent, then?"

"Perhaps we should talk to Ozzy about that."

Mercy scoffed. "I'm not interested in talking to him. I wholeheartedly believe he's toying with Mary Olive and still working for Lilith."

Levi pursed his lips for a moment before he sighed and slumped his shoulders. "Mercy, darling, I love you so deeply, but... I just don't agree with you. You're allowing your love for your sister to cloud your judgment. There's no mistaking the type of bond we share."

Mercy lifted her chin and gazed down her nose at him. "But a little bit of hellish magic might have Mary Olive convinced. I'm not. That guy put a stake through my mouth. Remember?"

"And I'm furious at him for that. But I also understand that Valefar set that direction. Remember that I can also control minds, Mercy, so I've seen firsthand how helpless that level of control makes people."

"But you're kind. You'd never hurt anyone with your power, Levi."

He turned his back to her. "Not anymore, love. But I've done things I'm not proud of in my time. And I do sympathize with Ozymandias."

Mercy bit her lip and studied his silhouette, her eyes moving over the cascades of his dark, curly hair. She had to shake off the memory of seeing dark-haired children lying in the hot midday sun. "Well, thank you for being vulnerable. I suppose I can start working on being more vulnerable with Mary and Ozzy. But until I'm ready, do you think you can take point on talking to him?"

Chapter Fifteen

Levi knocked and stepped back. He heard a few irritated whispers before footsteps approached. Mary opened the door a crack, and when she peered around it, her face lit up with a brilliant smile.

"Levi! Come in."

He stepped into the room, nodded in greeting to Ozymandias, and smiled at Mary. "I trust you're settling in well, yes?"

"I am," she said. "I'm enjoying this time with Ozzy. I can't believe you and Mercy have just quietly shared this for years."

Levi chuckled awkwardly. "Yeah, me neither. I wish we had more time to explore it."

Mary's look softened. "Oh, yeah. Because she's been running?"

"I don't hold it against her," Levi insisted. "I was a lot like her back when I was alive. She needs her freedom, and she needs to forge a path that's wholly her own. But she's also a scion, so she doesn't fully have the opportunity to explore that yet. It's an existential place to be. She deserves grace."

"I understand," Ozzy chimed in. He was seated across the room in a cushy high-back chair. "I don't know how much Mary told you, but I was compelled by my partner to live as I did. Valefar served Lilith. I, as his brother, was dragged into it."

"What is she like?" Levi asked.

"Well, she was the first vampire," Ozzy said. "So she's powerful. Most of us have a few powers, but she has many. I haven't an inkling of the full array of her abilities, but I've seen her take down other vampires with little effort. That woman is pure power."

"Other vampires? Did she... hunt them?"

"She didn't hunt them, no. When our species was initially thinned, she demanded that the especially ancient vampires serve her or die. Those of us she approached were given a choice, but she'd strike us down if we didn't answer the way she liked. Unfortunately for me, Valefar volunteered us as a hunting pair. And unfortunately for you, I've seen how easy it is for her to dispose of the vampires who defy her."

"Tell him why you were initially hunting vampires, Ozzy."

He glanced at Mary Olive, nodded, and returned his gaze to Levi. "I was a soldier ordered to perform a mass abduction of women in the Apennine Mountains. I was changed in the midst of that, alongside Valefar. I saw humans doing horrible things to other humans, and it..."

"It broke you?" Levi offered. "I understand."

Ozzy's eyes flicked to Mary again, then he cleared his throat. "I lost my compassion. I had only a tiny bit left, especially for my siblings like Valefar, which made me into the beast you saw previously. I see now where that compassion went and what it became, but I was angry at the time. Not just at the world, but at our species as a whole.

"I set out to hunt vampires, and Valefar was too happy to follow me down that path. Lilith noticed – we were among the vampires she scouted to serve her, purportedly, but Valefar approached her before she could come to us. I would have happily died there, standing before that witch. But Valefar was like you, Levi. He controlled me in that moment, and he made me commit to her."

"Commit to hunt down vampires with soul bonds, you mean," Levi said. "Like me and Mercy. And, ironically, like you and Mary Olive."

"Well, yes. Initially, I wasn't searching for soul bonds. I just wanted to punish our species for what they made me into and what they made me endure."

"It's funny," Mary said, moving to claim the other chair near Ozzy. "It's almost like being forced to walk this path brought him to me. Like it was meant to be, like I was meant to free him."

"From Valefar," Ozzy said. His eyes met Levi's confidently, but there was a sadness there. "I still serve Lilith, as far as she's concerned. And she wants Mercy. You, too, since she's still a fledgling."

"How can we stand against her, Ozzy?"

"Well, she's a vampire," he said. "Anything that can hurt us can hurt her... if you can get close enough. Beyond that, I've only heard tales. The angels tried to drown her once... she's still here, but they seemed to have reason to believe that would work. Other than that, it would take a holy weapon. And I'm not referring to holy water."

"Like a sword," Levi said knowingly.

"Like a sword," Ozzy echoed. "But aside from Samael, I've never seen an angel. I can ask around... someone may know something."

"You're not trying to run off, are you?" Mary asked, raising her eyebrows.

Ozzy fished a phone out of his pocket. "I don't need to take a trip around the world to do that, Mary. Phones and FedEx are much more effective."

She grinned at him, and he side-eyed her with a flirtatious smile. Watching them interact, Levi could see how they worked – he couldn't explain it, but they did feel *right* together.

Levi cleared his throat. "By the way, Ozzy, I am very sorry for what you went through. Having similar powers to Valefar, having seen firsthand what that can do... I sympathize with you. The thought of watching yourself commit acts you're opposed to is chilling."

Ozzy, to his surprise, looked up from his phone. "Oh. Thank you, Levi. I didn't think you would sympathize."

"I do." Levi glanced around, found an unclaimed chair, and took a seat. "When I first turned, I was left without a sire. I carried out some rather abhorrent acts. Fortunately, I snapped out of it and found my way back to myself. Mostly. I never felt quite whole until I found Mercy. You, having been under the control of another's will, must be going through the wringer. I'm so sorry for that, and I also apologize that my scion doesn't feel the same way."

"I feel so bad for Mercy," Mary muttered, crossing her arms. "I feel like I betrayed her, somehow."

"You didn't, dear," Levi said gently. "You can't help your situation, just as she can't help hers. Ozzy, my friend, I ask for some grace for Mercy's condemnation of you. She'll come around, but she'll take some patience. Unfortunately, she carries a lot of the trauma from my human life, and she's not wholly aware of it. She's learning and healing, but she's moving at her own pace."

Ozymandias tilted his chin as he gazed at the younger vampire. "How very diplomatic of you, coming to vouch for her like that. I can only imagine how deeply you love her. Of course I'll be patient with her. I know she'll come around – Mary is my missing piece, and she's said nothing but good things about you both. I trust her judgment wholeheartedly."

Mary nudged him with her foot and tucked her hair behind her ear. "Don't tell him that, honey. He's my boss until something better comes along. I don't want him to think I think he's worth tolerating."

As Levi chuckled good-naturedly, Ozzy laughed and reached out to take Mary's hand. Gazing up at her with sparkling eyes, he said, "I love you, Mary Olive."

They really are a good match, Levi thought again.

Fucking gag me. As Mercy's lone thought drifted to Levi, he realized she was approaching. He stood and turned to face the door, declaring, "Mercy's here."

"Mercy?" Mary bolted to open the door again, and then she embraced her sister with a half-hearted series of bounces. "Hey! How are ya settling in?"

Mercy smiled at her, but she pried her sister's arms away. "Good so far. Michael says he's prepared dinner for us, so Mary, you might want to wait until..."

"Until the people food comes out, got it. You kids scurry off. I'll be fine. Go bond!"

Gag.

Mercy, Levi silently pleaded. *Relax. We'll talk later... but Ozzy has some ideas for dealing with Lilith. We should discuss them with Michael.*

Fine. She started walking away without a word. Levi glanced over his shoulder to make sure Ozzy was following before he trailed after her.

LOOKING AROUND AGAIN, Michael's house wasn't anything Mercy would have expected for an angel. Were it lined in gold and outfitted with gaudy embellishments, she might have found it on-brand. Instead, it was minimalist, almost barren. The kitchen was gray and black, mostly, with a backsplash of diagonal tiles taking center stage as the main focal point.

Well, it would have been the star of the show. Instead, a cloaked figure stood with its back to them. Levi, Mercy, and Ozzy exchanged a cautious look. Levi, either the boldest or the stupidest of the bunch, cleared his throat.

"Michael?"

The being turned to them, greeting them with a perfectly blank mask. It wasn't just expressionless – this being *didn't have a face*. Dunes and valleys painted its visage with stiff highlights and shadows, but the ridge where its eyebrows might have been shifted as if acknowledging their presence. It lurched forward.

Levi pulled Mercy behind him as the creature took another wobbling step toward them. However, as if manifesting out of thin air, Michael appeared behind it.

"I hope you're hungry! Dinner is served."

"What the fuck is that thing?" Mercy demanded, pushing Levi aside just enough to glare at the archangel.

"A golem," he said fondly. "Made of clay – humans were made from earth, you know, so it's not quite different. But this one, not being made by God, isn't conscious. It has no soul or features. It's not *nephesh*. But it does have blood."

"I understand what you're going for here," Mercy said. "And that was very thoughtful of you, Michael. But sincerely, what the actual *fuck*, dude?"

"What Mercy means," Levi interjected quickly, "Is that this is a... *new* experience for all of us. And that thing tends toward terrifying if I'm being honest."

"Gertrude isn't scary," Michael said, placing a hand fondly on the golem's shoulder. "Think of her like a vegan turkey roast. It's *not* turkey, but it's shaped like one and comparable in flavor. Except, you know, this one is people-flavored."

Gertrude looked toward Michael and nodded, something that might have been enthusiastic if it had any intent or thought behind it.

Though the vampires were silent, Mercy stepped around Levi and faced the archangel with tight shoulders. "Alright, I'll give it a go."

"Wait," Ozzy said. Mercy almost looked relieved when he interjected, but her eyes widened when she saw how intently his gaze was locked on Michael. "You created something anthropomorphic from clay. You gave it something like sentience. You're an angel, aren't you?"

Mercy and Levi exchanged a look, fearing that Ozymandias might feel betrayed. Still not knowing him well, a sensation of shared fear passed between their psyches. When Michael nodded, however, the ancient vampire suddenly dropped to his knees.

"I need your help." His dark eyes glimmered passionately as he gazed at the heavenly being before him. "I was forced into a soul contract with Lilith. And yet, I've found my soulmate in Mary Olive. I want a future with her more than anything, but I genuinely believe it will take divine intervention to free me from the grip of that wretched demon."

Michael studied him, stroking his beard thoughtfully. When he finally spoke, it was in a calm, soft tone. "You don't need heavenly guidance, Ozzy. Mercy does. With my help, she can take the she-demon down. At the very least, Mercy can bruise her ego until she slinks back into whatever hellhole she's currently occupying. But it's up to her. She's more powerful than even you, you know."

"I've seen it," Ozzy said. "How is that possible?"

"Genuinely, I suspect it's love," Michael said. "We've both seen estries before, you and me. But one with her soulmate at her side and an untapped sea of ancient spiritual energy before her? Mercy can tap into powers the average vampire can only imagine. That's why Lilith wants her."

"And why you want her?"

The angel smiled at Ozzy mischievously. "That's why I want to *help* her, Ozzy. My Heavenly counterparts will not be extending any sort of contract at this time. Right now, this fight is Mercy's. We are mere onlookers."

"Michael," Levi interrupted. "Ozzy mentioned a tale of angels trying to drown Lilith. Is that something Mercy can replicate?"

He shifted. "Possibly. It's doubtful, though... she'd have to produce a *lot* of rain in a short amount of time. As powerful as she is, even a hurricane takes time to pick up steam. Logically, a flood of that magnitude is against the laws of nature. God is a stickler for His own laws."

"Ozzy also mentioned a heavenly weapon," Levi said slowly.

Michael grinned. "I knew you'd be asking about that soon. Let's train a little bit more, then we'll talk. Until then, eat."

The angel shoved his golem forward, sending it stumbling into Ozzy. He caught it and glanced at Levi and Mercy helplessly.

"SO... YOU GUYS *ate* this faceless thing?" Mary Olive asked. "And Michael is an angel. Where are his wings, then?"

"I mean, we didn't really *want* to," Mercy said. "But Michael was just *looking at us expectantly*, so, yeah. We tried it. I didn't really fancy it."

"The golem deflated like an empty Capri Sun," Levi said glumly. "I didn't think to ask Michael about his wings, though. It felt inappropriate given that he doesn't have them, or he *has* them, but they're not visible."

"Ah," Mary said. "So it might be one of those *it's not the size, it's how you use your wings* situations. I'm still really in awe, though. He doesn't strike me as particularly righteous."

Mercy shrugged. "I thought the same. Then he pulled out his flaming sword."

"Before Michael, the only angel I'd met was Samael," Ozzy explained. "But let me tell you, when his hip, modern persona finally peeled back, I could see it all around him. He's powerful. And Michael made it sound like Mercy has the power to challenge evil head-on, which is fascinating to me. In all my years, I've never heard of such potential existing in *anyone*."

"In every generation, there is a Chosen One," Mercy said. "She alone will stand against demons and the forces of darkness. My least favorite trope. As an author, I'd *never* lean into that crap."

Levi scoffed. "What about the Greek myth book you wrote?"

Mercy rolled her eyes. "Yeah, yeah, I get it. My debut sucked. You and Ann never let me forget it."

"And you also *love* Buffy," Mary added. "So does Levi; he literally quoted it when I staked Ozzy's hunting partner. You guys are both nerds with a soft spot for overused tropes. And while we're on the topic of nerdy things, *Café au Levi* is not a good name for a business."

"I have to agree," Michael said as the group approached where he was standing in the yard, waiting patiently. "But I'm just a food critic, and you did *that* right, at least. I stand by my statement that your food was heavenly."

Levi frowned, but Michael grinned at the group and ignored his impatience.

"Ah, an audience this time. This will be especially interesting with heightened stakes. Embarrassment is a very real possibility for you both. Did you do your stretches?"

Levi glanced at Mercy and cocked an eyebrow. "We're dead, Michael. We're not going to get a muscle cramp."

"What about a mental cramp?" he asked. "I expect you to take control this time, Levi. I want to see how that changes the playing field."

Fuck.

At the sound of Mercy's fleeting thought, Levi turned to face her. "You're not scared this time, are you, love?"

Mary shivered and snuggled into her flannel, and it momentarily distracted Mercy. However, when Levi mentally nudged her, red eyes crawled back to meet his gaze. "No. I trust you to act as the pilot for my powers. I'm just concerned that I literally won't be able to see what's going on. When I'm in that state, I only catch glimpses. And you still don't have a full grasp on my powers. It's even less than I have, really, as they're foreign to you. The only thing you have that I don't is age and groundedness."

Levi took her hands and nodded reassuringly. "And those are essential right now. I'll guide you through it, Mercy. Trust me."

She bit her lip for a moment, but he wasn't sure why – he could feel that she wasn't internally hesitating. "I do, Levi. Always."

The group waited in anticipation as Levi and Mercy turned to face the angel, their hands still intertwined between them. Michael looked them over with an air of both casual confidence and celestial authority while Mary Olive fidgeted with her beanie and Ozzy nervously cracked his knuckles one by one.

Facing down Saint Michael, Mercy felt herself mentally reaching out for Levi.

As soon as their consciousnesses brushed, it was as if microscopic currents of electricity were dancing over their skin. Suddenly, Mercy was aware of the sensation of weightlessness. It prickled against her hair almost playfully as she became one with the firmament, but then it was suddenly replaced by the crushing burden of gravity. The atmosphere had shifted, and a somewhat disconnected Mercy had the clarity of mind to realize the archangel had drawn his flaming sword. It was like she was caught in a different state, somewhere between airiness and being earthbound.

Michael gazed at her as if he could see her, and then a wicked smile tore across his face.

Before his eyes could burst into flames again, Mercy felt her silhouette flicker, almost, and a massive burst of wind pushed the angel across the yard. He landed on one knee, but he swiftly rose with his sword outstretched and his eyes locked on Levi. From there, Mercy only caught glimpses of the action.

Levi tumbled at one point, and the angel rolled onto his back and kicked him in the gut, a force that sent him soaring through the air. The power of Mercy's winds cushioned the descent, but when Levi's feet touched the ground, something shocking happened. Perhaps it was the rush of adrenaline from the freefall, or maybe a fight or flight reaction to the genuine pain Michael inflicted. Whatever the reason, it was like Mercy could suddenly see through Levi's gaze.

Levi narrowed his eyes, and Mercy wasn't sure if he was preparing for the next blow or if *she* was. The world around her was crystal clear, unfolding in real-time, no longer disjointed and coming to her in bursts. They were perfectly in sync, spiritually intertwined, grounded, and powerful. Perhaps as powerful as the angel before them.

Michael looked Levi over, then suddenly shifted and chucked his sword. Levi's head spun to follow it, and Mercy felt his dawning horror as he realized it was headed for Mary Olive.

Mercy, in that split second, severed her connection from Levi and reached out for the sword. In response, a single bolt of lightning descended from the heavens, striking the sword and sending it veering off course. When it embedded itself in the snow, Michael followed it with his gaze.

Mercy, corporeal once again, jammed her hand into Levi's. He looked down at their intertwined fingers with surprise, then met her gaze knowingly. Together, they raised their hands and created a wind tunnel – the force sucked the sword toward them as Michael dove for it.

As storm clouds brewed overhead, Mercy felt Levi urging her toward weightlessness again. She allowed her earthly connection to sever as she once again became wind, which Levi expertly used to pluck the burning weapon from the snow. It was so hot that as it rose, any lingering clumps of snow quickly dissipated as steam.

From there, the battle unfolded in flashes again – Levi dodging, deflecting, and occasionally retaliating against Michael's celestial prowess and unbelievably accurate marksmanship. Mercy, in her ethereal state, saw the action unfold in stills, like motionless fragments of a vivid dream.

Eventually, the battle seemingly reached its climax, and Levi and Mercy seamlessly synchronized their efforts. Levi's control became more refined, and Mercy's powers responded with heightened and intentional precision. Michael, though a force to be reckoned with, was struggling to fend off the coordinated onslaught.

When the heavenly weapon was once again sent flying, it seemed like it would impale the archangel. However, he lifted a single hand, and the entirety of the earth seemed to shudder in response. The brewing clouds overhead froze, the oncoming sword halted, and even Mary Olive's gasp seemed to die out. Michael stepped forward and claimed his sword from where it hung suspended, a motion that caused the air around him to ripple like gelatin.

The moment his hand wrapped around the hilt of the blade, an airborne Mercy became earthly in a sudden and shocking motion. After she slammed into the snow, Levi bent to help her up.

"Well played," Michael said. He sheathed his sword and crossed his arms. "I'm not easily impressed, but that was truly something. *You two* are truly something."

As Levi pulled Mercy to her feet, the exhaustion in their shared stream of consciousness was palpable. Though it clung to them heavily, there was also a sense of accomplishment and newfound confidence there that kept them wholly alert.

When Mary Olive clapped, the tense atmosphere dissipated. "That was incredible! I'm never buying a movie ticket again. I've never seen anything like that."

"Nor have I," Michael said. "Levi, I'm impressed by your coordination – I've never seen a dybbuk with such unwavering focus. And Mercy, your gift is unparalleled. Once again, the power of your love manifested in an incredible display of power – this time to protect your sister, shattering even the most formidable grip of control. The battles ahead might be daunting, but with your newfound coordination, we all stand a chance against the forces of darkness."

"With all due respect," Ozzy vocalized. "I don't believe this demonstrates in any way that we stand a chance. They haven't proven they can defeat an angel. Samael is every bit as powerful as you, right? It's going to take more than wind and a few flashes of lightning to defeat him."

"A valid point," Michael said. "And that's where a holy weapon should come in. Mercy, I'm sure you've forged a sword before?"

Mercy, believing him to be sarcastic, nodded. "Yep. I'm a regular blacksmith up in New York City. Known throughout Brooklyn and beyond."

Chapter Sixteen

In the catacombs beneath Michael's house (because finished basements are apparently overrated), they stood in a chamber full of metallurgy tools. Mary Olive picked up a cast curiously, but Ozzy nudged her and whispered something. As she grumbled and put it back down, Mercy shifted to watch while Michael drew his sword and used it to light the coals in the fireplace.

Levi fidgeted. "I do feel the need to clarify something, Michael – Mercy was being sarcastic. Ozzy might know how to make a sword, but the rest of us absolutely do not."

Michael sheathed his sword and turned to face them. "Fortunately for you, I have traditional blacksmith training from various different time periods. The key to this particular forgery lies in channeling your unique powers into the creation process, Mercy. I can guide you through the temporal tasks, but infusing yourself into this blade is solely on you."

Mercy exchanged a glance with Levi. "Okay, I'll accept some guidance. So, what do we need to do?"

"First, we need a base to serve as the foundation for your holy weapon." Michael gestured to Mary Olive, who was holding a hammer. When she caught his gaze, she quickly put it down and offered a smile. "Bronze is usually cast. Steel will have to be forged."

"How's a girl to choose?" Mercy asked sarcastically.

"Bronze!" Mary Olive exclaimed as she scooped up a cast and flitted to her sister's side. "Mercy, *look*. This hilt is beautiful. It almost ends in angel wings, right here."

Mercy nodded. "Sure, I like that. Bronze it is."

Michael grinned. "Great. Levi, grab a block of tin – yes, the silver blocks. Mercy, we need four times that amount in copper."

Mercy moved in the opposite direction of Levi and collected a few penny-colored blocks. When she returned to Michael, he and Ozzy were connecting a massive ceramic bowl to a set of tongs with a rounded holder tucked against its center. As the bowl slid into place, Michael straightened his back and scanned the workshop with an air of authority.

"Place the metals in," he instructed. Levi and Mercy followed his direction, and he nodded approvingly as their materials clinked against the stoneware. "Move the crucible into the hellfire now, Mercy, and let it sit until the metals have melted."

Mercy picked up the tongs and bowl that Michael had assembled and took a step toward the hearth, but she hesitated. She looked over her shoulder at Levi, who obediently stepped forward to help her manage the awkward balance of the metalworking tool. Together, they guided it into the flames.

After it settled, Levi glanced at Mercy, a silent affirmation passing between them. They stepped back and watched as the previously room-temperature metal began to glow.

"Hellfire is especially hot," Michael said. "So this will go quickly. Mercy, get your mold placed on a flat surface."

Mary Olive helpfully stepped forward to assist her sister in arranging the cast. They pulled the two pieces together, sat them upright, and fastened them in place with a clamp. Michael offered Mercy a ceramic funnel, which she affixed on the top of the mold.

"Okay," Michael said. "Looks like it's melted. It's time to pour it."

Mercy and Levi stepped forward to pick up the crucible, but she stopped and turned to face her sister. "Can you hold the mold in place, sis? I promise not to burn you."

Michael offered her a pair of fire-resistant gloves as the vampires approached with a ceramic cup full of red-hot molten metal. Mary steadily held the cast as Mercy and Levi cautiously guided the crucible toward the funnel. In tandem, they poured.

Michael stepped forward and shifted the cast, moving it so the funnel faced Mercy. "Alright, Mercy. Take the deepest breath possible and blow some wind in here."

"I can't do that!" Mercy protested.

"You *can*," Michael said. "I saw what you can do. Take a deep, *deep* breath, Mercy."

The warm, feathery presence of Levi's consciousness brushed against hers, and it oddly comforted her. Mercy took a deep breath, and when she exhaled, a gust of wind moved from her body. Michael ran his fingers through the gale, guiding it into the funnel.

The archangel nodded approvingly before he shifted the cast on its side again and hit it with a hammer. The two pieces split, revealing a stunning gold-hued hilt.

"Wow," Mercy marveled as she inched forward. "Can I pick it up?"

"You sure can," Michael said. "In fact, you're the only person who can – whoever forges a weapon in hellfire is its sole master. Try it out."

Cautiously, Mercy brushed the object with her fingertips. It wasn't hot, so she lifted it. She took a few playful swipes through the air before she grinned.

Michael offered her a leather sheath, so Mercy fit the hilt into it and admired its elegance. As soon as a blade was added, it'd qualify as one of the most beautiful weapons she had ever seen. While she admired it, Michael kneeled to light a candle with the hellfire before he ultimately stoked the blaze in the fireplace.

He handed Mercy the lit candle and started walking toward the staircase.

"Wait," Mercy said. "What about the blade?"

He looked over his shoulder with a mysterious smile. "That's your job, something we won't be completing down here in my metallurgy cave. I'll let you figure it out. A good meal will help you think. I'll replenish the golem and heat up more stuffing for you, Mary Olive."

The group smiled, but they all shared the same reaction – one of disappointment. Just as the vampires hadn't enjoyed their experience with the golem, Mary hadn't enjoyed the dry, gravyless stuffing, and she was dreading this next meal.

MARY OLIVE LOOKED OUT at the snowy landscape and let out an exasperated sigh before she began to pace restlessly. "That was terrifying. He *threw a blade at me*, Ozzy."

When she didn't receive a response, Mary turned and scanned the space. She didn't see the vampire, but when she lifted her gaze, she saw a large, black bat hanging from the ceiling fan.

"Hey, *Desmodus rotundus*. I'm talking to you."

His eyes opened.

"That's right, I Googled that so I could insult you. It means *common* vampire bat. I'm calling you basic."

Ozymandias spread his wings and stretched before he fluttered to the ground. He shifted back into a man and stood from his crouched position. "I speak Greek and Latin, including the ancient variants, and that is *not* a direct translation. In fact, it's not a translation, period."

She rolled her eyes and crossed her arms. "I'm literally panicking here. Can you please be present and listen?"

He grinned, exposing his fangs as he awkwardly shrugged. "I'm sorry, Mary Olive. You'll have to bear with me... I am not used to your company. When Valefar used to pace and rant, I was to avoid him."

Her expression grew gentler as she allowed her arms to drop by her sides. "Sorry, I forgot. The snippiness wasn't fair of me, either. I guess we're both learning."

He opened his arms to embrace her, stroking her hair as she buried her face into his mane. "Yes, we're both learning. And I'm listening, honey. Say what you need to."

She took a step back and nervously folded her hands together. "He threw a sword at me, Ozzy. Michael. The *good guy*. If he wasn't afraid to do that, what would Samael do?"

Ozzy ran his eyes over her face. She was an enigma to him – so soft and delicate while a barely contained wildfire blazed under the surface. Mary was his opposite in so many ways, but he could read her like a book. He could sense her fear, so he decided to attempt to assuage it. "It was a bluff, Mary. He didn't intend to hurt you."

"Right. But Samael likely intends to hurt Mercy when she turns Lilith away."

He winced. "Yes, he likely does. That's why Mercy is training, though. And why Michael had her start making a weapon."

"But things are looking *bad*. Right? There's no way she can learn to overcome a literal angel in however long we have left."

Ozzy walked to the window and gazed out at the icy world beyond the glass. If he hadn't met Mary Olive, he might be patrolling in that unforgiving cold right now. "I won't lie, Mary. I've been worried from the moment you staked Valefar. As soon as my mind was free of his influence, I suspected this would end badly. I'm hoping for the best, but I am not expecting it."

Her eyes widened, but her expression was stiff and unchanging otherwise. "I will not stand for that. No."

"Mary," he said sternly. "They haven't even made a blade yet. I simply will not let you intervene. Michael said this is Mercy's fight. It's not ours."

"I don't care. I am not letting my sister do this alone."

He glowered, and it was almost like his eyes faded to a deeper shade of red. Mary had never seen him mad, but the effect was downright terrifying. "I am going to be very straightforward. One, I don't want you to get hurt. Two, *I* don't want to get hurt. I am unashamedly selfish in that proclamation, but you don't know what happens to people who lose their soulmate."

Mary's jaw dropped for a moment before she looked away. "Actually, Ozzy, I do. We lose a part of ourselves and get kinda nutty. I know. Believe it or not, I've seen it. You still can't stop me from doing this."

He glanced out the window. With a resigned shake of his head, he began to retrace his steps back to her. With every deliberate stride, a sense of understanding seemed to be blossoming between them. "I used to be stubborn, too. I get it. You understand that you're making a decision for both of us right now, right?"

Mary lifted her chin. "I do. Are you okay with that?"

He studied her for a long moment, his eyes wide and passionate. "I suppose I am. I promise to stand with you until the very end."

"Let's hope they figure out how to forge that blade."

"Yeah, let's hope."

As Mercy and Levi entered their room, the warm, flickering glow of the gold candlelight painted dancing patterns across the walls. When Mercy sat on the bed, her partner seemingly manifested at her side. He brushed her hair behind her ear and kissed her cheek, then trailed his kisses toward her neck.

"Levi," she said, shrugging away from him. "I'm not in the mood."

He pulled away sharply. "We'll figure the sword thing out, Mercy. We're allowed to take a break, you know."

She sighed, her gaze fixed on the candle's flame. Hellfire. Flickering hellfire. What an odd holiday season this had become. "It's not just about the sword, Levi. It's everything – training with the archangel, knowing Lilith is coming, the fear of the unknown. It's all weighing on me. And it doesn't help that Michael is... he's *odd*. I didn't ever want this kind of responsibility."

"I get it. It's a lot. But you're not alone in this."

She leaned into his comforting presence, resting her head on his shoulder. "I know, but this isn't like you cheering me on when I went to pursue my career. It's different now. Lilith is powerful, and I can feel her darkness rolling in. It's suffocating. Don't you feel it? There's a heaviness in the air that wasn't there before, not even on Christmas when my family rejected me or when we all had to cohabitate."

Levi wrapped an arm around her, offering a temporary respite from the looming threats. "I certainly feel something. Though it might just be nausea after seeing my meal sputter out and flatten like an air mattress after a camping trip."

Mercy chuckled. "Yeah. I'm sorry I thought about killing you. Believe it or not, I'm really grateful you're here with me. We make a killer team, even though your Gertrude synopses are getting old."

"We do. And whatever happens, Mercy, I'll always love you. I'm sorry I haven't always been able to show you that wholly and authentically."

"Well, we have the rest of forever to explore that," Mercy said quietly. "You know, Levi, when all of this is over... well, I zipped from my apartment to your place in a matter of minutes. I wouldn't mind commuting to the city for meetings, so long as air traffic control isn't needed to help me land."

"I wouldn't mind commuting up there together," Levi said. "When my car is fixed, that is. And, you know, my house, too. *Our* house, I hope."

As the flickering candlelight cast shadows on the walls, creating an intimate space where love and fixity of purpose intertwined, they settled into a comfortable silence. Mercy's head was still on Levi's shoulder, and he stroked her hair while the tiny blinking flame bathed them in warmth.

Levi shifted away from Mercy. As he faced her, he took her hands in his. "About that sword. Michael made it sound like you have to channel your powers into the creation of the blade. And, well, it hit me – your lightning powers. I've only seen it in small spurts, but it awed even Michael. Maybe *that's* meant to be the blade. He carries something burning with hellfire, but maybe your weapon is meant to be much more celestial. Literally an energy you bring down from the heavens yourself."

Mercy frowned, deep in thought. "So, what? I'm supposed to create a whole ass sword out of lightning? How does that even work?"

"Not a whole-ass sword, love. Just the blade." Levi leaned forward. "I don't have the answer, but I know your powers are a force of nature. We've seen what you can do. Maybe, just maybe, you can channel that energy into a weapon. And Michael left us with an important tool – a bit of hellfire. He's hoping we'll figure it out."

"You think he expects me to experiment with hellfire on my own?" She looked down at their intertwined hands. "Sure, I guess that makes as much sense as anything else this week. Why else would he leave us with that stupid candle?"

"I say we try it, darling. What do we have to lose?"

Mercy glanced toward the window. Outside, it was as if an extra layer of clouds was rolling in, plunging the already inky night into a thick, velvety blackness. "A lot, I'd say. Hellfire sounds... Intimidating. What if it changes me? What if it works, but wielding such power corrupts me?"

"I won't let that happen. Let's take this candle outside and see what we can do."

"Alright," Mercy said reluctantly. *If I become a demon, Levi, I'm making you my first victim.*

Levi rose and smiled down at her, casting an ominous shadow across his mouth in the wan light. "That's why you're just a scion. Some would argue that estries *are* demons, but if you grow more devilish, I can correct your course. I promise, love, that I have your back."

Mercy was instantly skeptical of that confident statement, but she dared not voice her doubt. It didn't matter, she supposed. Levi doubtlessly heard the thought before it passed.

And he heard her very next suspicion, too: Michael might not have taught her how to forge the blade for a reason. Perhaps he was aware of her reluctance and skepticism. At the very least, God was. Perhaps these heavenly beings anticipated a fall from grace.

I don't know, and I can only imagine what banishment from the Garden of Eden means. Mercy had said those words mere days ago. Suddenly, they felt more pertinent than ever.

Chapter Seventeen

The door creaked open, and Mercy and Levi stepped out into the crisp night air. The moon hung high in the sky, casting a silver glow over the world around them. A soft layer of freshly fallen snow blanketed the earth, glistening like a field of diamonds.

Levi held the candle in his hands, its hellfire flame dancing and whipping about in the wintry air. He lifted a hand to shield it from the elements, stabilizing it as they slowly moved away from the house. Mercy, beside him, felt the cool touch of the snow under her thin boots, yet it didn't chill her. Nothing did nowadays.

They found a spot in the untouched snow, far removed from the house, where the moonlight bathed the landscape in an otherworldly glow. It felt right there, they both silently realized. Levi knelt, placing the candle in the center of the small clearing. The flickering flames illuminated snowflakes that fell like frozen stars. The night fell still, with not an ounce of breeze or movement in the icy world.

Mercy slowly knelt to join him on the ground. She pulled the hilt from its sheath, then leaned it against the pillar candle. The metal didn't quite touch the flame, but it hovered over it, just out of reach. She watched as the hellfire grew and stretched for it before she allowed herself to drop the tension from her shoulders.

She closed her eyes, meditating on the thought of channeling her inner power. In her mind's eye, it was like a blue orb – as frozen as the world around her, yet as warm as her own irises. As she mentally admired this ball of pure energy, Mercy tried her hardest to call on all the mysticism in the universe, pleading with it to heed her command and channel into the hilt she'd so carefully crafted. After a minute, she huffed. "This is stupid, Levi."

"Kinda," he admitted. "If you've got any better ideas, I'm open to them. Otherwise, I say you let me help you try to do this. You chose this method because something about it instinctually felt right. I trust that."

She offered her hands. "Alright, be my guest."

Levi reached out, intertwining his fingers with hers as the air around them suddenly crackled with energy. *Good,* he thought. *Focus on that energy, Mercy.* When the pair closed their eyes, they could still see tiny bursts of electricity sparking around her fingertips against the dark shield of heavy lids.

The weight of anticipation settled over them as Levi focused on the flickering of the candle's flame and Mercy focused on manifesting a bolt of lightning. As they slipped into a meditative state, each almost chanted their expectations in their minds. The sound of their internal monologues combined until it felt like a dark, ancient hymn, rhythmic and full of power. Finally, Mercy became aware of the creeping sensation of weightlessness.

This one, however, didn't penetrate to the core of her being like it usually did. When she opened her eyes, Mercy saw that she and Levi were suspended in the air above the candle. He kept his eyes closed, his focus unwavering.

Mercy instinctively extended a single hand toward the sky, watching as thick, dark clouds began to churn directly above her. Furrowing her brow, she focused on drawing a lightning bolt from the heavens. When it finally appeared, she moved her hand through the air before her to guide it toward the candle. The lightning, moving at an almost impossibly slow speed, crept down until it met the flickering flame. Then, it merged with the hellfire.

The tiny flame grew much larger, twisting and contorting, transforming into a radiant burst of bright blue energy. The intensity of the collision was enough to send a warm gale in every direction, emanating out like heat from a fire. It was enough to ruffle the vampires' hair, but Levi's focus was as rigid as ever, leaving Mercy alone as the moment's silent observer.

As the warm glow of the collision died down, the lightning bolt slowly retreated into the clouds, and Mercy and Levi lowered to meet the ground. When their feet touched down, Levi finally opened his eyes, and the pair watched in amazement as the amalgamation of hellfire and live lightning took shape before the hilt. It burned in a deep sapphire hue for a moment, and then it expanded in long, yellow streaks as the electricity snaked to meet and connect with the hilt.

The ensuing flash was even brighter than the first – this time, it cast a warm, otherworldly yellow glow across the landscape. While Mercy expected the glow to subside, it grew brighter and stretched toward the clouds. It became a solid column of light in the space between her and Levi, glowing at a brightness that – she imagined – should have blinded them. For a moment, though, it was like it was daylight outside, and Mercy could see everything. The entire world was fully lit, bathed in warm light and fully saturated color. In the next second, it was nighttime again, and streaks of multicolored light were left dancing in the sky above them.

"Aurora borealis," Mercy marveled. When her gaze fell back to the ground, her eyes widened. The lightning had seemingly fused to the hilt, but it snaked and contracted like live electricity. Slowly, Mercy leaned forward and scooped up the hilt.

"My God," she whispered. She lifted it to eye level and marveled as the lightning bolt expanded, bursting upward and extending threateningly. Slowly, Mercy hoisted herself to her feet. She swiped with the blade a few times to test it.

"Think fast."

Mercy spun as Levi tossed a snowball at her. The lightning sword sliced it in half, making the two halves of the snow chunk disintegrate as it melted mid-air. Levi scooped another handful of snow, patted it into a ball, and tossed it to Mercy. Once again, she swiped with her weapon.

Mercy chuckled as the melted droplets fell to the ground and the vibrant glow of the impossible blade cast a warm and almost festive atmosphere across the world around them. Holding this item forged in hellfire was the strangest sensation – it made her feel light and giddy.

"I think I failed you, Padawan," Levi said as he brushed his snowy hands over his pants. "We should have covered lightsaber training earlier."

"Qui-Gon would have covered that by now," she teased.

Levi laughed, the sound echoing in the crisp night air. Under the glimmering colors of the aurora borealis, clutching a heavenly weapon, Mercy thought back to her original Christmas wish – peace on earth for Mercy Mild Harker. Could it finally be possible?

"It feels tangible," she said, marveling at the sword. "Before, my powers felt disconnected from me somehow. But this puts at least one of them right in the palm of my hand, and it's invigorating. This is really, really different."

Mercy shifted her attention to a nearby tree. She stabbed forward with the sword, and its electricity obediently spanned the space between her and the tree, then enveloped it. After golden electricity sparked up and down the bark, she willed the lightning to return to the blade.

Mercy recalled Michael using the hellfire like a whip, so she focused on a single branch this time. She flicked her wrist forward, and a rope-like thread of lightning ensnared the branch. When she snapped the hilt toward the ground, the branch fell.

Before she could cheer, Levi's arms came around her, and his fangs brushed over her neck. She sighed and leaned into him as his teeth broke her skin. The contact lasted only a second – just enough for a small taste of her blood – before he pulled away and reached for the sword.

"Hey," Mercy said, pulling it out of his reach. "Michael said that only the creator of this sword can wield it."

"But I can control your powers," he said confidently. "And now that I've tasted your blood, they're temporarily my powers, too. Let's just *see*."

Hesitantly, Mercy allowed him to take the sword from her. She waited for him to burst into flame or *something*, but he just held and admired the sword wordlessly.

"Amazing," she whispered in awe. "So you can handle it if you've consumed my blood. Let's hope that isn't true for the average sword-using vampire."

He gave her a bored look before he turned his attention back to the same poor tree she'd been tormenting. Levi swiped the sword toward it, but nothing happened. Frustrated, he leaned forward and stabbed the air a few times.

"Levi," Mercy said. When he turned to her, she lifted a snowball. "Think fast."

While he couldn't cause the electricity to snake and expand as Mercy had, Levi had no issues slicing through each snowball she chucked at him. After a few rounds and a lot of giggles, he giddily returned the sword to her. Mercy cautiously sheathed it, then grinned as the holder contained the electrical charge without issue.

She shifted to return to the house, but Levi caught her hand. "Wait. It's not often we see skies like this in Connecticut. What do you say we stay outside a while?"

MERCY OPENED THE DOOR and peered around it, then cautiously tiptoed into the house. Levi trailed her before he cringed and stopped. "Okay, I'm sorry, I have to take off these boots. They're soaked."

Mary Olive, who had been sitting on the couch with a steaming cup of cocoa, suddenly stood and peered across the living room at them. Her blue eyes widened as she took in their disheveled appearance, and a mischievous grin crept onto her face.

"Well, well, well," she teased. "Look who decided to take a moonlit stroll. A little bit cold for a romantic rendezvous, isn't it?"

Mercy scoffed as she took off her boots and set them beside Levi's. "It wasn't romantic, Mary. Your knees must be sore from always jumping to conclusions."

"It wasn't much of a leap," Levi said. "I mean, there were sparks."

Mercy elbowed him as Mary squealed and inched forward. "I love a good love story. Do tell."

"We forged a blade," Mercy whispered.

"You did?" Michael asked, coming from the kitchen area of the house. "Mary, I was just making you some more stuffing for breakfast when I overheard, so do pardon the intrusion."

Mary's face fell at the mention of *more* stuffing, but she didn't say anything. Mercy touched the hilt of the sword proudly as she declared, "I forged the blade of the sword with live lightning and hellfire."

The room fell silent for a moment. Michael, ever composed, stepped forward with sparkling eyes. "Let me see it."

Mercy drew the sword from its sheath, bathing the space in the mesmerizing glow of the blade.

"I take back all the romantic rendezvous jokes. You guys are officially the coolest supernatural team ever."

"We certainly try," Mercy said as she returned the weapon to its sheath. "Let's just pray this weapon can do some damage."

"There's one way to find out," Michael declared confidently. "Let me ready Gertrude."

"The golem?" Mercy asked. "Michael, please don't make me fight that thing."

The archangel studied Mercy for a moment with his hands on his hips, but then he thought better of whatever he was going to say. "Well, there's one way to find out if it can do damage... wouldn't you say? And Lilith is coming. We can all feel the encroaching threat of her presence. It's truly now or never."

"Mercy," Levi said. "It's a decent idea to test out your new sword. I mean, sure, that golem is terrifying, but we have no idea what Samael and Lilith are going to unleash. We might as well prepare for the very worst."

"Great!" Michael exclaimed. "You three head outside – we'll put the sword to the test outside the house. I bought this furniture with money I earned myself, so I'd rather not destroy any of it. The yard is yours to do what you want with."

"Bundle up Mary," Mercy said. "I'm going to grab a dry pair of boots. Meet you guys outside."

AS THE TRIO STOOD TOGETHER in the early sunlight, Ozzy came jogging up. Levi caught a brief mental mumble from Mary as she enviously noted that he didn't have to control his breathing.

"Michael said you made a sword," he said eagerly. "A blade. Can I see it?"

"I'll draw it when the golem comes out," Mercy said patiently. "You'll see it in its full glory then. He's making me test the sword on... it? *Her* doesn't feel quite right, given that it's bald and featureless. Genderless, too, I'd assume."

"And mentally blank," Levi noted. "There's nothing there. She's soulless and thoughtless. Will be interesting to see if she can fight."

"Is your cafe open, Levi?" Mary interrupted. "I might DoorDash a sandwich or something. I'll keel over and die if I have to eat another serving of stuffing. I thought Michael was supposed to be a food critic."

The back door opened, followed by the appearance of Michael and the golem. He linked arms with Gertrude and guided her toward his friends, taking care to side-step iced-over puddles every here and there from where Mercy and Levi had tested the sword mere hours ago.

When he came to stand at the edge of the group, Michael drew his sword. The warm glow of its fire danced across the snow as he turned to Gertrude, casting shadows that seemed to waver and writhe.

"Gertrude," Michael said. "I am entrusting you with my most coveted heavenly weapon. Use it wisely and without mercy when I give you my command."

The golem, devoid of any facial features or expressions, simply stood there as Michael handed the sword over. Though blind, it reached out and accepted the blade. As the flames cast shadows against its featureless mask, Mercy felt a little bit uneasy. She remembered her thought earlier – that Michael might have been suspecting that Mercy would give in to Lilith and fall from grace like the vampires of Genesis – and studied Gertrude with genuine fear.

Without mercy wasn't exactly the kindest order, after all.

"Only the forger of a heavenly weapon can yield it," Ozzy said. "That's what you said earlier."

"That's true," Michael said. "If we're dealing in matters of the *nephesh*. Gertrude is neither alive nor dead, so she's exempt."

"Good luck," Levi whispered to Mercy. He kissed her cheek. "This thing isn't alive, Mercy, so don't hold back. Make me proud, love – this is all you."

"You'll be here if I need you?"

"Always."

Mary, Ozzy, and Levi watched with bated breath as Michael lifted a single finger before the golem. Gertrude lifted its chin as if following the motion with nonexistent eyes. "Gertrude, I want you to attack Mercy. Give her a challenge so she may test the full extent of her powers. I command you to carry out my will."

As Michael stepped back, Gertrude, now wielding the flaming sword, moved toward Mercy with an eerie and almost mechanical grace. With a sudden burst of movement, the golem swung the flaming sword at her. The blade arced through the air with deadly precision, but Mercy reacted instinctively, drawing her own lightning sword from its sheath.

The clash of the weapons felt like it shook the earth as Mercy struggled to hold her ground. As the pair stood locked, the distinct sound of steel meeting lightning filled the air with rolls of thunder. Mercy, in a moment of intuition, twisted toward Gertrude and managed to build enough momentum to push her away.

Gertrude slid across the snow, but the golem barely faltered. It locked its knees and twisted to face Mercy. Something about her eyeless stare made Mercy want to retreat, but she held her ground as the soulless creature charged her. Sparks flew when their swords met again, illuminating the snow with an icy blue hue.

Each swing of the swords created an intricate dance of light and shadow, an otherworldly display of strength and skill on the part of the golem and an instinctual and panicked response on Mercy's part. While Mercy was following her gut, Gertrude seemed to have inherited Michael's endless knowledge and practiced agility. It struck with aggression and precision, and it took everything in Mercy to focus on keeping the weapon at bay.

"Let me assist her," Levi pleaded as she nearly lost her footing. "Please. That thing could hurt her."

"If Gertrude draws blood, you may intrude. However, I want to see Mercy do this on her own. It's possible Lilith and Samael will be wise enough to separate you two."

Levi stepped back with a tight jaw and clenched fists as the vampire and golem continued slashing away in a loud and almost choreographed motion. Eventually, Gertrude cornered Mercy, and Levi nearly reacted before Mercy faded into a different state. Seeing her become wind from afar was a rare experience – the very essence of her person seemed to turn into grains of sand that floated off with the wind until she was no more. Gertrude, though presumably sightless, moved its head from side to side as if searching for her.

Mercy, however, manifested in a more solid form and dropped down from above, driving her blade directly into Gertrude's skull. The flaming sword clattered to the ground, still burning as the golem threw its arms back and slowly deflated, spilling blood all the while.

Mercy grimaced and plucked her sword from the golem's husk as its boneless remains slowly crumpled into something like a puddle.

Michael approached them, a satisfied expression on his face. He retrieved his sword and beamed at Mercy. "Well done. You're no match for me, of course, but you genuinely might give Lilith and Samael a run for their money."

Mercy sheathed her lightning sword, a newfound confidence in her eyes. "Thank you, Michael. Oddly enough, I do feel like I'm learning something from you. You've taught me well. You're a bit unconventional, but I respect that."

"Good," he said, turning his eyes to the sky knowingly. "Because they're coming. It's growing darker here."

"Mercy!" Mary called with sudden concern. "Mom texted me – Schnitzel was sick, so they're in town to see their vet."

"Shit," Mercy said with wide eyes. "How soon are they coming, Michael?"

"I don't know," he said. "But they're close. *Very* close."

"Stop standing around!" Mary snapped. "Let's go get them! I can't believe those idiots came back to town."

Chapter Eighteen

The small town had its usual characteristic air of tranquility as snowflakes began to gently blanket the streets. It was subtle at first, but the snowfall grew heavier as they approached the Commercial District in Winsted.

"Can you cut it out with the snow?" Mary Olive demanded from behind the steering wheel.

"I'm sorry!" Mercy exclaimed. "I'm nervous for them, sis."

Ozzy turned to meet Mercy's gaze. "They'll be okay, Mercy. Levi and I will back you girls up."

"Wait," Levi said, looking out the window. "Did they just go into my cafe?"

"They're at the cafe?" Mary asked. "Shit, let me pull into one of these spots. You guys cool with walking?"

Mercy and Levi were unbuckling and opening their doors before Mary could even veer off the road. They hit the ground running, but Mercy halted knowingly. She looked at the cafe up the road, then knelt to touch a single hand to the snow-covered concrete. A long slide of ice crept from her fingers and snaked toward Levi's business. He stopped walking and turned to face Mercy as she stepped back a few feet, then ran and jumped on the ice.

She slid all the way to the front of the cafe, then stepped off the ice just in time to miss Levi as he slid up behind her. Despite her urgency, he leaned down and touched the ice. It disintegrated under his fingertips.

"It's a good thing I drank your blood last night," he said. "That's an insurance liability."

Mercy glared at him as she opened the door. She entered with Levi trailing her, both eyeing the silhouettes standing across the room. Standing before the register, her parents turned to face her. There was warmth in their smiles, but something in their eyes hinted at a tension the vampires couldn't quite place.

Steve, rigid and uncomfortable, marched toward his daughter. "Mercy. I'm here with a message from Lilith and Samael. They claim they're interested in forging a truce."

Mercy's eyes narrowed skeptically. "A truce? I highly doubt that."

"That's what we thought, too," Beth admitted as she strolled up to stand beside her husband. "But they insisted on meeting you both at the old church on the outskirts of town. They said they'd release us if you agreed to meet them there."

"You're their prisoners?" Levi asked with wide eyes.

Beth and Steve raised their hands, gesturing to shackles Levi and Mercy couldn't see. As they stared at their bare wrists with wide eyes, the door opened behind them. Mary, in a blonde flash, darted past Mercy and Levi to embrace her parents.

"Good God, I was so worried about you! Are you guys okay?"

"*Mary!* You shouldn't be here. Leave this mess to the..." Steve trailed off and flicked his eyes toward Mercy before he dropped his voice. "Vampires."

Ozzy sauntered up and leaned close to Beth and Steve, examining them with narrowed eyes. They stared at him in confusion as he ran his eyes over their faces, then settled his gaze on their hands. His expression shifted toward one of surprise.

"Ozzy," Mercy whispered in awe. "Can you see the shackles?"

He nodded, his lips parted slightly. He reached forward to touch the invisible metal, then pulled his hand back as if he'd just touched something hot. Sure enough, his fingertips were smoking, but Mercy only caught a brief glimpse of them before he frantically buried them in his pockets.

"It's blessed," Ozzy explained. "By Samael, I assume. It'll take a holy weapon to remove them."

Levi studied Ozzy before he ushered the group toward the cafe's backroom. He waved to the cashier and called out, "I'm just going to chat with my relatives back here, Khalil. Please hold down the fort for me up here to give us a bit of privacy."

"That's not an okay thing to say anymore, Levi," Mercy said. "It has a history associated with European settlers and warring indigenous peoples."

"Thanks, Miss AP Style Guide," Levi grumbled. "Leave it to you to take a moment in an absolutely dire situation to educate me."

Mary grabbed her parent's elbows and led them to a baking station, where she promptly pulled over two stools.

As her parents settled, Levi moved close to address them in a hushed voice.

"Did they hurt you?"

"I... I don't rightly know." Beth blinked, wiping away the fog that had settled over her eyes. "I don't remember."

"Well, shit," Mercy said as she drew her sword. "I guess they wanted to keep us in the dark. Ozzy, do you think you can help guide me so I can cut these off?"

"Of course," he said, moving to her side. They approached Beth and Steve, and Mercy lifted the blade as Ozzy started offering direction. "Okay, we're going to ease that into the keyhole. Move slowly. Okay, a little to your right. Down, down, okay. Good. Keep moving it forward. You're about to make contact."

As Mercy followed his instruction, she felt something solid come into contact with the seemingly tangible lightning blade. She cautiously twisted her sword in what appeared to be empty air, then resigned to twist the bolt of lightning with her mind. As it twisted and snaked under her silent command, it eventually produced a resonant click from the device around Beth's wrists. She smiled with relief as the sound of falling chains was followed by a *thump* on the floor. Mercy stepped back with her sword turned toward the ceiling as her mother rubbed her wrists.

"It's right here, Mary Olive," Ozzy said, gesturing to a seemingly empty space on the ground. While Mary picked up and disposed of the blessed shackle, Mercy twisted her sword with admiration.

"Nifty, isn't it?" she said to her father. "Saint Michael the Archangel taught me to make it. Yeah, *the* Saint Michael. I told you I had a fucking soul."

"I stand corrected," he said as Mercy leaned forward and waited for Ozzy's direction to free Steve. "Now that I've seen a real demon, I know you're not one. I still don't like what you are, but if Saint Michael accepts it, I can admit my wrongs."

Yeesh, Levi thought. *Don't tell him we learned that vampires are descended from Lilith. Might as well bask in his bruised ego while we have the chance.*

Mercy cocked an eyebrow at Levi as Ozzy urged, "Okay, Mercy, angle it down."

While Mercy worked on unlocking the invisible shackles around Steve's wrists, Levi stepped forward to meet his gaze. "Steve, I can appreciate your reluctance toward what we are. I remember hating myself when I first turned. But you once loved a woman who was like us...?"

Steve's eyes quickly crept toward Beth before he averted them toward the floor. "Her name was April. She convinced me that we were... well, that we were meant to be together. Then she arranged for her own execution, and I was unfortunate enough to witness it. It took me a long time to overcome the damage that did."

Mary cleared her throat, and Steve's brown eyes flashed over to her as her nostrils flared. She shifted uncomfortably and clasped her hands together. "Sorry, Dad, no disrespect, but... did you deal with it?"

When he didn't answer, Beth slowly shifted in her stool. "He threw himself into religion instead. No, it wasn't enough. And now that we've met a fallen angel, we both understand what a folly that was."

"Religion is no folly," Ozzy said gently. "A little to the left, Mercy, you're getting close to moving away from the keyhole. Right, there you go. But I've lived a long time, Steve, and I've lived with a different sort of heartbreak. Finding comfort wherever you can is just a natural and very human response – there's no shame in that. Shame truly comes from defying your own morals. If it's true that you had a soulmate who was a vampire – as I'm understanding from the bits of conversation I'm catching – your discrimination against Mercy is beyond unfounded. Now more than ever, since an archangel has asked her to defend Heaven alongside him."

Steve was silent as Mercy managed to unlock his shackles. He rubbed his wrists gratefully as the invisible chains toppled to the floor. Mercy turned to Ozzy and nodded gratefully.

Pursing his lips, Steve said, "I suppose that's true. I've certainly never dealt with losing April head-on. And Beth, that's not to say I don't love you, because I do. Wholly and truly. But our connection..."

"It's different," Mercy said, glancing over her shoulder at Levi. "Words can't express what this connection is like. And the thought that you've lost this, Dad, is heartbreaking. But I also think the fact that you found Mom shows how fluid love is and how many forms it comes in. There's magic in that."

"That perspective is why I think you have what it takes to stand against Lilith," Ozzy said quietly. "She's..."

"Different," Beth said, echoing Mercy's earlier thought. "Terrifying."

A chill crept down Mercy's spine as she subconsciously shifted a hand to feel her sheathed sword. *And you still want to hear her out?*

I do, Levi thought in silent response. *If what they're saying is true, well... our connection is different. We have what it takes to stand our ground.*

I certainly fucking hope so, Mercy thought. *I just want peace, Levi. Desperately and truly.*

"Regardless of what she is," Levi said. "Mercy is a force of nature, and she knows everything she needs to. And I have her back."

"I do, too," agreed Mary Olive. "So, Mom and Dad, whatever happens... Tell Schnitz I love him."

"You won't go," Beth said quietly, staring at her human daughter with wide eyes.

"I will," Mary stated. "Mercy doesn't have a car, and Levi's was destroyed."

"She may drive us," Mercy said, "But she won't be involved. This isn't a job for any human."

Chapter Nineteen

Ozzy had opted to stay behind to keep an eye on Steve and Beth, who Levi had kindly set up with two steaming bowls of broccoli cheddar soup and baguettes. As Mary drove with intense concentration, Mercy leaned forward.

"He's actually a good guy," Mercy admitted. "I just wanted to say that now, you know, in case anything happens. I can tell you share something special with him. And while I had a pretty bad first impression of him, he's spoken on my behalf more times than I can count. I may not trust Michael fully, but I think Ozzy is a trustworthy guy."

Mary didn't take her eyes off the road, but she smiled. "Yeah, he is. I appreciate you saying that, sis. I love you."

"I love you, too, Mary Olive."

Eventually, the curtain of snow parted to reveal that lone church on the outskirts of town. Though time had aged and stained the tired white facade, its eggshell exterior nearly blended into the wintry landscape. Mary navigated her Honda in front of it, and Mercy and Levi immediately got out. Before Mary could even unstrap, Mercy leaned back into the car.

"Abso-fucking-lutely not, Mary. Sit your ass here while we deal with this."

"Why?"

"Uh, because you're *mortal*," Mercy growled. "Stay put. We'll be back."

Mary's eyes briefly flashed to Levi before she huffed and stared out the windshield. "Fine."

Mercy and Levi shut the doors in unison, and then he embraced her. "I love you, Mercy, and I'm so, so proud of you. You're braver than I ever was."

She kissed him briefly, allowing her lips to just barely brush his. It was fleeting, but still passionate... The type of kiss you might give a dying loved one at their bedside. Chaste. Haunting. "God, Levi, I love you *so* much. Thank you for everything you've done. Your encouragement, your patience, your unwavering love. I wish I'd had the words to tell you that sooner."

He smirked. "You can tell me after, *guerrera*."

"What does that mean?"

"Warrior," he said confidently. "Let's go face down the earthly embodiment of evil."

Mercy chuckled. "I should have known peace on earth was a high order. Next year, I'm asking Santa for an airfryer."

"You'd better stay off the naughty list."

The casual conversation was a pleasant distraction from the weight in the air. As they'd been noticing for a couple days, the air was heavy. The sky was dark, perhaps darker over the church than anywhere else in town. The atmosphere was undeniably ominous.

Snow crunched beneath their boots, filling the air with a cadenced beat amidst a heavy silence as they approached the looming church. Its massive doors grew closer, stretching before them like a shadow. However, these doors opened into an entire shadow world – one overseen by ungodly beings.

When they pushed through the creaking doors, the dim interior slowly revealed itself, lit only by faint, cloud-strained sunlight streaming through an array of stained glass windows. Dusty pews and one vast templon were bathed in rainbow light as the two vampires slowly crept further into the space.

In the center of the desolate church, two silhouettes seemingly materialized, clearly awaiting them. The figures stepped forward into a rainbow-hued patch of light, and as it illuminated their features, Mercy nearly hesitated. The impression they left on her was one she might have expected from Michael – she felt otherworldly awe.

The woman had stunning red hair, dark skin, and eyes that glowed gold even from a distance. The man beside her was as pale and unblemished as a cloud, save the two massive black-as-night leather wings that extended from his back. He pulled those spike-tipped wings close as he lifted his chin and gazed at the vampires. Mercy, mustering all her courage, met his eyes with unwavering confidence. However, he wasn't the being to greet her first.

"Mercy Mild Harker, my darling," Lilith purred, her eyes gleaming. "And Levi Romero, the loyal companion. How delightful to have you join us. It would be an understatement to say we've been waiting for you for many, many years."

Mercy's grip tightened on the hilt of her sword, but Samael's eyes went right to it. "A church is no place for weapons. Leave it at the door."

Levi met Mercy's gaze as they mutually realized that there was no way to defy an angel. Mercy unhooked the sheath from her belt, backtracked, and nudged it outside the church. Levi stood his ground against the immortal being as she slowly worked her way back to his side.

"Now, isn't that better?" Lilith cooed, her gaze shifting to Levi. "Ah, Levi. I recognize you. It's been many years, hasn't it?"

At that, Mercy looked at her partner as his eyes widened with horror. Though she couldn't quite sense his physical faculties, she almost knew his mouth went dry as his jaw slowly dropped in wordless horror.

Lilith's smile widened, revealing a wall of pearly white and razor-sharp teeth. "Ah, you're just now realizing, aren't you? I made you many years ago in the hopes that you might produce a scion of Biblical powers. My, how you've blossomed since I left you on that dirt road. I hear you've found your footing as a barista nowadays. And your dear scion is calling the shots. Isn't that true?"

Levi clenched his fists, attempting to coax his anger down. Mercy could hear his silent urging – he wanted her to speak, but his shock and fury prevented him from guiding her down a solid path.

"But I'm here for Mercy, truly," Lilith said, inching forward. As she stepped out of the rainbow illumination, her fiery hair seemed to lose its metallic sheen. "You have quite an impressive power in you, young scion. A lot of *anger*, too. It's justified, and I like that."

Mercy tried her best to block out Levi's anger as she met the golden-eyed gaze of the very first vampire. "My powers are Biblical, you say. I met with Michael, and he couldn't tell me what that meant. *Wouldn't*, I suppose."

Lilith scoffed, her lips curling back to reveal her fanged smile. "He wouldn't, as that would reveal mysteries that his Lord doesn't believe earthly beings are worthy of hearing. As when He first expelled His own creations from the Garden of Eden, knowledge is disobedience. He'll punish the harbingers of knowledge, and then He'll punish the recipients. My question, Mercy Mild, is if you're willing to accept that punishment."

Mercy waited for Levi to mentally whisper to her, but he stayed silent. She lifted her chin. "I am."

Lilith smiled gleefully. "There are two potential outcomes with powers like yours, Mercy. A great flood or a new bloodline. As a scion, you haven't made new vampires yet... but if you do, they'll be more like you than previous generations. And like the first humans, you're also already more mortal than other vampires. Once they stepped outside the Garden of Eden, they accepted mortality. It's a good thing you have your sword."

Mercy shifted, starkly aware of her sword's absence. "And that's why you've been searching for me? Because I'm more mortal than other vampires?"

"To the contrary, Mercy, you're more powerful than most. Perhaps more physically vulnerable, but that's only if beings can get close to you. And most can't, not with your powers and a weapon forged in hellfire. For that reason, I would like to invite you to join my army. I need a great warrior. A harbinger of knowledge, if you will. A bringer of floods."

"She's a scion," Levi growled, stepping in front of her protectively. "She doesn't have the freedom to make that choice. Ask me instead."

Lilith's smile faded into a scowl. "Very well, *sire*. I, your species' and your direct *lineage's* matriarch, invite you and your sweet scion to join my army."

Levi's face twisted with pure rage. Before he even spoke, Mercy could feel his anger bleeding through their shared connection. "Go back to Hell, you hag."

Lilith lunged at him with supernatural speed, her fingers elongating into claws as she reached for the cocky vampire. Mercy watched in horror as they disappeared into a blur of motion, moving almost too fast for her to see. Though she tried to catch them with her eyes, her gaze locked with Samael's. He smiled and stepped forward.

Her breath caught – even with the leathery wings, which she could tell were tattered, Samael's chiseled jawline accentuated his regal countenance. He was stunning. Silver eyes gazed at her with a mixture of melancholy and determination, flawlessly framed by a curtain of gold hair that was reminiscent of the auroras that doubtlessly paint the heavens. When he walked, a veil of iridescence almost seemed to shift in the air around him... perhaps hinting at the presence of infernal energies. While Michael felt mundane and unremarkable, Samael was the very essence of beauty. He was everything Mercy would have expected from an angel, and he was downright striking.

Intimidatingly so.

His eyes sparkled as he approached, his wings casting a shadow that almost seemed to devour the feeble multi-colored daylight that streamed through the church's windows. "For what it's worth, I know what it's like to stand as a second-class citizen. It's frustrating, isn't it? You just want to forge your own path, to find your own way, but you have someone eternally pulling your strings behind the scenes."

Mercy tilted her chin, informing him of her attention but offering no response.

"And that person is telling you to love them, that you'll be rewarded with eternity one day, that the very sands of time will bow before you... but that's not true. It simply isn't. It's up to each of us to forge our own paths. *We* must make the world bow at our feet."

"You're talking about my sire."

Samael smiled, and the effect nearly lit up the room. It made Mercy's heart flutter. "I know all about Levi and how you've been running from him. He's pathetic. Half a millennium and nothing to show for it... not wealth, not power, not love. Not even happiness. You need not be a scion, you know. You don't need him anymore. It's time you forge your own path, wouldn't you say?"

Nearby, several pews collided as Lilith and Levi finally slammed into them. She had him pinned, but he wasn't hurt – she was toying with him, Mercy realized. Buying time for Samael. While they momentarily captured Mercy's attention, Samael flexed his wings to draw her gaze again. When her eyes crawled back, he offered another devilish smile.

"Has he told you why you're still a scion?"

Mercy tilted her head. "It's for my protection."

"That's not true. You're more powerful than him. He knows that as a fully-fledged vampire, you'll see that. You're a threat to him."

"And you're not a threat to me?"

The angel before her smirked, and the effect was pure magic. His face, already perfect, was made even more beautiful by the supercilious expression. "As a being served by two million vampires, I am a threat to everyone. But your path, Mercy, is with us. Join us, for we shall inherit the earth." Samael raised his hand, unleashing a burst of flame that formed into a fiery serpent. It broke away from him and slithered toward the vampire. Reminiscent of the creature that once purportedly tempted humanity and nurtured its fall, it coiled fluidly in the air around Mercy and whispered encouragement to her.

Join us, Mercy.

Leave this place and never look back.

You'll finally be free. Finally. Free.

As the fire encircled her and slowly bled into a solid wall of flame, Mercy focused on the latent power hiding within her. She felt her tether to the earth sever, and she was rising in an instant. The serpent, however, caught her ankle as Michael's sword had and pulled her back against the earth.

As she collided with a pew, Mercy howled – a Bible fell loose and struck her leg. With tears slipping from her eyes,

Mercy grated her teeth and lifted her head to lock her eyes on Samael. He looked up as the roof cracked and a bolt of lightning tore through the ceiling. Before it could touch him, his wings stretched open and fluttered, pushing him back in one swift motion.

Samael's eyes gazed down at the smoking ground where the lightning had struck before they settled on Mercy with pure fury. "Was that your answer?"

"The answer is *Levi*, you asshole. How dare you call my partner pathetic? The love we share is more powerful than any being in the universe. Even you. *You're* the pathetic one."

He balked forward, clearly intending to strike her as the fire serpent slithered beside him. She was sure her bones would snap when his outstretched hand collided with her, but it was the snake that hurt her first. Mercy threw her head back and screamed as her skin started to bubble under the heat.

The pain triggered something in her, however, as it was soon replaced with that familiar pleasant warmth that came whenever Mercy became wind. Unlike when she was in that state, she could see every detail in the world around her. She saw Samael's eyes widen as his gaze combed over the air.

I'm fog, Mercy realized suddenly. She turned her attention to the fire serpent and approached it, encircling it as she focused on dropping the temperature. The serpent fizzled out, leaving a smear of black soot on the ground.

Mercy then shifted toward Samael, who was staring at the charred floorboard in confusion. He clearly couldn't see her. As she brushed past his ankles, she subconsciously deposited a layer of dew around him.

She manifested on her back with her legs angled above and her hands below her hips. She hooked Samael's ankles, kicked his knees in, and jumped to her feet as he toppled forward.

The weight of his wings took him down quickly, but he landed on his hands and knees. He stretched the leathery wings above him, casting an ominous shadow over Mercy as the sound of a snake's rattle surrounded him. His head jerked suddenly, rotating unnaturally on his neck until he was facing her. He met her gaze and blinked, flames suddenly flickering within his sockets. A massive flame serpent manifested and coiled between his limbs. Backward and contorted, he started creeping toward her.

Mercy shrieked when, once again, the snake sprang forward and encircled her legs up to the knees.

Samael, however, screamed next, and the serpent retreated. His head twisted back into its normal position as he collapsed, and Mercy stared on in shock as a bright flash of light separated his left wing from his body. The leathery mass thudded against the ground, making a sound that was almost wet. Drops of molten silver fell from the remaining stump as he forced himself to his feet to face his attacker.

Mary Olive stood before him, the lightning sword in her hands and her brow furrowed with intense concentration. A few specks of silver blood were splattered across her cheeks, glimmering as she met the angel's gaze with stormy blue eyes. "Get the fuck away from my sister!"

When Samael lurched forward toward Mary, the ensuing events almost seemed to unfold in slow motion for Mercy. Her hand was outstretched, and then there was wind.

It wasn't like any normal wind, though – this was electrically charged, sputtering with blue bolts of hot electricity, and its power sent Samael flying across the room. As he collided with a stained glass window, Mercy moved to her feet and scooped her sword from Mary's hand.

"Mercy!" Levi screamed. She spun in time to catch Lilith, practically airborne, as she collided with her.

The ancient vampiress had her pinned in an instant. Mercy, thinking fast, brought her knees up into the immortal's guts. Lilith stumbled, and though she didn't back down, the misstep gave Mercy a moment to tighten her grip on the sword and jump to her feet. When Lilith lurched forward again, Mercy sidestepped her and sliced.

Coppery red locks of hair fell to the ground. Lilith looked down at them in horror, then threw her head back and let out a primal scream.

In her moment of pause, Mercy jutted forward and struck Lilith across the belly with her sword. As it sliced her flesh, the electricity sizzled against wet droplets of blood. The vampiress, now weakened, retreated into the shadows with a haunting glare.

Yet, as Lilith faded away, a malevolent presence stepped forward. Samael, the fallen angel, unfolded his massive bat-like wing, casting a foreboding shadow that was darker than night. The silver streaks pouring from his open wound were the only things to break the darkness around him, glinting with a metallic sheen that only barely refracted the light.

"Get out of here, Mary Olive!" Mercy screamed.

Samael turned his silver eyes on Mary, who attempted to dart away. He scowled as his fiery serpent snaked forward and grabbed her ankle. She screeched in pain as she toppled, and an infuriated Mercy charged forward. She sliced mercilessly, almost instinctually carving through the air until her sword moved with a surge of divine strength. She found herself aiming for Samael's remaining right wing.

Samael suddenly fell to his knees, followed by a cascade of luminescent plumes that fell around him like falling stars. Mercy watched as his pitch-black batwing transformed into something that was the color of pure sunlight. The wing – perhaps like the former, though Mercy had been distracted – slowly folded in on itself until it burst into gold dust, leaving just a few luminescent feathers in its place.

Mercy, resolute in her mission, raised her sword before her as if to strike. Nevertheless, her voice came through as her weapon of choice.

"Samael, Lilith, I banish you both to the infernal realms from whence you came. O glorious Archangel St. Michael, Prince of the heavenly host, defend us in battle."

Mary Olive, injured but dedicated, managed to limp her way to Mercy's side. The girls intertwined hands and continued. "Oh, pray to the God of peace that He may put Samael under our feet, so far conquered that He may no longer be able to hold men in captivity."

Samael and Lilith screamed, their pained cries syncing like the howls of an entire pack of wolves.

"...Beating down the dragon, the ancient serpent, who is the devil and Satan, do thou again make him captive in the abyss, that he may no longer seduce the nations."

Levi took Mercy's free hand and started praying in Hebrew. As the three stood together, the floor split open, and hands slinked out and gripped the ankles of their injured adversaries. In the blink of an eye, hundreds of demons worked together to drag their beloved leaders into the depths of Hell.

Though Samael clawed at the floor, he didn't dramatically slow his demons. Lilith slinked into the slits of the earth first, but he soon followed, and the fissures shook as they came back together. Where each immortal had been dragged, a line of silver and red fluid sparkled in the wintry light that streamed through the broken window.

The structure of the church was clearly impacted beyond the broken window, though, as it started to sway threateningly. Mercy and Levi exchanged a look and dragged Mary Olive toward the door.

The trio had only stumbled outside before Mercy keeled over. She pulled her hands away from her abdomen in shock, realizing they were covered in blood. A deep gash marred Mercy's side, the result of an apparently cunning and subtle strike from Samael.

"Why isn't it healing?" Mercy asked as she met Levi's panicked gaze. He instantly moved to support her weight. "Oh my God. This is the cost of victory. He got me."

"Mercy!" Levi exclaimed. "Look at me. Hey. *Look at me.* Jesus Christ, your eyes are getting foggy. Mary Olive! Say something to her!"

"*Mercy!*" Mary pleaded. "Fuck. Come back. Come back. Do you hear me? Don't fucking do this. Mercy!"

Her fingers twitched for a moment, feeling the thickness of blood between them, before she ultimately succumbed to her wound. The world went black.

Chapter Twenty

Mercy sat up and gasped. She was in a dark void, surrounded by luminescent feathers. She fumbled blindly and found her sword tucked neatly inside its sheath. She drew it and illuminated the space with golden light.

As the light brushed against the darkness, it began to fizzle and fade. Slowly, it dissipated and broke, blossoming into a verdant sea of greenery. Massively lush leaves emerged, and each seemed to give off some sort of luminescence. The world around her slowly opened.

She was standing in a garden.

Now that the world was well-lit, she sheathed her sword and hooked it to her belt. As she stared down at her midriff, a thought bloomed in her mind.

I was struck. There was blood.

But who'd hurt her? And if someone *had* hurt her, where the Hell was the wound? As she took in the surrounding world, she wasn't quite sure. The last thing she remembered was wrapping her presents and hopping on a bus to Connecticut to celebrate Christmas at her childhood home.

No, she thought. That wasn't right – her sword was the last thing she remembered. She had forged it herself using hellfire under the direction of an angel. She'd done so with Levi and Mary Olive at her side.

They were there when I died.

The thought came to her before she wholly processed it. *They were there when I died.* She was dead. Mercy had been standing against Samael and Lilith, two dark immortals who wanted to use her as a weapon. She'd banished them, it seemed, before she discovered a mortal wound.

"Hello?" Her voice danced through the air in an unexpected visual – golden dust sparkled as the sound projected. "Anyone there?"

All at once, sound suddenly followed. Birds chirped all around her. A babbling brook somewhere nearby infused the air with the sweet sound of flowing water.

Almost overwhelmed, Mercy began to wander.

Oh, Mercy.

"Levi?"

His voice didn't respond. She shivered, believing she'd imagined his presence, and continued her trek.

Come to me, Mercy. I'm here.

Mercy halted. This time, his voice seemed to dance across the wind, emanating from a solid source on the strange yet definitely tactile plane. As the gentle breeze ruffled her hair, she reached out and ran her fingers through it. The wind glittered, and she realized with a start that it felt almost tangible. Furrowing her brow, she wrapped her fingers around it.

The air, wispy and velvety, became almost like a ribbon between her fingertips. As she held it, she realized that she was an estrie – she *was* wind. Focusing all her strength, she became one with the atmosphere and glided across the wind, moving perfectly opposite to the direction it flowed.

Eventually, she came to a tree and solidified again. As soon as her feet made contact with the earth, Mercy craned her neck to gaze up toward its branches. It stretched higher than any she'd ever seen.

"Hello."

At the sound of a voice, Mercy jumped and spun around. Her eyes widened. "Kaitlyn?"

The woman laughed. "No, I'm sorry. I'm Lailah. I just took a form that I thought may be familiar and, therefore, less distressing to you. Welcome to Eden, Mercy."

Mercy ran her eyes over the woman suspiciously. "Who are you, Lailah?"

"An angel." The woman unsheathed a sword of her own and lifted it, watching with sparkling brown eyes as it lit with flickering flames. "You've found the Tree of Life, or the Tree of Mercy, as you've referred to it. This is the very spot where souls are created. They're nurtured within the roots, and when new flowers blossom near the top, those souls come into existence. Your soul was nurtured here many centuries ago."

Mercy turned back to gaze at the massive tree in awe. "Wow, incredible. So I'm dead, then?"

Lailah laughed and sheathed her sword again. "As I understand it, Mercy, you've been dead."

"I mean, like, *dead* dead?"

The angel laughed again, and the sound sent golden sparkles flying through the air around them. "Oh, you are charming. You're not quite *dead* dead, Mercy. You're in a space that is extant and apart from time, yet in step with it and co-existing alongside its eternal stretches. Our friend Michael sent you here."

Mercy raised an eyebrow, not quite sure what to say.

"That's a good thing," Lailah said. "You were in a lot of pain, so we stepped in to help you out. It's the least we can do – you chose to fight on the side of Heaven, a choice that may have prevented a war for control of its divine plane. I hope you understand that Michael has been guiding you in the hopes that you'd make the right choice, but he couldn't force or even encourage you to make it. It had to be you, dear.

"And now, you have the choice to come with me and live in paradise until we must continue that fight again, or return to earth as you were. I cannot promise, however, that your return will be as painless as your journey here."

Though she didn't wholly remember the pain that had sent her reeling, Mercy reached down to touch where her wound had been. Lailah nodded as if understanding what Mercy was silently asking.

"Either way," Mercy slowly ventured, "You're expecting me to stand alongside Heaven again?"

The angel smiled, which made Mercy's stomach lurch. It was so strange to see a stranger with a familiar face bearing a smile she'd known for many years. If she stayed in paradise – or continued to paradise, if it wasn't this place – she may never see that smile again. At least, not in the context of the person who actually owned it.

"Let me ask you, what brought you here? To this tree?"

"A voice," Mercy said quietly.

"A loved one's voice?"

"You could say that, yes."

The angel looked up at the tree, following its height with her eyes. Mercy followed her gaze and saw that some of the lowest branches had a few flowers on them. While most were covered in leaves and miscellaneous fruits, those flowers taunted Mercy's gaze. As the angel stood silently, the vampire shifted. "Are those vampires?"

"The flowers are, yes. As you can see, the branches around them are largely empty. Most of their peers have moved along the soul's eternal journey, but a few still linger. I like to think love keeps them abloom, just as it keeps their lives going."

One flower caught her eye – it was golden, and it shimmered like words did in the Eden air. Mercy studied it for a moment and took a deep breath. "I have to go back, then."

"If you believe you're fighting for love rather than Heaven, then yes," Lailah said. "But this is about your beliefs, Mercy, and where you find your strength."

"My strength is *them*," Mercy said. "My loved ones. Levi. Mary Olive. My parents, Kaitlyn, even Ozzy, I think."

Lailah produced her sword, lifted it in the air, and whipped with it. In response to the rope of fire that extended from it, a single apple fell down from the tree. She offered it to Mercy.

"If I eat this," Mercy said, "I'll have to leave paradise."

Lailah poked her sword into the ground and leaned against its handle, gazing at Mercy as the flames lit her face from below. "And I'll tell you exactly what Michael told the last beings to leave Eden. You'll find a paradise within. In fact, I think you've already found it, and I think you know that it's better."

When Mercy extended her hand, the angel humbly offered the apple again. It iced over, frozen under Mercy's touch. As she gazed down at it, she felt her fangs pricking her lower lip. When she looked back up at the angel, Lailah was smiling.

Mercy raised the apple to her lips.

MERCY GASPED AND ATTEMPTED to sit up, but pain blinded her and she fell back against a soft surface. When her eyes fluttered open again, the haze of pain slowly receded enough for her to look around. She found herself lying in a soft bed, and the room was dimly lit. There was a figure on the bed beside her, just outside her peripherals, so her hand snaked over to meet theirs.

Levi instantly sat up, hovering over her with a tender smile curved on his lips. "Hey, little warrior. You did it."

"I'm alive?"

He chuckled. "Well, you certainly gave it your best shot, but the Angel of Death didn't take you down. An injury from a holy weapon or an angel can block our healing abilities, so I'm sorry to say that you'll be healing like a human for the course of this one."

Mercy touched her abdomen and winced. "Oh, fuck, this *hurts*."

"Yeah, he got you good."

"How are you? How's Mary Olive?"

"Oh, I'm fine. I had a few knicks, but I've healed up. Your sister was burned pretty badly where Samael caught her on the ankle, but she'll make a full recovery, too. Apparently, Michael was an EMT before he was a food critic, so he fixed you both up. Mary Olive told him he should be a chef in his next career change so he learns to make something other than stuffing. She suggested gravy as a starting point."

Mercy cracked a smile. "That sounds like my sister."

"She's downstairs celebrating with Ozzy and your parents. Michael said the victory was worth a toast."

"My parents are celebrating here? Okay, now I *know* I didn't survive."

"Har-dee-har, doofus. I told you I'd protect you."

She met his gaze and bit her lip. "Levi, I... I went somewhere while I was unconscious. I found myself in the Garden of Eden, and I was asked to make a choice. The angel I spoke with led me to believe that I've been fighting for love this whole time."

Levi considered her words, his gaze deep and contemplative. "When I found my coven and had to find an ounce of my humanity again, I myself came to the same conclusion. I found myself reflecting on the people I loved, and I realized that if anything happened to me, the memory of them would cease to exist. To a degree, I kept living for them. And today, I find meaning in being with you, in the connection we've forged. Life might be chaotic, and love might be complicated, but it's worth it, don't you think?"

Mercy nodded thoughtfully. "It is. Sacrifices are part of the journey, but they lead to something greater. Like the blade we forged, a lightning strike shaped it into something powerful. Maybe our battles and sacrifices are shaping us for something greater, too."

He grew grim. "Yeah, they are. Michael said we've banished Samael and Lilith for now, but they'll be back. And a Heavenly War will still happen, eventually. You've proven yourself as a warrior, so he may be calling on you to assist again one day."

"I'll be stronger then," she said confidently. "I'm still a fledgling now, but I'll be so much more as a fully mature vampire. I'll be like you – you held your own pretty damn well in that church."

He grinned. "Well, sure. It helps when your girlfriend has a heavenly weapon in her arsenal and Buffy for a sister."

"The sword!" Mercy exclaimed in surprise. "Wait, how was Mary able to wield that? Michael said only the maker could use their respective holy weapon."

"Turns out, he was being politically correct. We helped you make it, Mercy. You called on me and Mary Olive to help. Any of us can wield it – not to the extent *you* can, but we can touch it. That part was up to us to figure out, lest he stir up heavenly tensions or something."

"Can we go see everyone? Am I allowed to move?"

"Sure." Levi wrapped his arms around Mercy and pulled her to a sitting position, and she gasped and winced through the process. Once she was sitting up, her fingers tightly gripped his shoulders for a moment. He stared at her red eyes before he turned his head away. "Go ahead, Mercy."

She leaned forward and sunk her teeth into his neck, and he winced – it usually didn't hurt, but she was ravenous. She drank greedily until the wound healed, and then she punctured the skin again, and this time, she didn't let go. Levi let her cling to him for a minute before he finally said, "That's enough."

Mercy gasped and pulled away. It took everything in her to stop – the injury made her more predatory, more reactive. Nonetheless, she regained her composure as Levi stood, wiped her mouth with a tissue, and pulled her to her feet.

As they made their way out of the bedroom and down the stairs, the sound of clinking glasses and laughter floated to them. Levi steadied Mercy as they stepped down from the staircase and headed toward the dining room.

When they approached, Mary Olive squealed, jumped up from her chair, and darted for her sister. Levi stepped in her path. "Ah, ah, ah, Mary – she's still hurt. No bear hugs."

Mary, practically vibrating in place, tip-toed forward and gently wrapped her arms around her sister's shoulders. "Mercy! Thank God you're okay. Don't ever scare me like that again."

"You're a fucking badass, Mary Olive," she said. "I wouldn't be here if you hadn't hopped in. You're *so* brave."

Mary shrugged. "Eh, that was nothing. You ever worked a food service job? You should see my customers before they've had their coffee. They make Satan look like a cuddly bunny."

Beth and Steve approached behind Mary, and they were next to embrace Mercy. She squirmed in their embrace before her mother finally relinquished her. Her father held her just a moment longer before he also stepped back.

"Saint Michael told us everything," Beth said. "We're so proud of you, Mercy."

"We are," Steve agreed. "And we're sorry for how the holidays played out. *I'm* sorry. I... I have a lot to work through, and taking it out on you was cruel and unfair of me. I promise I'll work on myself, and I'm so sorry I let it get to this point. And I promise this year's celebration will be better if you'll still come."

"Of course I'll still come! No offense, Mom, but I won't be eating food anymore, so please don't cook for me. And I will respectfully refrain from the holy water blessing."

She chuckled. "That's fair. You don't have to put on a show to fit in with us, Mercy."

"You're *so* much more than us," Steve added. "We're very proud to have you as our daughter, honey. We love you."

"I love you guys, too." Mercy glanced over her shoulder at Levi, suddenly very aware of his presence. His eyes sparkled, and she grinned at him before she turned back to her parents. "Speaking of love... If you guys don't mind, I'd like to bring someone special to the next family holiday."

"Of course," Beth said. "I think Mary's going to be bringing someone, too."

Mercy glanced across the room at Ozzy, who grinned and lifted his hand to wave. She waved back, silently noting that Schnitzel was curled up in his lap and purring. As the two vampires smiled at each other, Mercy let go of any lingering doubts about the former hunter. She was now certain that their paths were meant to cross, that he was meant to help her prepare to face her greatest battle. Hell, maybe he was meant to inspire Mary Olive with fearlessness.

Whatever the reason, he was now family. After all, Schnitzel accepted him.

From the head of the table, Michael caught Mercy's gaze and raised his glass.

"A hard-fought victory," he acknowledged. "I respect you, Mercy. Thank you for standing alongside Heaven in defending this realm against evil. But remember, the Heavenly War is an ongoing struggle. Samael may be defeated for now, but his return is inevitable. Stay vigilant, for the battle between light and darkness never truly ends. I may call on you again."

"I hope you do," Mercy said. "I'll be stronger next time. Oh, and better with my sword. Just give me a bit of time to heal up first."

He chuckled. "I'll do my best to fend off darkness until then. I think I, the greatest warrior in Heaven, can manage."

"Perfect." Mercy winked at him. "Because training's not over, big guy. You may be a weird dude, but something tells me I still have a bit to learn from you."

Michael grinned. "If that was a formal request to continue as my student, then I accept. I look forward to seeing your skills grow."

"If you guys don't mind," Levi said. "Mercy and I are going to take a little walk before we join you."

"Give us a holler if you need help," Mary offered.

"We will, sis. Ready, Levi?"

He steadied his arm against hers and led Mercy to the back door. When he opened it, she shivered.

"Oh," she breathed. "I'm cold. This injury must be messing me up."

He glanced at the coatrack where Mary Olive had tossed a few flannels, then scooped up a fleece-lined one and helped her put it on. He also grabbed an oversized one and pulled it on himself. Levi looped his arm back into Mercy's and led her outside.

The snow crunched beneath their boots as they strolled through the winter-kissed yard, the air filled with the scent of pine and the distant promise of more snow. This one wouldn't come from Mercy's fury, though – just a natural January snowfall. Clad in cozy flannel, they were a picture-perfect scene straight out of a Hallmark movie.

"Never thought I'd see the day when Mercy Mild Harker is wandering around in a basic white girl flannel," Levi remarked, a mischievous twinkle in his eyes.

Mercy chuckled. "Times change. So do people."

"You mean you're cold now?"

"*So* cold," she huffed. "I'd forgotten what it's like. Thank goodness Mary was prepared. Next Christmas, I'm gifting her black towels *and* some nice black jackets, though."

"I'm sure she'll appreciate that, knowing Mary." Levi's gaze softened as he looked at her. "Speaking of change, I've been thinking about something."

She arched an eyebrow, a hint of curiosity in her eyes. "Oh?"

"You've changed." He stopped walking and turned to face her. "When we met, I saw the potential for who you'd become. I knew you were special. But throughout all these years as my scion, I've seen you face down adversity time and time again. From your writing career alongside that ghastly Ann character to dealing with your dysfunctional family for traditional holidays despite the changes vampirism brought, you've proven you have grit. And it culminated into this absolute warrior of a woman I'm now standing before."

"I couldn't have done it without my sire."

"Perhaps, but you've proven you don't need one anymore." Levi reached for her hand, intertwining their fingers. "I set you free from your scionship, Mercy. You're no longer bound by necessity, and you can make your own choices from now on. Congratulations, darling. I'm proud of you."

"Levi, I..."

"No need for words."

Tears welled up in Mercy's eyes, overwhelmed by the magnitude of the moment. There was *power* in it. She could physically feel the confines of his authority drifting away, freeing her thoughts and emotions from its confusing grasp. For the first time in ages, she was *her*, wholly and authentically. She pulled Levi into a tight embrace. "Thank you," she whispered.

Levi kissed the top of her head before he buried his face in her hair. The pair stood locked in an embrace for a long moment before they broke apart and started strolling again, hand in hand.

Scanning the snowy landscape, Mercy leaned into him. "It'll be an adjustment, moving back to town."

"I seem to recall a certain business lady from the big city who once claimed to hate small-town life."

Mercy laughed, the sound echoing in the crisp winter air. "Oh, I do. But it's not about where you're at. It's about who you're with. And, well, *maybe* I've developed a soft spot for this small town."

"And me, too?"

She bumped shoulders with him and winced at the pain it sent shooting through her midriff. "Don't push your luck, Levi Lestat. You're starting to sound a bit obsessive."

He grinned as he looked down at the ground. As they walked through the winter wonderland, surrounded by the quiet beauty of snow-covered trees and the promise of a fresh start, Mercy felt a profound sense of gratitude. The snowy landscape, the cozy flannel, and the comfort of Levi's hand in hers painted a picture of a future filled with endless possibilities.

"DON'T EVEN LOOK AT the Audis."

"I *wasn't*." Levi jammed his hands in his pockets as they walked through the car lot. His trench coat danced around his knees as he strolled. "I know, you hated the last one. I just... Whatever I get, I'm getting a custom paint job."

Mercy huffed. "Fine. Just don't make it matte again. You looked like a sporty suburban mom picking up her precious angels from school every time you rolled around town."

"Ouch," he said. "What are you getting? A Jaguar?"

"What makes you think I'd want that?"

"Isn't that one of the coveted pets? A Jaguar parked outside, a mink around the shoulders, a tiger in the bed, and a jackass who pays for it all?"

"Let me guess – you're the jackass."

"I'm the *tiger*, thank you very much. The jackass is whatever your pen name is."

"Don't pretend you don't know it."

"Mercy?" The sound of a new voice in the conversation made the pair pause. Just a few cars away, Kaitlyn waved at her and excitedly approached. She spread her arms for a hug, but Mercy lifted a hand.

"Hold on," she said. "Really, really gentle with this – I just had a surgery, so I'm fragile."

Kaitlyn hugged her gently, then respectfully stepped back. "I thought you were just staying until the New Year!"

Mercy touched her wound and shrugged. "Yeah, well, this changed things. Really put into perspective what life is all about. I decided to stay in town with my partner. Kaitlyn, this is Levi."

Her eyes landed on Levi. She lit up. "I know you! The coffee shop guy. *Now* I see why you gave us free drinks."

Levi chuckled. "That's me, coffee shop guy. I had a bit of car trouble that's led me to look for a new one, and since Mercy's staying in town and needs a car now, we figured we'd shop together."

"I'm shopping with my fiancée, Melissa. I'd love to introduce you guys to her. Since you're staying in town, Mercy, maybe we can plan a double date?"

"You know, I'd really like that. We definitely need more time to catch up, and I'd love for you to get to know Levi."

"It's a date," Kaitlyn said. "By the way, I saw a car that's *so* you. It's near the front of the lot. White wheels, red velvet interior. Mercy to the core."

"I'll look for it."

"When you make your way up there, flag us down! I'm going to head back that way now, Melissa's up there preparing for a test drive."

"See ya," Mercy said with a wave. When Kaitlyn disappeared from sight, Mercy turned to Levi. "It's going to be weird with Mary Olive being out of town so often. I might as well start making social connections now."

Levi was examining the price tag on a Jeep, but he moved to Mercy's side and fell into step with her. "Yeah, I can't believe Michael encouraged them to hunt down vampires with soul bonds and help them find control."

"Yeah, with those nine hunting pairs still out there and with Mary Olive very much being human, it's certainly a creative decision. But I trust his judgment, I guess."

"Well, Ozzy is ancient and fearless, and Mary Olive is an absolute badass. They'll do great, nonetheless. Maybe they'll carry the torch and chase the rest of the remaining evil out of the world."

Mercy smiled as they continued walking. "Who woulda thunk I'd be the sister to settle down?"

Levi chuckled. "Well, I certainly thunk it. Since the moment we met, I knew you were mine."

"And *you're mine*," she said, bumping hips with him. She winced slightly at the motion, but smiled convincingly when her partner cocked an eyebrow at her.

He suddenly stopped, admiring a red Cadillac sedan.

"Take it for a test drive."

"Sure," he said. "Let's go look at that Mercy-car Kaitlyn suggested. Better make sure it has enough room in the backseat for Gertrude."

"I hate that Michael gave that thing to us," Mercy muttered. She slipped on a bit of ice, but Levi caught her arm and steadied her. "Thanks."

"I'll always catch you. You're not just my partner; you're my everything."

"You're not just my everything, you're my forever. I promise to stand by you, to love you endlessly, and to be your partner in crime, no matter how many Audis with bad custom paint jobs come our way."

"Forever is a long time. That's a *lot* of custom paint jobs you're going to hate."

"I know, and I hate that thought. Don't be surprised if I parody it in *Vampnado*."

"Oh God, Mercy. Tell me you're not actually writing that."

As they resumed their walk, Mercy's hand intertwined with Levi's, sealing the promise of a future entwined. It felt like the perfect conclusion to an adventure in which the extraordinary and ordinary intersected in a quaint, sleepy town in Connecticut.

Finally, for the time being, there was peace on earth for Mercy Mild Harker.

Also by Nikki Elizabeth

Industrialized
Poor Vinnie's Valor
Part One: Experiment

Standalone
Peace on Earth & Mercy Mild

Watch for more at https://authornikkielizabeth.com.

About the Author

Since 2007, Nikki Elizabeth's written work has been featured in publications across North America. At her day job, Nikki works as a copywriter serving corporations in the home improvement sector. In January 2024, she expanded her professional presence as a writer by publishing her debut novella, *Industrialized, Poor Vinnie's Valor*, with her first debut novel, *Industrialized, Part One: Experiment*, following in April 2024. Find more of her work at authornikkielizabeth.com.

Read more at https://authornikkielizabeth.com.

9 798227 224606